# Contents

# French Kisses

# Part One: September–November

# Chapter 1: The Encounter

"It's just so bloody predictable, that's what gets me."

Rachel had the phone clamped uncomfortably against one ear as she stomped up and down the kitchen, unpacking the contents of her shopping bags with fury.

"First he has a midlife crisis aged forty and dumps me, and then he goes and gets the poor girl pregnant."

An aubergine broke loose from her grip and wobbled down the old wooden table to collide with an opened bottle of red wine, fortunately with the cork still in it.

"Buggeration."

She set the bottle upright again and sat down with a sigh.

"Look Jilly, I'd better go. I'm not up to multitasking at the moment. Yup, pop round later and I'll give you the full story. Ciao, bye."

Rachel was in the kitchen of the stone house she had renovated with her soon-to-be ex-husband Michael more than a decade before. Over the years they had acquired odd bits of furniture – some of it, like the table, given to them by neighbours when they had first settled in southeastern France in their twenties.

When Michael started to earn a decent wage from his property business, they could easily have afforded newer smarter things, but neither of them wanted to change anything about the home they had painstakingly created together. Rachel liked to think about the generations of children who had hidden themselves in their cupboards and built dens under the heavy French table, just like her two had done when they were younger. It was furniture that was built to survive – unlike her marriage, she thought, as she flung bags of pasta and cereal packets into cupboards.

Fortunately, Michael's new squeeze – being a mere slip of a girl – was a fan of chrome and MDF, so there had been no fighting over furniture when Michael moved out.

When she'd finished unpacking, Rachel made a cup of coffee, grabbed a couple of madeleines and went upstairs to her studio. This was her place of work and her sanctuary. It was here that she worked on the prints of birds, animals and landscapes that she sold to local galleries and shops.

It was a warm September day and from the window she could see the red-tiled roofs of the houses lower down the slope, beyond the edge of the village walls. In the distance, the lumpy tops of the far-off hills were turning sage green and grey as the sun moved around them. Normally the view would inspire her and she would dash down ideas in crayon on the thick creamy paper of her sketchbook. Discovering that Michael was about to start a new family had knocked her sideways and she wasn't feeling the least bit creative.

"Damn the man," she muttered to herself. "Paperwork, that's the answer." She picked up a folder full of receipts and invoices, but the morning's encounter had rattled her and she couldn't even concentrate on basic admin tasks. She turned on the radio, hoping to distract herself, only to find that they were playing what had been "their" tune. Exasperated, Rachel twirled the dial until she reached a talk show and let the chatter wash over her as she dislodged a cat from the chair and sat down with her coffee.

Looking offended, the cat jumped back onto her lap, curled up and went to sleep. Rachel ran her fingers through the amber twirls of his fur and gazed absent-mindedly out of the window.

It had been just over a year since Michael had announced to Rachel that he was leaving her for another woman, if you could call her that. Amelie was in her late-twenties and taught dance at the local arts college. She was skinny, blonde, athletic and altogether annoying.

Eventually, Rachel had grown used to the idea and coped with it so long as Michael's new domestic arrangements were not shoved in her face too often. Unfortunately, he had moved into Amelie's apartment in the neighbouring town – Dreste – so they ran into each other with depressing regularity.

Rachel had had a few months of peace because the lovebirds had gone down to the coast near Nice for the long summer holidays. Michael had texted the kids to say he would be back soon, but she had been unable to get a specific date from either Alice or Charlie.

The household was running low on supplies of all the heavy boring stuff, so that morning Rachel had decided to pop into Dreste while she was fairly sure the coast would be clear. As a rule she avoided supermarkets like the plague, preferring to support the shops in Pelette. However, it had got to the point where she needed things like industrial quantities of tinned tomatoes and cat food that she didn't want to lug up the hill on her bike.

So, there she was, piling washing powder and loo roll into her trolley at the big Auchan store when she glanced up to see Michael and Amelie holding hands by the baby food section. Her stomach sank like a stone because she knew it could only mean one thing.

The cat on her lap stirred, bringing her back to reality. "She's welcome to him, eh Fudge?" she said, unwrapping a sweet, fluffy madeleine and sipping the coffee, which, she noticed, had gone cold. The tepid liquid gave her a shock. "Get a grip, woman," she said, standing up and carefully replacing the cat on the warm cushion. "We've got work to do." Slipping an ink-covered apron over her head, Rachel selected a cutting tool and set to work on a new print.

* * *

That evening, Rachel rehearsed the horrors of the morning with Jilly, a fellow Brit and neighbour. She had worked with Michael for a few years and was annoyingly even-handed when it came to any conflicts between her former colleague and his wife. Jilly had recently married the local garage owner, Thierry. He was besotted with his new wife, who was a few years older than him.

Being naturally kind and sympathetic and in a soppy state didn't make her ideal company for a rant about Michael. Rachel's first choice would have been Margot – a much tougher cookie – but she was out of town, so Jilly got to hear about the supermarket encounter first.

Rachel grabbed a bottle of white wine and some crackers and led the way to the top terrace, by the house.

"So," said Jilly, once they were settled. "I want to hear all the gory details. You said you ran into them in Auchan?"

"'Fraid so," said Rachel, filling her friend's glass.

"And? What did you do?"

"I was in *Détergents* so I tried to hide behind a stack of Toilet Duck, but Michael spotted me."

"Go on," said Jilly, wincing.

"I thought I might get away with it or that the bloody man would just ignore me, but no." Rachel munched thoughtfully on a cracker. "He actually called my name and waved at me across the store!"

"Ouch!"

"You can say that again. I was trapped."

"How awful," said Jilly, entering into the spirit of things. "He should have done the decent thing and stayed in *Bébé et Maman*."

Rachel nodded furiously. "You're right," she said, topping up their glasses. "But when I pretended not to hear him, the two of them came right over. God, it was awful."

"What did they say?"

"Well, it was all very civilised. After the usual kissy-kissy greeting, Michael said they had planned to tell me properly, whatever that means," Rachel took a swig of wine. "But that 'they' were pregnant and so excited, but hadn't wanted to say anything before the summer hols because it was too early and blah, blah, blah."

Jilly gave her a sympathetic pat on the hand.

"And Amelie just stood there looking sweet and proud with the teeniest of bumps as if she was the only bloody woman he had ever got up the duff."

Jilly got a misty look in her eyes and opened her mouth to speak, but shut it again when she saw her friend's fierce expression.

"Don't you dare say anything *nice*!"

They were both silent for a minute, glancing out at the twilight and listening to the clicks and buzzes of insects in the garden. Although it was nearly autumn, the ground was still warm and busy with life. Rachel had planted jasmine and its sweet scent occasionally wafted over to them.

Eventually, Jilly spoke. "It sounds like Michael hasn't told the kids yet, then?"

Rachel sighed and pulled the cardigan she was wearing tighter around her shoulders. "Nope. And he'd better get his skates on because Junior will be making his appearance in a couple of months' time, apparently."

"How do you think they'll take it?"

"What, losing a father and gaining a sibling twenty years younger?"

"I thought Alice was not quite fifteen?"

"Details, details. Top up?" asked Rachel, proffering the bottle.

"Better not. Thierry is cooking, so I mustn't be late."

Jilly was still quite starry-eyed about her new husband, a trait that Rachel and battle-hardened friends like Margot sometimes found a trifle irritating.

They both stood and Jilly went over to hug her friend.

"Will you be okay? You're welcome to join us for supper."

Rachel smiled and shook her head, thinking she didn't fancy being the gooseberry that evening. "That's really sweet of you but I've got things to do."

"Well, if you're sure."

"Quite sure. Give my love to Thierry."

Jilly nodded and squeezed her hand. "Of course."

They walked together to the end of the terrace, then Rachel watched as her friend headed down the path to her adoring husband and his lovingly prepared casserole.

Rachel gathered up the glasses and went back inside. The kids were both out somewhere and there was nothing on TV so she decided to head back to her studio. She didn't trust herself with a lino-cutting tool after she'd had a glass or two of wine, so instead she pulled out the prints she had finished that week and laid them out on her work bench.

She had promised to deliver a new batch of work to the gallery in Dreste and wanted to select some pieces to have framed. She enjoyed everything about the creative process, including making her own frames when she had the time. She switched on the radio and listened to Europop for a while until the incessant chatter got too much and she turned it off.

"How can people bear that twaddle?" she asked the dusty grey cat who lay curled up on a pile of rags. She tutted as she watched it try to pull a streak of vermilion ink off its tail.

"That's what happens if you insist on sleeping up here, Mousey." The cat opened a lazy eye, yawned, turned and went back to sleep.

# Chapter 2: Summer in England

Rachel's life post-Michael had developed a routine in which she worked every day in the studio, creating her prints and greetings cards. When she was involved in a new design she was inclined to lose track of time, so she had an old-fashioned alarm clock in the studio that buzzed and clanked when it was time to do important stuff like lock up the chickens or feed the kids.

In the morning, she accompanied Charlie and Alice to the main square where they were collected by the village bus and taken into town to school. They were grown-up enough not to need a chaperone, but Rachel enjoyed the walk. Mid-afternoon, she downed tools and went to meet them or they ambled back themselves, sometimes calling in on friends in the village. The shrill ring of the alarm clock now showed her that it was home time.

"It's time to go and fetch the offspring, pusskins. Want to come?"

Rachel took off her apron and dashed downstairs. The cats sometimes liked a walk and would follow at a distance then sit on the church wall to wait for her to return.

Rachel knew she was lucky: despite all the changes and the new developments that had happened in the nearly two decades since they had pitched up,

Pelette hadn't really altered. There was a core of local people who knew her well.

They had watched Rachel and Michael arrive, restore their house and have the children. When Michael took off with Amelie, the villagers had quietly and discreetly come together to look after Rachel and the children.

She couldn't say what had changed, but she felt protected and knew that Alice and Charlie would never come to harm in the area. It was partly the fact that everyone knew everyone, but it was more than this: her children had been the first to be born in the old Seurat farmhouse for many years and that made them special.

Now the kids were gradually settling back to school after the long summer holidays. This year, like every year since they were born, Rachel had taken them to England for four weeks to visit their relatives in Devon and Yorkshire.

When the children were little, she and Michael would watch and worry about them. They were eccentric – English kids who chattered away together in French – but after a while they would be bounding around the Dales or across Exmoor with their cousins, picking up the local accents.

After the split, she had dreaded the trip back. What would people think of her? Surely they would wonder what she had or hadn't done to make her husband look for love elsewhere. In fact, family and friends – including Michael's friends – had been sympathetic and understanding.

One of his oldest mates had sidled up to her rather drunkenly at a barbecue and said Michael was a stupid sod to leave her. She managed to extract herself before his wife came over and dragged him back to the chicken thighs.

That was in Harrogate, near the ex in-laws' place. What she really loved and looked forward to most was being back in Devon at her childhood home.

One evening after a long day exploring rock pools and sunning themselves at the beach, she had left Alice and Charlie with their grandfather, Harold, and hiked up to the cliff top. The tangy sea air was the one element she really missed from her home. She felt the pull of it every time she visited: there was a strong, physical connection with the ocean that she guessed only people born on an island ever developed. A love of the sea was one of many things she had shared with her parents.

When her mother Jean passed away, Rachel had tried to persuade her father to live with them in France, but he had refused. She was disappointed, but she understood.

Taking her hand, Harold had spoken to her gently. "I'm too old and set in my ways, sweet pea. The move would probably finish me off, anyway."

"Don't say that, Dad," said Rachel, a lump in her throat. "I'm too young to be an orphan."

Harold had laughed. "As long as I take my daily totter along the sea front, I'll be fine for a few years yet."

She had cried when the family returned to France, leaving Harold alone in the house. Her brother Henry lived in America and visited as often as he could, but they both wondered how Harold would cope on his own after decades of marriage. They needn't have worried: a handsome man, he was soon scooped up by Connie, a merry widow from London, and had never looked back.

Rachel smiled to herself, remembering that evening in Devon, when the pair had agreed to skip their Tai Chi class and look after Charlie and Alice so she could go for a walk and enjoy her brief time back in England.

She hadn't kept up with many people, but she had arranged to call in at her friend Mary's house for tea after her walk. They had been at secondary school together and had kept in touch even during the years when Rachel was completely absorbed in Michael and their new life together. Mary was the person Rachel felt closest to from the old days. Over strong tea and Jaffa Cakes, she brought her friend up to date with Michael's romance and her own life with the kids.

Rachel thought she had made her experience as an artist in rural France sound rather fun and exciting, and had been surprised by her friend's reaction.

"It sounds a bit lonely, Rach," Mary had said with a frown.

"I'm not lonely. I'm just, well, busy."

"You could come back and live here, you know?"

Rachel shook her head. "No, I couldn't. Not any more. The kids are more French than English. And there's the house, my friends and my work ..."

"Kids are adaptable and you could easily find some studio space in town." Mary smiled. "But I understand." She got up and walked over to the kitchen window where a band of drizzle was starting to blow in off the sea. "Who would exchange all that lovely French sunshine for this?"

"Oh, we have our fair share of bad weather, don't you worry. Some of the storms are real humdingers." Rachel stood and joined her friend by the sink, putting an arm around her shoulder. "But it is my home."

Mary patted her on the hip. "I know. So, do you fancy a quick drink at the King's Head for old times' sake or are you expected back at Harold's?"

"Nope, I've got the night off. Dad has promised the kids fish finger sandwiches for tea so I said I might give supper a miss and see what you were up to."

"Great. Two large Chardonnays and that fine English delicacy, scampi and chips, coming up."

"Yum, my favourite!"

A few hours later, when she had tottered tipsily back to the house, Rachel found everything quiet and assumed that everyone had gone to bed. Instead she discovered the entire household plus a couple of local kids playing darts in the kitchen.

"It's good for hand-eye coordination," her father had said when she'd expressed concern as the sharp objects whizzed across the room and pinged off walls.

"And I insisted they all wear cycle helmets to protect their heads," added Connie, who was safely positioned by the door.

Knowing when she was beaten, Rachel shook her head, laughing. "Well, there's not much I can say to that. Goodnight all."

Now, sitting under a plane tree in Pelette waiting for the bus to arrive from Dreste, Rachel smiled at the recollection. She knew her children didn't yet appreciate how lucky they were to have friends and family in two countries. She had enjoyed her time in England more than she had expected to this year.

Michael's relatives had been kind, agreeing with her that it was important for the children not to lose touch with their cousins just because their parents had split up.

A creak and rattle indicated that the bus was about to crest the steep, narrow street and make its way into the square. It drew to a halt opposite where she sat. Rachel was always fascinated as she watched the youngsters get off – the girls looked so much more glamorous than she and her friends had been at that age. She'd never had the big hair and perfect skin these girls had. Alice was turning into a young woman and was worryingly gorgeous. Charlie was only two years younger but he was still a boy. As she saw him slouch towards her, Rachel was overwhelmed with love for her children.

The three of them walked home together, the cats joining them when they reached the church and running alongside.

Back at the house, she prepared supper then went into the studio to carry on with some birthday cards she was designing. The rhythm of work always helped her to think. She wasn't quite sure how things were going to turn out, but she was determined that her little family would be okay. And was she lonely, as Mary had suggested? Of course not. In any case, she was far too busy with her prints and the kids to think about finding a new man.

She'd had offers, of course. As soon as Michael had left her, she had been surprised when all kinds of unsuitable men – men who had been friends of theirs for years – rushed around to offer help, and sometimes more. The fact that every available male in the local area turned up at her door was one more reason for her to be angry with Michael.

Things hadn't been going too well between them for some time; they didn't not get on, things had just become a bit boring. Rachel had secretly imagined that she might make her own bid for freedom when the children were older, though she doubted whether she would ever really have done it. She loved her husband and it seemed to her that marriage was bound to be unexciting sometimes, so she was furious when Michael decided to jump ship. Whenever she thought about it, all the frustration came rushing back.

* * *

Rachel had been clearing out one of the sheds at the side of the house to use for storage and was dusty, tired and thirsty. The children were out with friends so she was on her own. Michael had gone into the village and come back with only half the things she had asked him for, looking rather sheepish. That's when he'd broken the news: he hadn't been to the village, he'd gone into Dreste to see Amelie and – Rachel guessed – to make sure the girl really did want him.

That moment was frozen in time and Rachel could remember every detail: the chickens preening in the dust that swirled around the courtyard, the church bell striking 3pm, the sound of children splashing around in a neighbour's swimming pool. She had stood there, open-mouthed, not making sense of the words that washed over her. Then Michael had put on his reasonable voice, the one he used to clinch a property deal. The one that made her cringe.

"Are you saying what I think you're saying?"

Rachel's brain couldn't take it in for a minute. "That you're leaving?"

Michael nodded, looking sorrowful. "Of course I still love you and the children ..."

"But you love this girl more than us."

Michael had paced around the terrace, rubbing the top of his bald head as he tended to when he was upset.

"Rach, this isn't easy for me either."

"Pah!" Rachel almost spat the word at him. "Not easy for you? How dare you say that! You're walzing out of my life with Miss Tippy-Toes leaving me with two kids and this bloody great house to manage on my own. With no money."

Michael raised his hands in a gesture of submission and looked pained. "I'm sorry, sweetheart ..."

"Don't bloody well 'sweetheart' me!"

"Rachel, you'll be fine. We'll sort out the money – I won't let you starve." He had stopped pacing and was looking from the sun-baked terrace towards the kitchen, where Rachel had put a pile of new prints that she planned to have framed.

"With the maintenance and the money from your work, you'll be fine." He smiled weakly. "And I'll pay you rent to use the garage, of course."

That had been the final straw.

"I don't want you anywhere near the garage. You can keep that geriatric vehicle of yours in Dreste. Or, better still, take it to the wrecker's yard where it belongs."

For the first time, Michael looked shocked. He shook his head, sounding pained. "How can you say that about Di-Di?"

Rachel felt the teeniest sense of remorse bubbling under the fury as she pictured the old mustard yellow car, a Citroën Dyane, which had been pretty ancient when they'd acquired her and the house from their canny neighbour all those years ago. He, Monsieur Seurat, had looked about ninety then but was still going strong, unlike the car. Despite the fact that Di-Di had a tendency to conk out at inopportune moments and they now had a proper car, they had clung on to her.

"I've got things to do here," said Rachel, fearful that she was about to cry over a darned metal box.

Michael nodded and looked relieved to have an excuse to leave. "I'll go now, but perhaps we can talk again tomorrow. You know you can call me any time."

The look he got made him beat a hasty retreat. "Okay, I'm off." And with that he turned, got into Di-Di and drove off, the engine stuttering and farting as it went.

The details of the next few days and weeks were a blur. After some initial tears, the children had been remarkably sanguine about it. All their friends' parents seemed to be divorced. Amelie had taught Alice ballet, so it was not as though she was a complete stranger to them. Her parents were clearly embarrassed by their daughter turning into a home-breaker and went out of their way to be generous to their newly acquired grandchildren.

Michael was as good as his word about the money and Rachel got a regular lump of cash every month to help with the children. But she found herself more and more uneasy at the idea of being a "kept woman". She also discovered that losing a husband – unsatisfactory though he might have been – left a big hole in her life. She seemed to have more time on her hands for some reason. She channelled a lot of energy into her work, occasionally stabbing right through the sheets of lino and imagining Michael's sensitive parts under the roller as she worked the heavy press.

# Chapter 3: An Unexpected Proposal

It was the beginning of November and Rachel was busy completing orders for her regular customers. That morning, she decided to drop off a box of small framed prints and greetings cards at Jolies Cadeaux in Dreste. After the usual polite chitchat the shop's owner, Madame Piquot, caught her firmly by the wrist.

"It is time for lunch. Come with me."

Rachel was surprised. She knew Madame Piquot quite well, having supplied the gallery for many years, but they had never socialised. Now, Madame indicated to her assistant that she was going out and led Rachel to a quiet restaurant in the next street.

The owner greeted her warmly and led the women to what was clearly Madame's usual table in the window, from where they could watch the world go by.

"Pastis for Madame and what may I bring the young lady?"

Rachel didn't really like the old-fashioned aperitif with its strong anise flavour, having got very drunk on it with Michael many years before, but she ordered one to be polite.

The two women sipped their drinks and Rachel ate an olive and looked across the square aimlessly, wondering what Madame wanted to speak to her about. After several minutes of silence, she couldn't bear it any more.

"Madame, is there something you wanted to say to me?" She suddenly felt anxious. "Is there a problem with my work?"

Monique Piquot put down her glass and looked at her steadily.

"There is nothing wrong with the work, my dear. But I am worried about you."

"Worried? About me?" This was not at all what Rachel had expected to hear.

"I can see from the prints that you are not happy."

Rachel looked puzzled and said nothing, waiting for her to go on.

"Your work has taken a somewhat, let's say 'Gothic' turn lately. Fortunately people like black and white prints, and your starlings and crows are very striking."

Rachel ran through some of the recent work in her mind's eye and had to concede that she had become rather fond of stormy skies, jagged mountains and black, silhouetted birds. She bit her lip, but before she could speak Madame went on.

"The work is strong, but it is not … " she looked up to the ceiling, searching for the word. "The pictures are not *joyeux*." She raised her hands as if grabbing something. "Your work used to be joyous!"

Rachel felt her throat tighten and feared she was going to cry. Madame Piquot saw this and patted her hand.

"You have had a difficult time, I know."

Rachel never discussed her personal life with any of her customers, but Dreste was a small town and

Madame Piquot was at the centre of it. As well as the gallery, she also ran a *pension* that was always full of regular guests who loved its old-fashioned charm. With all her contacts, it was inevitable she would have heard about Michael and the new baby.

"I have a proposal for you." Madame waved over the waiter and ordered a carafe of chilled rosé wine and two omelettes. Rachel had an agonising wait until their meal was brought out and Madame was ready to continue with her speech.

"I can no longer manage the gallery and the *pension*. My guests are always delightful – I choose them well – but I am too old to be nice to people all the time."

Rachel nibbled on a rocket leaf, intrigued by what was to come. Madame took a dainty sip of wine and nodded to a passing gentleman. "Your house would be perfect."

Rachel was puzzled. "Perfect for what, Madame?"

Monique raised her eyebrows as if she had made herself quite clear.

"Perfect as a *pension*," she said at last. "The house is a good size, the village is not too far from town and my guests would find it charming." She smiled at the young waiter who tipped the last of the rosé wine into their glasses and refreshed the bread basket. "And – most importantly of all," she added, waggling one immaculately polished nail under Rachel's nose, "it will bring you joy."

* * *

After lunch Rachel wandered around town and attempted to do some shopping, but found it hard to concentrate. Her imagination had been fired up and her head was spinning with questions about the *pension*. Madame was right: she had fallen into a rut with her work and what she needed probably was a brand-new project. But, what did she know about running a guesthouse? "Precisely nothing," she said to herself.

On the other hand, how hard could it be? She had plenty of experience skivvying for her own household, after all. "Paying guests" would bring fresh, exciting people into her life – and keep the coffers topped up. She couldn't depend on Michael forever, especially now he had a new family to support, she thought ruefully.

What she needed was a second opinion. As the town hall clock chimed the quarter, she realised that she had time to drop in on a friend before collecting the children.

A former catwalk model, Philippe had retired when he hit thirty and work started to dry up. He retrained as a florist and now ran a shop that made beautiful floral arrangements and, at certain times of the year when business was slow, he also did some light gardening for a select bunch of clients. Rachel was lucky enough to be one of the chosen few. They had gradually come to know each other as they worked side by side to create an approximation of an English garden in a corner of her otherwise ungovernable plot of land.

The shop was empty as she went in, the old-fashioned doorbell tinkling behind her. Philippe put down the bouquet he was making and wiped his hands on his apron before greeting her with three kisses.

"So, what's up?" He looked her up and down. "You look different."

Rachel dropped her bags on the floor and slumped into a chair by the counter. "I've just had the most wonderful lunch," she said, kicking off her shoes.

Philippe raised a quizzical eyebrow. "With a man?"

"Good heavens, no," she said laughing. "With Madame Piquot and she has given me a great idea. Actually, it was all her idea, but I think it could be great for me, for us and ..."

"Wooah! Hold on. Let me make some coffee, then you can tell me all about it."

"Okay, but hurry up!"

Rachel played with a ball of raffia and thumbed a magazine, impatient for Philippe to return so she could tell him the news.

It seemed an age before he reappeared with two tiny cups of strong coffee and a plate of petit fours. "I'm ready – tell all."

It didn't take Rachel long to outline Monique Piquot's startling suggestion. "So? What do you think?"

Philippe said nothing for a moment, just looked thoughtfully at her as he sipped his drink.

"I think it could be exactly what you need, though we'll have to do something about the lower garden and the pots on the terrace will need refreshing."

"You're teasing me now!"

"Not at all. I think it's a great idea."

"Really? Could I really do it, do you think?" Rachel had risen to her feet and was anxiously picking the petals off a gerbera.

"Oh!"

"Sorry!" She put the flower back with the others on the counter and sat down guiltily, chewing on her nails instead.

"Of course you could do it – your home is like a guesthouse anyway, with the children, their friends and your visitors from England."

"That's true, but I couldn't expect paying guests to put up with Pokémon bed linen, creaky beds and cupboard drawers that come apart in your hands," she said, nibbling on a biscuit. "Do you think anyone would come? We are in the middle of nowhere."

Philippe smiled. "I think in a brochure they would call that rustic charm in a tranquil location." Rachel looked at him doubtfully. "Which is not to say that you won't have to make a few tiny improvements here and there."

Rachel stared out of the window at the shoppers going by. There were definitely a few tourists among them, come to visit the medieval church and walk the city walls. Some also hired cars to visit the local villages, including Pelette.

"I suppose I have nothing to lose. And I can bribe the kids to help get everything ready." She looked at her watch. "Anyway, I'd better go. It's nearly chucking-out time at school."

Philippe embraced her again and opened the door onto the street.

"Thanks so much," she said, manoeuvring past him with her shopping bags. "I think I'm probably definitely going to do it."

He laughed. "Let me know what you decide and I'll come over to the house and attack that wilderness of yours."

She smiled and attempted a wave as she ran backwards along the road. "How are you with a paint-brush?" she asked.

Philippe raised a perfectly groomed eyebrow in a way that conveyed deep disdain. "Terrible. I leave all the DIY to my darling Albert, but there's no one better with a trowel and a pot of pelargoniums."

"In that case, it's a definite maybe."

Leaving the shop, Rachel collected the car and drove around to the school where Alice and Charlie were lolling around with their friends on opposite sides of the road. Her children tolerated each other – much like the cats – but were not exactly the best of friends. Rachel hoped they would become closer when they were older, just as she and her brother Henry had done. He had moved to the States some years before, which improved their relationship no end.

Rachel waited until they'd got through the school traffic and were heading towards Pelette before mentioning the guesthouse to the kids.

"So what do you reckon?"

"Cool."

"That's it? 'Cool'?"

Charlie shrugged without lifting his eyes from the game on his phone.

"And what do you think?" she asked her daughter, who was curled up in the front seat next to her. "Is it cool with you?"

Alice had her eyes fixed on the dusty road that headed out of town and up the hill. Eventually, a similarly Gallic shrug came from the girl, who was pulling dark blonde curls between her fingers and watching them bounce back in place.

"What does Dad say?"

Rachel sighed and fixed her eyes on the road. "I

haven't spoken to Dad yet." And he was far too obsessed with the baby business, though she didn't want to say that. "Anyway, I wanted to see what you two thought of the idea first."

"But it's his house," said Charlie from the back seat.

"Yes, yes it is. Partly. But it's your home." Rachel could feel some of the earlier enthusiasm start to fade. "And Dad wants us to be happy."

They drove on a little further in silence apart from the crunching and pinging of stones hitting the car.

"Okay."

Rachel looked at her daughter. "Okay?"

"If Dad says it's okay, then okay."

Rachel turned and smiled. "That's great. Good. Cool!" She felt relieved and surprised by how much the guesthouse scheme had come to matter to her in just a few short hours. "I'll ring Dad later and see what he says. I'm sure it won't be a problem."

She waited until after supper, when Charlie was out at a neighbour's and Alice had retreated to her room, before ringing Michael. She said she had something to ask him and could he come over for coffee to discuss it?

The next morning he turned up at the house looking tanned and relaxed with a big grin on his face. The baby had been born a week before and it was clear that he was still full of adrenaline. Rachel could see it was a good time to speak to him about the guesthouse because all his attention was focused on becoming a father again.

After she had listened to a full report about the health and well-being of the new arrival, Rachel outlined the plan.

"I think that's a marvellous idea, Rach," said Michael, beaming. "It will give you something to do when the children are at school."

"You mean apart from painting my toenails and watching daytime television?" God, he was infuriating. "I do already run a business you know!" Rachel was trying – and failing – to keep her temper. "You really can be a patronising bastard sometimes."

No one admired Rachel's prints and paintings more than Michael, but he worried about her financial sense: she was successful but he had always managed the money aspect for her. He was also very good at the promotional side of things and every home they went into seemed to have a print of hers on the wall or a greetings card propped up on a bookshelf.

Some years before, Michael had even got Rachel a commission to do some book illustration, but that work had dried up when the publishers turned to artists who could create designs on a computer more quickly and cheaply than she could manage on paper.

"My work is important enough to feature in *Belle Dimanche* magazine or have you forgotten that?"

Michael's smile indicated that he hadn't forgotten it and was still amused – as they had both been at the time – by the description of her as a leading British artist who had been compelled to move to France because of the superior food and weather. In fact, Rachel had never worked as a print-maker in England, but the magazine was not about to let facts stand in the way of a good story.

"That is not what I meant and you know it," he said, soothingly. "I just think it would do you good to have a new focus in your life."

Can this man be any more patronising, she asked herself. Yes he can, she thought, as he patted her hand and smiled his drippy smile.

"And I will help, of course," he added. "Once the baby is a little bit older and life has got back to normal again."

My goodness, you really have no idea, Rachel thought to herself. Instead she smiled and poured him more coffee. "That's a very kind offer, but I think Amelie might need you more than I do."

Michael shook his head and looked serious. "This is important for you and the children, Rach, and I won't let you down."

She couldn't help herself as the word "Again" slipped from her lips. Michael looked hurt.

"Okay, sorry! Thanks for the offer. I'm sure we'll be fine, but it's good to know you're prepared to help in between changing nappies and wiping up sick."

Michael chuckled. "You forget that I have been through it before."

He really was exasperating. "I'm hardly likely to forget! I was there, too, remember?"

"What I mean to say is that I've got experience of the whole baby thing, so nappies hold no fear for me."

Rachel could tell nothing was going to dent his conviction that he was going to sail through late fatherhood unscathed and still have the time and energy to help his ex with a brand-new venture. She decided to smile sweetly and say nothing.

Taking her smile as a sign of encouragement, he kissed her, swallowed the last of his coffee and drove back to Amelie and the baby.

# Chapter 4: Summer 1997

After Michael had driven off, Rachel sighed as she picked up the coffee things and put them in the dishwasher. Drying her hands, she noticed a photo at the back of the dresser, where it had slipped under a shelf and was half hidden behind some mugs. Somehow it had survived the whirlwind that had followed Michael's desertion of her, when she had flown through the house, tearing up photos and throwing mementoes into a black bin bag before hurling them into the dustbin.

She picked up the photo and peered at it. It showed her and Michael standing by a pile of rocks in a field, squinting into the sunshine. They were both wearing grubby jeans and Michael had his long blond hair – now long gone – tied into a low pony tail and was holding a scythe. She was wearing a floral top and gardening gloves and was smiling at the camera. Before she turned over the photo to check the date, she knew what it would say: "Summer 1997".

She had met Michael in her early twenties when they were both on their gap years. Unlike many of her friends who had gone off to Thailand and India, Rachel had decided to stay in Europe and work on her French.

Michael, who had embraced the "drink-your-way-around-the-world" option with gusto, washed up broke in Marseille and was gradually hitching back across Europe to Yorkshire. He had got as far as Chevandier when he heard that locals in a nearby village had received funding to restore their medieval walls and were looking for willing volunteers to help in return for living expenses, food and the corner of a warm barn to sleep in.

Rachel had signed up because she was interested in history and decided that it would look good on her CV to have been involved in a community project. Their companions were an assortment of other young Europeans, one or two local kids and an American pretending to be Canadian. As the only Brits on the project, they naturally fell in together and Rachel provided Michael with a shoulder to cry on when his then-girlfriend dumped him for one of the East Germans in the group.

They all worked side by side under the direction of Guillaume, a civil engineer who broke a few hearts that summer. They rose early to clear the ground and move stones before the sun got too hot, swam in the slightly smelly pond in the afternoons and had long political discussions in a mixture of languages over campfires in the evening.

It was here that Rachel discovered her talent for drawing and she would often wander off with a sketchbook and some watercolour crayons to capture an especially beautiful sunset.

. Sometimes Michael would join her, which she put up with so long as he promised not to chatter. He was fascinated by Rachel's intense concentration as she captured a scene in a few fluid marks. When she was satisfied with the work, they would walk back to the group and sit and smoke and – if they had any money – split a pack of beers.

It was Michael who first realised that he was in love. They had been clearing nettles and pulling out weeds near a particularly crumbly section of the wall when a large stone broke free and grazed the length of Rachel's shin. Her cry of pain and alarm cut Michael to the core and he had an intense feeling that he wanted to protect her.

At the time, this had involved running to fetch Guillaume and helping to carry Rachel to the village café where she was numbed with brandy as pieces of grit were carefully extracted from her damaged leg with tweezers.

By late August, the project was coming to an end and everyone was making plans: the East Germans were getting a train to Prague; the American was heading north to start a postgraduate degree at the Sorbonne; the Spanish boys had linked up with the Austrian girls and were all going south to find bar work at the coast.

Rachel didn't know what she was going to do, but she knew she wasn't ready to go back to England – not yet, at least. She didn't know what Michael's plans were. Since the accident his behaviour towards her had changed – he had become distant and no longer joined her when she went drawing. She was sad and puzzled that Michael now avoided her, realising how much she missed his friendship.

It was a fortnight after the accident when he came to search her out where she was trying to paint the lichens that grew over the famous wall. Her heart skipped as he came bounding over, assuming it was to say his goodbyes. Instead, without saying a word, he grasped her by the shoulders and kissed her full on the mouth. Startled, she pulled back, gasping.

"Michael, what are you doing?"

He had stepped back and was pacing up and down with his hands on his hips.

"I've figured out what was wrong with me," he said, dragging his hand through his hair. "It's because I love you. I'm sorry, I didn't know and then ..." He broke off to kiss her again, "... and then, you had the accident and I couldn't bear it."

He smiled and frowned and kissed her once more, and this time she didn't pull away.

"You've done something to me, Rachel."

He looked at her the way he had never looked at her before, as though he was trying to commit every detail of her eyes, her mouth, her nose, her skin to memory. Then he threw his head back and laughed. "I love you!"

Rachel couldn't help laughing as well, as relief and excitement and surprise bubbled up inside her.

"Well, I am pretty fond of you, too, of course."

For a second, Michael looked anxious. "You do love me, don't you? I don't think I could hack it if you didn't feel the same."

She put her hands to his face and kissed him gently. "Do you know what? I think I might love you, too."

With that, she took his hand and led him to a barn at the edge of the sunflower fields where they made love on a pile of canvas sacks until evening fell and the bats began to swoop and dive above their heads.

Now, as she stood in the kitchen with the photograph in her hands, she wondered what would have happened if she had gone back home the way she should have done. Lots of girls in her situation had fallen in love during their gap years, but most of them did the sensible thing and returned to their normal lives.

Instead, she and Michael had decided to stay in France at the end of the project. She managed to blag her way into a college that taught English to local business people and he got a job as an assistant in the estate agents he would eventually own. They stayed in Pelette and bought an empty farmhouse for peanuts from Monsieur Seurat and set about restoring it with the help of friends they had made in the village.

The first winter had not been easy, but they were young enough to enjoy reading by the warm glow of paraffin lamps and washing in water hauled from the well, carried with chattering teeth back to the house and warmed on top of a wood burner.

To begin with, some of the locals had kept their distance, sure that the young couple would give up and go home. But eventually, seeing how determined the pair were, their neighbours had dug around in their attics for unwanted furniture to help the couple to furnish the place. The result was what Rachel's friends in England were calling "shabby chic", although at her house the emphasis was very much on the shabby.

Their daughter Alice had come along almost immediately and Charlie followed a couple of years later. Having two small children at home made it difficult for Rachel to work every day at the college. It was then that Michael suggested she sell her sketches.

She had started in a small way, selling bits and

pieces in the village shop. The turning point had been when Michael came home one evening with the postmaster, Monsieur Lambert, in tow. Beaming from ear to ear, Michael had explained that he had encountered George Lambert on his way to the municipal tip with a hand-printing press and had offered to take it off his hands for 300 francs. Rachel had thrown her arms around Monsieur Lambert's neck and kissed him, making him blush with pleasure.

Rachel's eyes watered and she felt a lump in her throat. Where had the time gone? That must have been at least ten years ago. And how had she let them drift apart when she and Michael had been such good friends and passionate lovers?

A persistent tap, tap, tap on the kitchen door brought her back to reality and she wiped her eyes on a tea towel.

"What's done is done, eh ladies?" she said to the chickens as she slid the photo into a drawer, put a bowl with kitchen scraps into her basket and walked out into the garden.

Standing by the coop, feeding the chooks, she could see the roof of a small red car as it wound its way up the road towards the house. It was driven by a smart woman in her fifties who waved a lazy arm out of the car window as she screeched to a halt in the courtyard.

"What's this I hear about babies?" she shouted, before switching off the engine.

Wiping her nose, Rachel smiled and walked over. "It's true. Michael is a daddy again. Little Olivier has made his appearance and mother and baby are both doing well, so I'm told."

Margot got out of the car and hugged her friend. "And how are you?"

Rachel shrugged. "Oh, you know. I'm fine. Come in and have tea and I'll tell you all about it."

"And cake," added her friend, holding up a box from the local patisserie.

Margot was one of Rachel's oldest friends. She and her husband Hervé had bought a house in the village from Michael, soon after he had taken over the estate agency business. They had moved down from Normandy with their two boys and completely transformed the crumbly old house into a warm, welcoming home. Then, six months after the work was completed, they were out hiking when Hervé dropped dead from an undiagnosed heart condition.

The two families were already close and Michael had felt terribly guilty, as if it was entirely his fault that Hervé had left the rolling fields of the north for the hillier country of the Rhône-Alpes.

Her friends had expected Margot to pack up and head back to Caen, but the boys had already settled at school so they all stayed put. She was an attractive woman and over the years Margot had had affairs but had never remarried. Recently, she had developed a steely demeanour that some people found off-putting, but underneath it she was kindness itself and Rachel counted her among her closest friends. She found Margot's hard-bitten attitude a healthy counterpoint to Jilly's determined optimism. Despite their different approaches to life, the three women were good friends and it was Jilly who had sent Margot over to see how Rachel was coping with news of the baby's arrival.

Once inside the house, Margot went straight to the dresser, selected some plates and carefully lifted the delicate cakes from their box. "So. Tell me everything."

Rachel put out the tea things and cutlery. "Ooh, bagsie the apricot tartelette."

"All in good time, my dear. Bring me up to date with the news first." She looked at her friend and frowned. "Have you been crying?"

Rachel nodded, opened the drawer and placed the photo of the smiling young couple on the table.

Margot picked it up and studied it. "You and Michael, I assume?"

"I just found it and it got me thinking again about us and where I went wrong."

Margot sighed. "You didn't go wrong, Rachel. You just grew up and grew apart. Take this," she said, handing her a plate.

Rachel put the fruit tart on her plate, licking her fingers. Margot selected a chocolate millefeuille. For a moment, the women were silent while they teased apart the pastries with their forks.

"So, go on."

Rachel took a sip of tea and wiped a buttery flake from her lips. "I know you're right. People change over time."

"But?"

"But I still feel it was my fault that I couldn't hold things together."

Margot added a pink macaron to her plate and sighed. "Utter nonsense."

Rachel grabbed a mini éclair. "Is it? My life is a complete disaster area while Michael's has just started all over again."

Margot put down her napkin with an air of exasperation. "You are responsible for your own happiness, Rachel – no one else. You must stop feeling sorry for yourself."

Rachel paused with her fork midair, shocked by her friend's sharp tone.

Margot patted her hand. "Forget Michael," she added, more gently. "He has a new life now and you know what they say: you won't find the right love until you let go of the wrong one."

"Who says that?"

Margot shrugged and took a sip of Earl Grey. "I read it in a magazine at the dentist's. But it's true – it's time for you to go back out into the world."

"And find a new love, just like that?"

"Maybe not love, not at first anyway. But a new man, for sure."

"Ha! Where am I going to find one of those in Pelette? The only available men around here are single for a good reason."

"That, my dear, I will leave to you. Now, would you like to share the fig tartelette?"

"Where do you put it all?" asked Rachel, laughing.

Margot looked at her flat stomach. "It's a matter of evolution. Over many centuries, we French have developed the ability to eat patisserie and not gain weight. Of course, being perennially anxious and smoking too much also helps."

Rachel patted her belly. Although splitting from Michael had taken pounds off her, she was still curvier than Margot who was all smooth lines and sharp edges. "I guess I'm not anxious enough."

"I'm very glad to hear it."

"But you are right, Margot …"

"When am I not?" she responded with a shrug, placing a sliver of tart on each of their plates.

"It's time I gave up on Michael and made a new start."

"*Très bien*. Now eat."

After Margot had gone and Rachel was back in her studio, she thought about what they had discussed. "Damn it, Fudge. If Michael can have a brand-new life, then so can I."

The cat paused from cleaning its belly and looked at her with its amber eyes. "I can tell you agree," said Rachel. "So that's what we're going to do: open a guesthouse and – just maybe – find ourselves a new man."

# Chapter 5: At the Picture-framer's

Since her discussion with Madame Piquot, Rachel had had a burst of energy and created a new batch of work including sun-baked landscapes and images of cats with eyes the colour of sea glass that she knew people loved.

There was too much for her to frame herself, so she decided to take it to Monsieur Callot's shop. She loved her visits to the picture-framer's because she knew that, if she was stuck, Bernard Callot would always find just the right mount and frames for her prints. She had been coming to him for years and told anyone who asked that his beautiful frames were responsible for many of her sales.

She went in now, with a portfolio of prints under her arm. She was looking forward to getting Bernard's opinion on the new work she had produced: sinuous trees, mysterious-looking animals and meadows with jewel-like dots of colour that were a far cry from her jet-black rooks.

She was examining the tall rack of mouldings when she heard an unfamiliar voice asking if she needed any help.

She turned, startled by the question – she knew the contents of the shop almost as well as Monsieur Callot did – and by the unknown grey-haired man she saw there. He stood in the doorway to the workroom wearing a red shirt with the sleeves rolled up – despite the chilly weather – under Monsieur Callot's work apron, with a pencil tucked behind one ear. She was so surprised by the presence of a stranger in the shop that she was momentarily lost for words.

"Oh, I came to see Monsieur Callot, to discuss the frames for my new work." She didn't really want to leave all her prints with someone she didn't know. "It's okay, I can come back later."

"I'm afraid he won't be in for a while," said the man, walking into the shop to greet her. "He had an accident and needs to rest for a while." The man saw Rachel's evident alarm. "It's okay – he had a fall and has dislocated his shoulder. He has been told to rest, but he will be back."

He smiled and extended a hand, having first wiped it on his apron. "I'm his nephew, Paul Callot. And you are?"

Rachel shook his hand and introduced herself. "Thompson, Rachel Thompson," she said, digging out a rather dog-eared business card from the depths of her coat pocket.

"Ah, yes. My uncle mentioned you. So, may I see your work?" he asked, pointing at the portfolio she was clutching by her side.

She lifted it onto the workbench and slowly unzipped it, not sure that she wanted to entrust her prints to a stranger.

"It's okay," he said, smiling. "I am a picture restorer, but I also make bespoke frames. My uncle taught me everything I know."

Rachel smiled back, relaxing a little at the thought

that all might not be lost. She lifted out the prints and handed them to Paul Callot who spread them out on the table. She watched him as he rubbed his chin for a moment then went to the plan chest and pulled out different-coloured mounts for her to see.

"I think a dove grey mount for that one, don't you? And perhaps this for the frame," he said, reaching for a length of pale oak.

The new Mr C had a good eye and Rachel found herself nodding in agreement, impressed with his choices. Gradually, they worked through the stack of prints, finding mounts and frames for all of them.

They had pretty much finished when Rachel pulled out a watercolour from the side pocket of her portfolio. It was a seascape she had painted on a visit to England years before and then forgotten about. Finding it again recently, she'd decided it would look nice in one of the guest bedrooms. She hadn't known what to do with it and had intended to ask Monsieur Callot his opinion.

"Ah, that's a tricky one," Paul said now, taking the painting and walking over to the window with it, obviously enjoying the challenge. He put the picture down and rummaged in a drawer by the counter. "What about this?"

Rachel wrinkled her nose when she saw the ruby red mount, thinking that it would overpower the image, but in fact it was perfect. The colour brought out the details on the sides of the boats on the pebbled beach and echoed the flecks of red she had put in the evening sky.

"Gosh – well, I would never have chosen that, but it really works."

He grinned at her. "So, do I get the job?"

"Absolutely."

His eyes crinkled into a smile. "Good! If you're happy to leave everything with me, I'll tot up the costs and let you have a total at the end of the week." He went to the counter and made a note in the diary. "Do you want to come and collect them or shall I deliver them to a gallery for you, Madame Thompson?"

"Call me Rachel, please." Even after all her years in France, she still sometimes found the formal way people addressed each other stifling. "If you could bring them to the house, that would be great."

He looked at the address and frowned.

"You'll have to help me out here," he said, passing a hand through his thick mop of grey hair. "I'm from Paris."

"Oh sure," she said smiling. "It's easy: go twelve kilometres out of town on the Chevandier road, turn right at the Auchan supermarket and continue for about ten minutes. Go left into the village, carry on through and we're past the old mill on the left."

She thought for a second. "Or put the postcode into your sat nav, ignore it when it tries to send you down past the vineyard, take the second turning, come up the hill and ask for us at the *tabac*."

Taking the pencil from behind his ear, Paul frowned as he jotted the instructions in his diary. "Fine. I'll be over in a week or so."

# Chapter 6: Getting Organised

Arriving back in Pelette, Rachel strode into her house determined to sort the place out. How difficult could it be to transform the old farmhouse into a tourist paradise? Having decided that she was going to move into the B&B business, it was time to get organised.

"Right," she said, to no one in particular. "I need to make a list." She dug out a notebook from one of the kitchen drawers. Flicking through it to find a blank page she found an old shopping list:

knickers (Alice)
vodka
white envelopes
cat food
Vaseline (Michael)
Chicken Kievs x 4

She wrinkled her brow, trying to remember why Michael had been in need of Vaseline but failed.

Rummaging around a bit more, she found a pencil and was sitting at the kitchen table chewing it and wondering where to start when Irina came in.

Irina was probably the same age as Rachel, but no one had ever dared ask her. She had turned up at the house after Michael advertised in town for a cleaner. There had been other applicants, but Irina stood out from the pack, and not just because of her hair, which was a fetching shade of aubergine.

Since then it had been jet black and blonde, but was now a less excitable shade, a little like the bottom of a copper pan. To begin with, Michael had held a theory that she was on the run from Russian gangsters. As the family got to know her better, it became clear that Irina was not the kind of person to run from anyone. She was a woman of few words and had the kind of facial expression that said "Don't mess with me".

Over the years, she had acted as nanny, cook, gardener and confidante, as well as cleaner. These additional roles had never been discussed: Irina simply saw a gap and filled it. Because Alice and Charlie had grown up with Irina in their lives, they could curse quite impressively in Ukrainian.

Her relationship with Rachel was half housekeeper, half stern friend. "Tea, Rachel?"

"Ooh, yes please. That's what I need to get the brain cells firing." So far all she had written was "Legal stuff, tax, etc. Ask Michael."

Well, he had said he wanted to help and it was his line of business after all. Michael had made his money selling crumbly ruins to pink-skinned Brits in search of "The Dream" and he was good at it. Clients were inevitably charmed by his genuine enthusiasm for their often bonkers schemes and some of them had become friends of theirs.

"Is short list, Madame," said Irina, peering over Rachel's shoulder as she placed a mug of tea down by her side. "Kiev, beautiful city," she added, before heading back to the utility room and her stack of ironing.

Rachel sighed. This is hopeless, she thought. She grabbed the phone. "Hi Jilly, are you free? I need help!"

When her friend arrived ten minutes later looking perky, Rachel was doodling on the notepad on which she had now added "Buy paint".

"You okay, Rach? You look a bit tense."

"I'm fine," she said, nodding towards the utility room. "It's just … well, you know."

"Ah, enough said." Jilly smiled. She knew what Rachel meant. Skinny and fierce, Irina could be an unnerving presence. She was able to convey the impression that she didn't approve of whatever it was you were doing by the subtlest of signs. However, she was a boon to the household as well as a staunch friend who saw it as her duty to defend Rachel in her new single life.

"Shall we get started, then?"

"Sure. Er, what do you suggest?"

Having worked with Michael for a while, Jilly knew a thing or two about how to present houses. She now ran a shop selling "antique" furniture to incomers looking for period charm.

"I think we should walk through the house and make notes of what needs doing."

"Splendid! That's just what I thought," said Rachel, handing the notebook to her friend and leading the way out of the kitchen and up the stairs to the top of the house.

The building was in two parts, shaped like an "L". The shorter section of the "L" was where the kitchen and the small sitting room were. Above, were the family bedrooms. The other, larger part of the house had become somewhere for the kids to play when they were little, a storage area and emergency accommodation for guests who didn't mind saggy mattresses and cobwebs.

A walk through the house revealed that the "Big End", as it was known, was in reasonable condition but full of stuff. Rachel's heart sank as the list of accumulated junk lengthened, but Jilly bounced from room to room opening the shutters and cooing over the space and the light, just like the estate agent she used to be.

After half an hour, the notepad was full and Jilly was looking pleased with herself. "It's really not that bad, Rachel. What you need to do is throw away anything that's broken, dust the beams and titivate the old furniture," said Jilly, investigating a wonky chair. "Then, you give everything a good scrub and a coat of white paint and you'll be all set."

Looking around, Rachel was beginning to see that Jilly might have a point. The whole building had been properly renovated when they'd bought it; it had just been unloved for rather a long time.

"For example," said Jilly, warming to her theme, "this room would make a lovely guest bedroom and you could put an extra bathroom over there in the old dressing room."

Rachel looked at her doubtfully. "Won't that cost lots of money?"

Jilly sighed. "You have to 'speculate to accumulate' as they say. And I'm sure one of Irina's cousins could sort it out for you fairly cheaply."

Irina had a never-ending supply of relatives who had pretty much cornered the market in plumbing.

"Here you go," said Jilly, handing the stack of neatly written lists to Rachel, who flipped through them, reading. "Bedroom 1: fit bathroom, replace shutters, mend gap in floor, repaint windows." She looked up. "I'd better ask Irina to bring the whole family round."

Jilly laughed. "They're the best. You won't regret it."

* * *

Rachel set out her plans for the guesthouse on the phone to her father that evening. "So there you are, Dad – I'm going to be a landlady. Do you think I'm mad?"

Harold went quiet for a moment, obviously mulling the idea over in his head. "No, I think it sounds like a super plan, darling."

Rachel had always been close to her father and they had taken to speaking on the phone every day after her mother Jean had died. These conversations had become less frequent since Harold had found what his grandchildren referred to as "lurve" with Connie. One of the many things the pair had in common was children who had spent time in France, although Connie's daughter, Eleanor, had gone back to England after a year or so.

"You don't think I'd be taking on too much, then?" asked Rachel. "On my own, I mean." She could hear muffled voices at the end of the phone and knew that Harold was conferring with Connie.

"If you open a guesthouse, sweet pea, it will be number one in all the travel guides before you know it."

Rachel could hear more mutterings as her father turned away again.

"And we'll come and help, you know. We're good at decorating and Connie makes wonderful breakfasts."

Rachel smiled to herself and wanted to cry a little bit at the same time.

"Thanks Dad – and Connie," she shouted down the phone. "I appreciate that vote of confidence."

"Okay darling. Just let us know if there's anything you need. Better go now. Connie's making margaritas to get us in the mood for our salsa class."

Rachel chuckled and wiped a tiny tear from the corner of her eye – whether it was of sadness or amusement at the picture of her octogenarian father shimmying across the dance floor in his Cuban heels, she wasn't sure.

Her parents had known Michael almost as long as she had, and Harold had been hurt and disappointed when he had left the family "in the lurch". Her brother Henry had snorted and pronounced Michael a prat.

She was glad that her mother hadn't been around for the break-up, though she knew Jean would have been fascinated to see how Michael was dealing with his second go at fatherhood.

It was time for an early night – she had a major sorting-out project ahead of her.

# Chapter 7: Operation Guesthouse

Rachel had lined up a gang of people to help with the clear-out that weekend. She had promised to lay on sandwiches and beer for willing volunteers and was offering cold hard cash for the Ukrainians and her children, who were less easily bribed with food.

It was 8am on Saturday morning and Rachel was ready for action. She had donned an old pair of shorts and a shirt and had her hair twisted up under a scarf to protect it from the dust. She looked at her watch and frowned – where was everyone?

Just as she was thinking that no one was going to come, the throaty rumble of a vehicle cheered her up. Irina had arranged for her "cousins", Alexei and Gregor, to supply some muscle and make a start on the repairs. The two of them appeared now in an ancient pick-up truck, ready to remove any broken furniture. Their exact relationship to Irina, much like everything else about her, was a mystery.

Alexei was in his twenties, stick thin and – Rachel couldn't help noticing – rather attractive, though far too young for her. Gregor was a much older man, with an impressive moustache and a dour expression.

Hand in hand behind them came Jilly and Thierry, her drop-dead gorgeous husband who, according to Michael, had the brain power of a gnat with dementia. Rachel sniggered to herself at Michael's *bons mots*.

He, too, had offered to help in Operation Guesthouse, but she had turned him down – this was her new venture, after all.

After everyone had exchanged greetings, Rachel brought out coffee and they discussed tactics whilst munching on the buttery croissants and warm rolls that Jilly had brought from the village *boulangerie*.

Rachel had decided that she was going to empty her storeroom then help Irina with general cleaning duties; Jilly volunteered to paint and make notes of how they might "dress" the rooms later, and Thierry was going to join Alexei and Gregor in humping furniture and doing DIY.

Armed with Marigolds, bin bags, dusters, paintbrushes and assorted tools, Rachel and her trusty helpers trooped off into the Big End.

Rachel headed upstairs to one of the smaller bedrooms that had become a storage room for her kit. It had – she now realised – been years since she had looked at the contents. Rootling through the drawers and dusty shelves, she found broken tools, dried-up tubes of paint, ancient reference books and prints that hadn't quite worked but that she had fully intended reusing one day. These she carefully put in a box, but the rest was junk.

"Right," she said. "It's time to say goodbye to this lot."

It was quite liberating, she decided, chucking broken odds and ends into a bin bag then hurling the bags out of the window into the courtyard, causing the chickens to squawk and scatter in alarm.

Next door, Thierry cranked up the radio and sang along tunelessly as he mended wobbly shutters and Alexei carried broken chairs down to the truck.

After about an hour of activity, Alice appeared from her room, looking bleary-eyed and grumpy.

Rachel looked over and smiled. "You're up nice and early! Have you come to help?"

Her daughter grunted. "S'pose I might as well. I can't sleep with all that noise going on."

The raucous tones of Alexei and Thierry could now be heard singing along to a U2 classic in the next room: "With or without you, ooh ooh!"

Rachel grimaced, "I don't think Bono has anything to worry about."

"Who?"

"He was a singer in the olden days," she said, handing Alice a stack of cardboard boxes and a duster. "Give those books a wipe and put them in the boxes, love."

When the shelves had been cleared, she got out a screwdriver and dismantled them for Alexei, who had offered to carry away the bulky furniture. With his dark eyes and high cheekbones, he was the male version of Irina who appeared now and shooed him out of the room with her mop.

Empty, with the wooden floorboards shiny and clean, the room looked quite respectable. When they had originally restored the house, she and Michael had decided to leave some of the walls unplastered, so the original stone was visible. Now, Rachel walked around the room stroking the pale stones. She called Jilly up to see it.

She looked around approvingly. "Lovely!"

A curly head appeared around the door: Charlie had risen.

"Mum, I'm hungry."

"There's food in the fridge and Irina will be making sandwiches for the workers later."

Charlie frowned, evidently trying to make sense of this information and failing. "Workers? Er, why is everyone here?" He went around the room, submitting to a kiss from Jilly and a hug from Irina.

Rachel sighed. "I told you last night. Our friends have come to help me – help us – turn this end of the house into somewhere fit for human habitation."

He shrugged. "I like it the way it is."

"You might like it all dusty, dirty and full of broken bikes, but it won't do for paying guests."

Alice rolled her eyes. "He is such a slob."

Turning, Charlie acknowledged his sister's presence by sticking out his tongue and blowing a raspberry.

"Come and have some croissants," said Jilly, handing her paintbrush to Rachel and whisking the boy away before he got a sharp slap from his sister.

"And don't disappear," Rachel shouted after him. "You promised to help, remember?"

"Yeah, whatever."

Rachel pulled off her rubber gloves with a sigh. "I think it's time for tea."

Irina nodded. "I put on the kettle."

On her way down to the kitchen, Rachel peeked into the other rooms. In between murdering rock classics, Alexei and Thierry had managed to empty the big bedroom of its furniture and were slapping white paint on the walls and ceiling.

"Wow, this is looking great!"

Alexei's dour face broke into a smile, enhanced by one gold tooth. "Rachel, we do good work for you."

"You certainly do. Come and have a cup of tea."

Gregor appeared from the bathroom where he'd made a start on the new fittings. The cousins exchanged glances. "Is best we finish the job, I think."

"Or perhaps you'd prefer a beer?" she suggested.

Thierry shrugged and came down from the ladder while Alexei treated Rachel to another flash of his golden gnasher.

Gregor nodded. "For a beer we can stop."

Everyone downed tools and went out onto the terrace with mugs of tea or bottles of cold beer. Alexei went indoors to chat to Irina who was slicing ham for the baguettes.

Thierry had found a football and he, Gregor and Charlie were having a knockabout in the courtyard.

"I think there's a bit of a 'bromance' going on between your husband and the Ukrainians," Rachel said to Jilly over biscuits.

Jilly laughed. "They've bonded over football and soft rock."

Alexei came out of the kitchen with trays piled high with baguettes stuffed with ham, cheese and pungent local salami, salads and olives. Irina followed him out with jugs of apple juice and more beers. Everyone grabbed some lunch and found a comfortable spot for a snooze. No one was prepared to work through the middle of the day, even in November.

It was a couple of hours before the gang got back to their feet and returned to their duties. By the end of the day, all of the rooms had been cleaned, work on the new bathroom was going well and the whole of the upstairs had been painted. Rachel was amazed by what they had achieved in such a short space of time.

The next day, Charlie was dragged out of bed to help Jilly and Thierry to paint the downstairs rooms; Rachel and Alice painted the shutters and the Ukrainians finished the new bathroom.

When they gathered for a celebratory pizza in the village that evening, it was with the feeling of a job well done. Rachel rose to her feet and made a short speech thanking everyone for helping.

Gregor responded with a toast. "We wish you and the children success, health and happiness," he said, as they all raised their glasses.

"Here's to friendship," added Rachel, as they all stood to clink glasses and embrace.

# Chapter 8: Special Delivery

After a call to Rachel to okay the costs of framing her prints, Paul Callot had carried on with the work, promising to deliver everything to her home that week. Rachel was in her studio sorting through the reference books they had found during the clear-out when a blue van with the words "Picture Perfect" emblazoned on its side drew up in the courtyard.

Looking out of the open window, she saw Paul Callot emerge from the vehicle and go to the heavy front door. When she'd first met him at the frame shop she'd guessed he was quite old, but looking at him now she decided that he was probably only in his mid-forties and in pretty good nick. As if feeling her gaze upon him, he looked up and smiled, raising one hand to shade his eyes from the sun.

"Good morning," he said, with a wave. "I hope I've not caught you at a bad time?"

"No worse than usual. I'll be down in a second." She stopped at a mirror on the way downstairs, straightening her shirt and checking her teeth for crumbs from the toast she had just polished off.

Paul could hear the flip, flop of her sandals as she dashed downstairs to the hallway.

"Hi, thanks so much for coming," she said, shaking his hand. "Do you need help bringing in the pictures?"

"Sure, that would be great," he said, heading back

to the van, which now had a skinny brown cat on the bonnet. Paul paused to give Fudge a scratch behind the ears before opening up the back.

"I haven't quite finished, but I thought I'd drop this lot off as I was passing." He handed Rachel a box and took a second, larger one himself.

"I love getting work back," she said. "It feels like Christmas every time." Rachel led the way through the sitting room and upstairs to her studio.

"Nice space," said Paul, glancing around the bright room with its windows that looked out over the garden and sunflower fields beyond.

"It was a sitting room, but I commandeered it so I could concentrate on my work."

"Good choice," he said nodding.

They took out the prints and stacked them on the work bench.

She lifted each of them up and held them against the wall. "I'm really hoping these will help to give the guest rooms a more homely feel."

"I'm sure they will."

Rachel carefully examined each of the prints, occasionally stopping to rub a finger along a frame or tilt the work towards the window to catch the light. It was almost as if she was seeing each print for the first time and she was quite absorbed.

Paul leant against the bench, watching her for several minutes with a half-smile on his face, then looked at his watch. "Well, if you're happy with everything, I'll leave you to it."

"Oh, I'm sorry! I didn't mean to ignore you. The work always looks so different, so much better when it's been framed." She smiled. "I was just thinking about which print I should put where." She looked at him thoughtfully for a moment. "I don't suppose you'd like to look at the guest rooms and give me your opinion, would you? Only if you've got time, of course."

Paul looked at his watch again. "I'd like that," he said with a smile.

"Great! Would you like coffee or the tour first?"

"Tour first, I think."

They went from room to room carrying batches of prints and leaning them against walls and placing them on furniture to see what would fit best where. Again, Rachel was impressed with Paul's eye. After half an hour they had found places for all the work he had brought over. Back in the kitchen, he sipped his coffee while Rachel wrote out a cheque , which he slipped into his back pocket.

"You know, if you had a card or a poster for the guesthouse that we could put in the shop, we could perhaps send you some customers."

"Could you? We need everyone to spread the word," said Rachel, chewing her lip. "Madame Piquot is passing on her bookings for the next couple of months, but after that I'm on my own." She looked gloomy. "I suppose I'll have to get a website designed, so new people can actually find us."

Paul smiled. "I might be able to help you there."

"You could, really?"

"Sure. I set up a website for my uncle's shop last week." He dug around in his "man bag" and drew out a shiny new postcard with the framer's website address on it.

"That's very impressive."

He laughed. "Don't be too impressed – it's really simple to do. You just choose a template then upload the images and format the text."

Rachel frowned. "You might as well be speaking Greek – I'm hopeless at that sort of thing."

"If you can take a few photos of the guesthouse and write a short description of what you're offering, directions to the property, that kind of thing, I'll help you put it all together."

"Really? You're a lifesaver."

"Uncle has told me you are one of his oldest customers and that I should do my best to keep you happy." He looked at her with his dark eyes all serious, but she had the distinct impression he was flirting with her.

"Well, that would make me very happy indeed." She opened the front door, admiring his long legs and neat bum as he strolled over to the van.

"Better check underneath for more cats," she said, as Fudge stretched and hopped down from the bonnet.

He raised an eyebrow but turned away, knelt and looked under the van anyway. "All clear."

"You can never be too careful."

Paul smiled, obviously unsure whether she was serious or not. "Let me know when you have something ready for the website and I'll come over if you'd like me to."

Rachel nodded enthusiastically. "Yes please!"

As the van pulled away and trundled off down into the village, Rachel picked up the cat that had ambled over to her. Everything was coming together with the guesthouse and she'd met a man who might yet become a friend. "Things are looking up, eh scraggy?" she said, scratching the scrawny beast under the chin.

\* \* \*

That afternoon, she decided to cycle across the village to meet the children off the school bus. Neither of the kids approved of this motherly attention and Charlie quickly jumped on the bike and peddled away, leaving Rachel to wait for Alice who took ages getting off the bus because she had to say farewell to all the friends she wouldn't see for hours.

The bus was owned and managed as a co-operative and the villagers had a strict rota for who was doing the school run. This week it was the turn of Madame Lambert in the morning and Claude le Taxi in the afternoon.

It was Claude who now gave them a toot as the bus pulled away. As he drove past, he winked and gave Rachel an approving look.

"God, Mum," said Alice. "I wish you wouldn't come out to meet us looking like that. It's *so* embarrassing."

"Everyone should have embarrassing parents. It toughens you up for the future," said Rachel, giving Alice a hug. "You can imagine what I had to put up with from your granddad."

As far as Alice was concerned, her grandfather Harold could do no wrong. Sighing dramatically, she wriggled away from her mother's embrace.

"Anyway," said Rachel, jogging alongside her to catch up. "What's wrong with me today? I think I look perfectly respectable." She looked down at her cotton shirt and trousers, which had barely any paint on them at all.

"Yeah, right. Apart from the fact that everyone can see your underwear."

"What? Nonsense," said Rachel, before patting the back of her trousers.

It was only then that she realised she was wearing her favourite cargo pants, which just happened to have a gaping hole under the left buttock where the fabric had ripped and she had never got round to sewing it up. She blushed inwardly at the thought that Paul Callot would have had a full view of her rear end as he followed her up the stairs to the studio that morning.

"Oh oops!" Pulling down the waistband she saw that, fortunately, she had put on a pair of flowery pants so she was decent. She ran a couple of steps to catch up with her daughter, who was striding ahead, and looped her arm through Alice's.

"It's okay, I'm wearing my best undies so there's no harm done. So, tell me about school."

# Chapter 9: Something in the Post

Madame Piquot had been right: having a major project to focus on helped to lift Rachel out of a rut that she had fallen into without even noticing it. She had been going through the motions, but the fun had gone out of her work. Now, she felt inspired again and keen to get going. At 8am, she went down to the kitchen for coffee and a slice of toast. Irina had collected the post from the box at the end of the drive on her way in and handed it to Rachel who sighed.

"More rubbish," she said, flicking through the brightly coloured stack as she finished her breakfast. "Junk, junk, junk," she said, putting most of it directly into the recycling box. "Oh, what's this? Not junk."

Among the flyers for supermarkets and local traders was a large white envelope with her name and address carefully inscribed on the front.

"How exciting, real post," she said to Irina, turning the envelope over and tearing it open. Inside she found several sheets of paper with lists of names, dates, contact details and notes. She squinted to make out the copperplate handwriting:

*M. & Mme Reiss, 3rd visit, marmalade not Nutella*
*M. Neave, Scottish, 4th visit, snores so put him at the back*
*M. & Mme Holz, 2nd visit, will want breakfast at 6am . . .*

She laughed, waving the pages in the air. "Look Irina, we have the history of everyone who ever stayed at Madame Piquot's guesthouse."

Irina took the pages from her and carefully looked through them before extracting the last one from the pile and holding it out for Rachel to see.

"Your first guests are coming very soon, Madame."

Rachel spluttered with alarm. "What? No, they can't be." She took the paper and scanned the list. "Oh crikey, you're quite right. It says here 'M. & Mme Karlsen, 15–23 November, 2nd visit. Monsieur can't manage stairs.' Can't manage stairs, what are we going to do with him?"

"Bedroom 3, Rachel. On the courtyard."

"You're right, of course," she said, tapping her head. "I must remember that the bike room is now Bedroom 3." She ran her finger down the list.

"There are two more bookings for November then we've got 'Professor Perry, 6–13 December, 1st visit.' The only note Madame Piquot has made about him is that he's an American." She slurped her coffee. "If he's a professor, he's probably ancient and decrepit, too."

She got up from the kitchen table and went to peer at the calendar next to the fridge. "Yikes, 15 November is only a couple of weeks away."

Irina shrugged. "All is ready, Madame. You tell Mr Claude to collect the people from town in taxi and bring them here."

"Yes, I guess so. Unless they're coming by car, in which case they'll need a map and directions. Damn – I'd forgotten the website!"

She grabbed her phone from the bowl by the door and called the number of the picture-framer's shop.

Much to her relief, Paul Callot was there and agreed to come over that evening.

"Perfect!" said Rachel, thinking it would give her time to take the photographs she had promised and then completely forgotten about. "And maybe you can stay for supper?" she added, realising that they hadn't agreed a fee yet and she needed to be nice to him.

"That would be very nice." Paul hesitated for a moment and she could hear him flicking through the pages of his diary. "I think I may try a different route this evening. Last time it was a little scenic, shall we say. So I ignore the vineyard, turn right – then who do I ask for directions if the *tabac* is closed?"

"Oh, it's not that bad really. After the *tabac*, you carry on up the hill past the pizzeria, then go left and carry on for five minutes. If you get stuck, call me and I'll send out a Sherpa."

"A Sherpa? Okay. See you later."

"Right," she said, draining her coffee. "Any idea where my camera is, Irina?"

"In box at bottom of wardrobe, Madame."

"Great," said Rachel. "Better get snapping."

She went from room to room with the camera, opening and closing the shutters, shifting the furniture and moving vases of flowers around to make the place look fresh and inviting. She got quite carried away, snapping views from the balcony of the garden and the surrounding countryside.

In the courtyard, she photographed the chickens and the cats asleep in separate patches of sunlight on the back terrace.

"I take picture of you, Madame?"

"Good heavens, no Irina! No one will want to come if they think I'm in charge."

Irina shrugged, but was not – Rachel noted – disagreeing. "It is normal for you to look like this," she said, indicating her boss's clothes. "You are an *artist*," she added, putting great stress on the last word. Although she wouldn't admit it to Rachel, Irina was actually rather proud of working for her.

Rachel was wearing a long tunic in swirly patterns of purple and green over cropped trousers and had a pair of paint-spattered plimsolls on her brown feet. She plonked the camera into Irina's outstretched hand and sighed.

"Okay, but this is just for us – not the website."

Irina made her move to a sunny spot by the side wall, close to a pot of roses recently planted by Philippe. Rachel held out the hem of her tunic like a little girl in a party frock and pouted at the camera.

"How about this?"

"Very beautiful," said Irina, snapping pictures as her boss leapt around and adopted various silly poses. "You should be a model, Madame."

Rachel laughed. "I think not!" she said, taking the camera. "Right. Better get on. I've got lots to do today."

# Chapter 10: Some Technical Assistance

Back in the studio, Rachel spent the afternoon finalising the drawings for a range of Christmas cards she had designed. At 6pm she stopped and went downstairs to prepare supper. She had decided to make a gigantic lamb casserole for them all. She had just finished and had stashed the pans in the dishwasher when she heard a car on the drive. Looking out, she saw Paul Callot approaching with a bottle of wine in one hand and a flat canvas bag in the other.

"I thought you might like to have this back," he said, handing the bag to her as she ushered him into the cosy sitting room. Taking the bag and peering inside she saw that it contained the small seascape – now with the ruby red mount Paul had picked out and a pale oak frame.

"Goodness, I'd forgotten about this one! It looks lovely," she said, walking around the room with it, holding it against different sections of the wall. "You know, I might keep it for us rather than letting it go to the guests."

He smiled. "I'm glad you like it. I'll have the last couple of pieces ready next week, if that's okay?"

"Sure," she said, thinking it would be nice to see him again. "Shall we get started? I don't want to keep you too long."

Paul shrugged, "I'm all yours."

She led the way to the office where the family computer lived. Paul sat in front of it and opened up the website template he had chosen for Rachel.

"What do you think? Smart isn't it?"

"Wow, yes!" she said, feeling completely out of her depth. "What do we do now?"

"Well, we choose which of your photos to use and put in some words about the guesthouse. You know – where it is, what you offer, costs, contact details, directions," he smiled. "Oh, speaking of which, I wasn't sure that I was on the right road so I asked a guy in the village where you were."

"Really? Who was that?"

"I didn't catch his name."

"What did he look like?"

"Chubby, about sixty, pot-belly, stubble."

"Hmm, that could be half the population of Pelette."

Paul laughed. "He was sitting outside the grocer's shop with an old gentleman in a serge suit." He stroked his chin thoughtfully. "I'd no idea people really wore serge. And they had a three-legged dog with them."

"Oh, that's Fred the Bread, his father Monsieur Bertrand and Fifi."

"'Fred the Bread'? He's the baker, right?"

Rachel smiled brightly and handed him the camera. "You got it. Well, you make a start with this and I'll fetch us a drink. Beer okay?"

"That would be great."

When Rachel returned with their drinks, Paul had all the house pictures on the computer, ready for her to look at. She peered at the screen as the slide show started and the images swept by.

"Kitchen, Bedroom 1, Bedroom 2, view from the balcony, back terrace, chickens, Fudge and Mousey – ooh, better delete those. We don't want to frighten the anti-bird people and cat-phobics."

"I think you should keep them," said Paul, taking a swig from his beer. "It suggests that this is a homely place to stay."

"Hmm, maybe. Ah, here's Bedroom 3, the big courtyard, more chickens. What's next?"

The photos that Irina had taken of Rachel prancing around on the terrace flashed up in front of them.

"Oh, definitely delete those!"

"They're lovely. Keep them," said Paul, putting them into the "Website" folder.

"Are you familiar with the English concept of 'beer goggles'?"

Paul shook his head slowly. "'Beer goggles'? No, I don't think I am," he said, tipping the last of the beer into his mouth. "But another of these small beers would be nice."

"Coming up."

They spent the next half an hour making pages for the website and choosing pictures for each of them.

"It looks great," said Rachel. "We're nearly done!"

"Er, not quite. You have to put some words in yet."

She groaned. "I do pictures. I'm rubbish with words."

"It's not hard. Just tell me about the rooms and I'll write it down."

So that's what they did. They looked at the photographs and Rachel explained which room was which, how many people each of them could take, what the views were like and so on. After another half an hour, they had filled most of the web pages and finished their second beer.

Rachel, who was bored by this time, yawned and stretched. "Thanks so much, Paul. I could never have done it without you."

"Don't thank me yet, you've still got to write a description of the guesthouse for the Home page that will persuade people to choose you."

"Have I? Oh dear." She blew across the top of her empty beer bottle making it whistle and gazed up at the ceiling. "What about 'Nice house in the countryside'?"

Paul frowned. "Don't you think that's perhaps a bit boring?"

"Probably. What about 'Peaceful country retreat'? No, that makes us sounds like Buddhists."

"How about 'Traditional guesthouse in, er ...'?"

"In the middle of nowhere? Hmm, I'm not sure that sounds right either." She peered into her empty bottle. "I'm going to put supper on and get us another drink." As she got up from her chair, she patted him playfully on the thigh. "You carry on."

He gave her an amused look. "Okay boss."

Feeling quite wicked, she skipped down to the kitchen past her son, who was watching a film on TV.

"Will you set the table for me, sweetheart? And tell Alice that supper won't be long. I'm just finishing off with Monsieur Callot."

Charlie grunted, stopped the film and hoisted himself up from the sofa. "Good. I'm starving."

Rachel put the casserole in the oven and kissed her son as she headed back to the office.

"Why are you making that noise?" he asked.

"What noise, love?"

"You're humming."

"Am I?" she laughed. "Yes, perhaps I am."

She was definitely humming when she got back to the office and sat down in her place next to Paul, who was concentrating on the screen.

"Okay, I think I've got it," he said. "'A warm welcome awaits you in rural France'. What do you think?"

Rachel screwed up her face. "It's a bit cheesy, but I guess it will do."

"Let's put it up there for now," said Paul, bending over the keyboard and tapping in the words with two fingers. "You can always change it later." He gave her a sideways glance. "If you can think of anything better, that is."

Rachel reclined in her chair and studied the back of Paul's head, thinking that the separate curls of his hair were the colour of wood ash, ranging from black to the palest of greys. The evening was cool and he had put on a textured purple sweater that reminded her of moorland heather. She was thinking what nice shoulders he had, when he turned and caught her looking at him. He held her glance for a moment with his blue-grey eyes.

"Anything else?"

"Sorry?" she asked, realising that her mind had wandered far away from the matter at hand.

"Is there anything else you'd like to say about the guesthouse? Does it have a name, for example?"

"A name? Golly, I suppose we do need a name." She spun on her chair, biting a nail. "Well, the house is called *Tournesol* – sunflower."

Paul nodded and typed. "'A warm welcome is

guaranteed at the Tournesol Guesthouse.'" Next to it, he put a photo of Rachel in green and purple smiling at the camera.

Rachel laughed. "How could anyone resist that!"

He spun around to face her, his expression suddenly quite serious. "Impossible," he said, quietly.

Rachel felt an unexpected thrill run through her as their eyes met and didn't know what to say.

Paul smiled and clinked his bottle against hers. "Do I get supper now?"

"You do!" she said, coming back to reality. "I hope you like lamb casserole."

"Love it."

Rachel left Paul in the sitting room with Charlie while she went to make a salad. Alice joined her in the kitchen.

"Who's that man?"

"That's Paul Callot from the picture-framer's and he has been helping me with the guesthouse website." Rachel looked nervously across at her daughter. "Is that all right with you?"

Alice shrugged. "Okay."

"Good," said Rachel with a smile. She wasn't sure why she cared what her children thought about Paul, but she did. "Can you call them in, please love?"

Charlie came in with Paul, the two of them in a dense conversation about computer games.

"I'll show you sometime, if you like?"

"That would be great, Charlie. I've heard a lot about RuneScape but I don't know how it works."

Rachel smiled and handed Paul a plate, mouthing a silent "thank you" as she did so.

* * *

After the meal, the children went back to their TV and texting, and the adults lingered at the table, nibbling on hunks of local cheese and finishing the wine.

Paul looked up at the clock. "We're not going to get the map and the pricing information on there tonight, I'm afraid."

Rachel nodded. "I guess I'll manage the rest."

"I don't mean to be rude, but …"

"Okay, okay! I know I'm hopeless." She looked at him, emboldened by the red wine and conversation. "I don't suppose you'd consider coming back to help? For a fee obviously."

He leant back in the chair and raised his glass to her. "For a supper like that and your charming company, I would be very happy to help."

"Good, great," she said, pouring out the coffee and offering him pralines. Was he flirting with her? She looked at the second empty bottle on the table.

"You know, I really can't let you drive home after all the beer and the wine. You are very welcome to stay – I mean, we have plenty of beds," she added, in case he thought she was after him.

Paul hesitated for a moment then smiled and nodded. "If that's no problem, it would probably be wise."

Rachel stood. "Good. Well, pick a bed – er, I mean a room – and I'll just tidy up here."

"Don't go to any trouble. I know the rooms are all set up for your guests. I'll be fine down here."

She was torn between being a generous hostess and the thought of having to strip the brand-new linen off one of the beds and remake the darned thing. Laziness won.

"Well, if you wouldn't mind, the sofa in the sitting room is ever so comfortable ..."

"I wouldn't mind at all. Really."

"And there's a downstairs loo. So, okay," she said, smiling nervously. "I'll bring down some bedding. And something for you to wear."

He caught her by the wrist and gave her a lazy smile. "I'm in your hands."

Blimey, she thought, skipping up the stairs. If the kids weren't here I don't know what might happen. She went to the linen cupboard and pulled out a single duvet, a sheet, pillows, towel and a toothbrush and threw them downstairs to where Paul was waiting.

"Sorry," she said, wrestling with a pillowcase. "This is 'house' bed linen for the kids and me. I'm keeping all the good stuff for paying guests. God, that sounds awful!"

Paul laughed as he stuffed the duvet into its cover. "That's fine. I'm just happy not having to drive home past the local gendarme."

Rachel could have told him that the local gendarme was based sixty kilometres away and only came anywhere near Pelette on high days and holidays, but decided not to.

"I do hope you'll be comfy," she said, dislodging a plastic toy from down the side of the raspberry red sofa as she shook out a sheet and threw down a pillow. "I'm afraid the bed linen is rather garish."

"It's fine, really." Paul lay down on the duvet, his hands folded behind his head. "I'm a big fan of *My Little Pony*."

She handed him one of Michael's old T-shirts to sleep in. "And Metallica?"

"My favourite band."

She laughed. "You are a very easy house guest."

He got up from the sofa and came towards her. She held her breath, half-hoping that he'd press his mouth on hers, but instead she felt his lips against one cheek and then the other, his hands on her arms.

"Goodnight Rachel. And thank you for a very nice evening."

She opened her eyes to find him ever so close. He had taken off his sweater earlier in the evening and she could see one or two curls from his chest through the gap in his shirt.

"Sleep well Paul."

Controlling the urge to grab and kiss him properly, she said goodnight and went upstairs to her room. There, she couldn't sleep for thinking of him lying below her. Okay, the *My Little Pony* bed linen was a bit of a passion killer, but she still felt excited at the thought of a man who wasn't Michael coming into her life.

# Chapter 11: The Morning After

The next morning, Rachel took extra care getting dressed before going downstairs to find her guest. She hesitated at the sitting-room door, wondering whether or not to knock. What was the etiquette when you had a man you barely knew but definitely fancied sleeping on your sofa? What would Paul think if she tapped and opened the door? Yikes – what if he invited her in to join him? Her imagination was running riot. She walked into the kitchen and got a glass, deciding that she really wanted to know whether he was awake or not. She held the glass against the heavy wooden door and pressed one ear to it. She stuffed a finger in the other ear so she could hear better, but it was hopeless: all she could hear was her own heartbeat and the blood swooshing around her body.

"Darn," she muttered, deciding that she would have to be patient and wait for Paul to get up when he was ready. She was just about to tiptoe away, when she remembered the lock low down on the door. Sinking down into a squat, she placed an eye against the keyhole and squinted into the room.

Ahead of her she could see a mound of lurid pink and purple duvet and the sole of one brown foot sticking up over the arm of the sofa. She chuckled at the thought of going in and tickling it, but decided that the sensible thing to do would be to make a big pot of coffee and see if the aroma would lure him out.

"You drop something, Madame?"

Irina's voice at full volume made Rachel swear and topple backwards onto the floor. "Oh, you gave me a fright!" she said, bringing a hand to her chest where her heart was pounding.

Irina stood over her, arms folded across her chest looking a bit miffed. "I wipe the door and I polish the handle every week."

"Your work is immaculate," hissed Rachel, from where she sat with her back against the wall, the empty glass clutched in her hand.

"You have problem with throat, Madame? Your voice is sounding funny."

Rachel patted her throat. "I'm fine, really."

Irina raised one sharply defined eyebrow. "And why you sit on the ground?"

"No particular reason," whispered Rachel, shrugging her shoulders. She then watched in horror as the beautifully polished brass knob slowly turned and the door opened to reveal Paul Callot in Michael's Metallica T-shirt and a pair of blue and white striped boxer shorts.

From her position on the floor, Rachel was at eye level with his shorts. Lifting her gaze to preserve his modesty, she gave Paul a wave in what she hoped was a casual manner.

"Good morning. I hope you slept well?"

Paul looked blearily from Rachel to Irina, who had a barely suppressed smirk across her face. He ran a hand across his chin, which now sported a rather attractive sprinkling of salt-and-pepper stubble. "Are you all right down there?"

Rachel smiled and got to her feet. "Yes, yes. Just checking for, er ..." Her mind went a complete blank as her mouth opened but no words came out. What possible reason was there for her to be on hands and knees directly outside Paul's room?

After what seemed like an age, Irina broke the silence. "Spiders, Madame?"

The woman was worth her weight in gold. "Spiders, yes! I can't stand them, you see," she added, turning to her guest. "Have you met Irina, my wonderful housekeeper?"

Paul extended a hand to Irina, both of them ignoring the fact that he was in his underwear.

Rachel grinned desperately. "Yes, excellent work. There are definitely no spiders to catch down here." She handed the glass to Irina. "Do carry on."

Irina turned and headed back to the laundry room from where she could be heard trying and failing to suppress a laugh.

Rachel got to her feet, dusting off her hands. "Is there anything you need?" she asked brightly. "Coffee?"

"Could I have a shower, perhaps?"

"Sure, help yourself." She pointed him in the direction of the bathroom then went into the kitchen to feed the cats. She stood at the sink, her head in her hands, groaning. "He's going to think I'm completely mad." She sighed deeply. "But we must carry on as normal, pusskins. It's the only way."

Twenty minutes later, Paul came into the room, his damp hair brushed back in unruly strands on his head. He smelled fresh and clean and Rachel had a vision of herself nuzzling his neck. Instead, she smiled and asked him again how he had slept.

"Not too bad, thanks." He dug in his jeans pocket and dug out a plastic soldier and a tiny pink shoe that he placed on the kitchen table. "You might be needing these."

Rachel picked up the shoe and smiled at it. "You know, Barbie has spent years looking for that." Grimacing, she poured them each a coffee. "Oh dear – was the sofa really uncomfortable?"

Paul accepted the mug gratefully and pulled out a chair. "No. Once the cognac kicked in, I was fine."

"Sorry – I should have given you one of the guest rooms."

He gave her a rueful grin. "It was fine. Really. I never sleep well in a strange place."

"Can I make it up to you with an FEB?"

"A 'nefeebie'?"

"FEB – 'full English breakfast'. Speciality of the house."

He shook his head and smiled. "That would be very nice, but I have to get back and open up the shop." He put down his empty coffee mug and stood up. "Thanks for supper and everything. It was fun."

"You're welcome." She chewed her lip, thinking that she really wanted to see him again. "And if you could help me finish the website, I would be ever so grateful. You've seen how useless I am with computers."

"Of course. But perhaps we could do it at my place? If you don't mind the spiders, of course."

She laughed nervously. Had he sussed her out? "Whatever suits you best," she said, leading the way to the front door. In the doorway, she wasn't sure how formal to be with a man she had seen in his boxers just half an hour before. Paul ignored the hand she extended, grasping her lightly by the shoulders and kissing her on both cheeks.

"Why don't you come over to the shop on Friday evening and we'll finish everything off?"

"Perfect," said Rachel, making an effort to remain reasonably business-like. "I have to drop the kids off at their father's, so I'll come over after that."

Halfway to his van, Paul stopped and turned to face her. "If you're free all evening, perhaps you'd like to have dinner with me?"

Rachel could still feel the pleasant sensation of his stubble tickling her cheeks and did her best not to beam from ear to ear. "That would be lovely, thank you."

"Good." Paul nodded and got into the van. "See you on Friday, then."

Rachel stood in the doorway until the van was out of sight. If Paul had looked back, he would have seen a thirty-something woman in a green dress dancing a jig around the courtyard.

* * *

The fact that there was an attractive new man in her sights was just one reason for Rachel to be in a pretty good mood. Project Guesthouse was going well. The Big End had been cleared, anything that didn't work had been mended or replaced and all the new prints were up.

Jilly had announced she was coming over mid-morning to help Rachel put the final touches to the rooms. "It's called styling," said Jilly after coffee, "and it makes all the difference."

Laden with an armful of scatter cushions, Rachel followed her friend through the house as Jilly plumped and tweaked pillows, and draped throws artfully over the backs of armchairs. Irina followed behind, muttering darkly about dust mites.

When they were done, Rachel walked her friend down the drive towards the village. Turning back, Jilly looked at the front of the house and pulled a face. "Perhaps you need to call Philippe. Those pots look rather tatty."

The courtyard had been neglected recently and the flowerbeds and planters suffered frequent assaults from the chickens who liked to dig in them.

"Hmm, you're right," said Rachel, looking at her watch. "I'll give him a call and see if he can do a mercy dash this afternoon."

Philippe had offered to come over one day when the florist's was closed to assist where needed. Mid-afternoon, he arrived with his van laden with pot plants and miniature shrubs. Rachel waved as he arrived and was surprised to see Margot emerge from the passenger seat. "Since when have you taken up gardening?" she asked, after greeting her friends.

"Darling, you know that grubbing around in the soil is not my thing, but I happened to be passing when Philippe was loading up his vehicle, so I offered my help."

"An offer I obviously declined," added Philippe, with a wink. "But Albert wasn't free and she was determined to come."

Margot pursed her lips. "Hand me a plant, a trowel and some instructions and I shall be fine."

Rachel gave her a hug. "That's very thoughtful of you." She hesitated, looking at Margot's beautifully manicured fingernails. "I'll get us some gloves."

With gloves on their hands and the sun on their backs, the women set to at one end of the courtyard, while Philippe dug out the beds at the other end. They worked in companionable silence for a while.

"So, what's this I hear about a new man?" asked Margot eventually. Rachel sat back on her heels.

"What new man?"

Margot shrugged. "Philippe heard from Albert's sister that Monsieur Claude had told Madame Lambert that you had had a visitor."

"Did he indeed?"

Philippe looked across from where he was pretending to concentrate on the *Buxus sempervirens* and smiled.

"A 'handsome' visitor according to Madame Lambert."

"Really? Do go on."

"And Philippe and I thought it might have been Monsieur Callot's nephew from the frame shop."

"Did you, now?" Rachel kept her eyes focused on the deep-blue pot that she was filling with compost. "How fascinating."

Five seconds ticked by. "So, aren't you going to tell us?" Margot and Philippe were now sitting up like meerkats, eager for gossip.

Rachel sighed and put down her trowel. "Your information is correct."

Margot clapped her gloved hands together in excitement. "Excellent!"

"But, there's no need to get excited. Paul just dropped off some work and helped me out with a new website."

"Ooh, they're on first-name terms already," said Philippe.

Margot nodded eagerly. "That is very promising."

Rachel looked from one to the other of her companions. "I think you are both getting ahead of yourselves here."

Philippe shrugged and went back to his flowerbed. "So you won't care that Madame Piquot also heard from Monsieur Seurat's sister that Paul Callot said he really enjoyed meeting you?"

"What?" Rachel shrieked.

"It's just what I've heard."

"You're making this up."

Philippe solemnly raised a hand to his chest. "I swear on my Alexander McQueen toe cap boots that that's the gossip in Dreste."

Margot took off her gloves. "Darling Rachel, I think this is splendid news," she said, lighting a cigarette.

Rachel smiled. "Paul delivered my prints and told somebody he enjoyed meeting me. That hardly amounts to a betrothal."

Margot waggled a finger at her. "Not yet. But it is a good beginning."

"Exactly," added Philippe. "You are back on the road to love!"

Rachel laughed, but inside she was just a little bit pleased at the discovery that Paul liked her. She wasn't about to tell her friends he had spent the night on her sofa or that they had a "dinner date" lined up for later in the week.

# Chapter 12: An Evening with Paul

On Friday morning, Rachel was up early to check that Philippe's new plantings had survived the attentions of the chickens, before hurrying into her studio to complete a print of a sunflower she had decided on for the guesthouse business card.

She was restless, looking forward to seeing Paul again that evening but also aware it was a business meeting, not a date. Having the print to concentrate on helped to distract her, but she found herself checking the clock several times during the day.

Rachel was unusually prompt collecting Charlie and Alice from the bus that afternoon. Back at the house, she went upstairs to change out of her work gear ready for her evening out. When she came downstairs, her daughter stared at her in silence.

"You're wearing your best dress," said Alice, a furrow forming across her usually smooth brow.

"I've got a meeting with Monsieur Callot and I want to look respectable." Rachel looked down at the red velvet frock she had chosen. "Don't you like it?"

"It looks like you're going to a ball or something."

"Does it?" This was not the effect Rachel had intended at all. "Oh dear. I'd better change."

Dashing back to her room, she flung open her wardrobe and pulled out various garments, eventually settling on a loose sea-green top that set off her auburn hair nicely and a long black skirt.

Back in the sitting room she did a twirl in front of her children. "Better?"

Charlie looked up from his phone and grunted in what Rachel took to be an expression of approval. Alice pursed her lips, thought for a second, then nodded. "Yup, that's better."

Rachel smiled. "Right, kids. Let's get you over to baby HQ."

\* \* \*

Rachel left the children with Michael as arranged, then walked round to Picture Perfect for her meeting.

Paul smiled and looked at her approvingly when she arrived, then led her into the back office where the computer lived. Rachel was properly prepared and had all the prices, maps and other bits of information ready in a folder. Paul was equally well organised, so the official Tournesol Guesthouse website was completed in a couple of hours.

When they had finished, Paul leant back, stretching his arms behind his head. "I think we deserve a drink after that. What do you think?"

Rachel nodded. "That would be lovely."

"Come upstairs to the flat and I'll see what we've got."

Paul turned off the lights in the shop and ushered her through a back door and up three flights of stairs. At the top, Rachel was surprised to find a large living room under the eaves. From the window she could see right across town to the squat tower of the fortress on the hill opposite.

"Wow, what a great view."

Paul smiled. "Pretty impressive, isn't it? That's why my uncle chose to put the sitting room up here and the bedroom downstairs."

Rachel caught his eye at the word "bedroom". Control yourself woman. "Good choice," she said, smiling demurely.

"So, white wine? Or I could rustle up a gin and tonic if you're feeling homesick."

"That's a really kind offer, but I tend to steer clear of gin. It makes me peculiar."

Paul raised an eyebrow. "Sounds intriguing. Explain."

"Oh, I don't dance on tables or anything like that."

"Shame."

"It makes me sad and gives me bad dreams." She shrugged her shoulders. "That's all."

"Well, we don't want to keep you awake all night," said Paul with a smile. "Not for bad reasons, anyway."

Rachel winced. "Have you forgiven me yet for making you sleep on a sofa booby-trapped with plastic toys?"

"Forgiven and forgotten," said Paul, selecting a bottle of Viognier. "Oh, I should warn you I don't cook," he said, handing her a glass of wine.

Rachel was enjoying his company so much that she didn't really mind what she ate. "Pizza, then?" she said, following him into the kitchen.

Paul shook his head and began extracting delicious-looking dishes from the fridge. "No, much better than that. I called in at the *traiteur* next door!"

"Oh yum." Rachel went over to join him as he placed the cartons on the counter. "This is such a treat," she said, as Paul brought out aluminium dishes filled with slices of duck, meaty terrines, coquilles St Jacques, fish stew and stuffed artichokes. "I daren't go into that shop because I spend so much money."

"I'm glad you approve of my choices," he said, with a smile.

"I do. I most definitely do."

"Have a seat in the living room while I put these in the oven, then we can eat." Rachel was more than happy to obey Paul's instructions and sat on the sofa by the window, gazing out at the rooftops in the moonlight.

It wasn't long before he called her back into the kitchen where he had added to the shop-bought goodies with a salad and some local cheeses. They chatted easily over the meal, although Rachel felt there was something quite business-like about Paul's conversation that evening.

She wondered what would happen next between them – if anything. Her prints were all framed and the website was done, so there would be no real reason for Paul to see her again. Unless romance was on the cards, of course.

Rachel had come prepared and was wearing her best frillies, just in case Paul fell for her powers of seduction. She was aware of being quite flirty over dinner but, although Paul seemed to enjoy the attention, he was definitely keeping his distance.

After the meal, she took her glass and went back to her place on the sofa while Paul cleared up the plates and made coffee. Rachel found his behaviour rather perplexing. He had invited her to stay for dinner and had definitely been flirting with her when they had worked together at her house. Here in the flat, he seemed to be backing away. Paul had gone from what she thought of as potential boyfriend material to a "colleague" again.

What had she done to put him off her? Was she not making it plain that she really rather fancied him? As she sat in the sitting room, feeling nicely woozy after the wine and dinner, she wondered what to do. Perhaps strip down to her smalls and drape herself over the table with the words "Come and get it!" tattooed across her chest?

She was gently chuckling to herself when Paul came into the room. As if reading her mind, he came and sat by her side and gently smoothed her hair back from her face. "You are a very attractive woman, Rachel."

She held her breath waiting for the kiss, which didn't come. "But?" she asked, the hint of frustration obvious from her tone.

Paul leant back and sighed. "I have heard from my uncle. His shoulder is better and he plans to come back to the shop very soon."

"That's good, isn't it?"

"It is, in one way," he said, smiling. "But it also means that I won't be needed here any more, so I'll be going back to Paris."

Rachel drooped for a moment, disappointed that the one man in Dreste who she actually found attractive was about to leave.

Paul had got up and was standing by the window, gazing at the view. "And there's something else," he added, turning back to face her.

"Oh dear." Rachel knew what was coming. "Don't tell me – you're married?"

Paul nodded. "Technically, yes."

Rachel raised an eyebrow. "Explain."

"It's a bit like you and your husband. We are almost divorced, but not quite."

"I see."

"I'm sorry, Rachel. I've really enjoyed the time we've spent together and would have liked to get to know you better."

It might have been the wine or the good food or the conversation they'd had, but Rachel felt bold that evening. "So, it's not that you don't find me attractive or think I'm mad or anything like that?"

Paul laughed and came back to join her on the sofa. "You are definitely attractive and only moderately mad."

"Cheeky!" Rachel picked up a cushion and whacked him with it, playfully. "Now I don't know whether to be offended or not."

"You should be flattered that I don't just want to sleep with you then disappear."

She looked at him with the hint of a smile on her face. "When did you say you were leaving?"

"Probably in a week or so." He looked at her quizzically. "Are you saying you don't mind?"

Rachel put her hand behind his head and gently pulled him towards her. "I don't if you don't."

He pulled back and looked at her. "I won't be coming back to Dreste, Rachel. You do understand that, don't you?"

She nodded then kissed him. "Let's not waste the time we have."

He brushed the back of his hand gently down the side of her neck, running his fingers across the top of her breasts and making her tingle. "If you're sure."

"I'm sure," she said, grabbing the front of his shirt this time so he couldn't pull away.

* * *

Rachel hadn't slept with anyone else since she'd married Michael, so she was surprised by the ease with which she'd fallen into bed with Paul – having first dragged him onto the sofa. Even though they barely knew one another, it had seemed like the most natural thing in the world to explore each other's bodies. After his initial reluctance, Paul had launched himself on her with passion and they had had an enjoyable romp.

For Rachel, the oddest part had been waking in the early hours and thinking that she was back in her own bed with her husband. The sensation had lasted just a split second and she chuckled to herself because the two men had such different builds: Michael was short and stocky while Paul was wiry and tall. Paul had masses of grey hair while her ex had lost his blond curls before he reached thirty. Despite their encounter essentially being a one-night stand, Paul had been sweet and attentive, enfolding her in his arms as they fell asleep.

Knowing that Paul was shortly to be heading back to Paris made them both subdued in the morning. It was understood that their relationship had no future and that this encounter was a one-off. There was no question that Rachel would go north with Paul and she wasn't about to ask him to abandon the bright lights of the capital for their sleepy backwater.

As Rachel showered, Paul went out to get some fresh bread for their breakfast and they chatted about this and that over warm brioches and bowls of milky coffee. It was all very civilised and no mention was made of what had happened between them; it was almost as if they hadn't made love together that night.

Despite being very grown-up and sensible about it, Rachel did feel a bit sad when she kissed Paul good-bye and trotted off down the narrow street to fetch the children. At the same time, she was aware of a new spring in her step. She felt buzzy and alive, as if a switch had been turned back on in her head – and deep inside her body.

She was still smiling to herself when she arrived at Amelie's apartment building, a place that generally filled her with gloom. When she had dropped off the kids the evening before, she had been invited in for a drink and to meet the baby. She had declined the offer, explaining she was on her way to dinner with a friend, but really not feeling strong enough to cope with Michael's scene of domestic bliss.

She now rang the bell to their apartment then waited on a bench across the road, the autumn leaves swirling around her feet. Opposite, Alice appeared on the balcony and waved. "We're just coming, Mum."

A couple of minutes later, the kids came to the door followed by Michael, who was holding Olivier.

"I thought you might like to meet him," he said, sheepishly.

Rachel peered at the baby with his scrunched-up face, bald head and bright blue eyes and smiled. "The poor child looks a lot like you."

Michael laughed. "Hopefully he'll grow out of that. Rach, won't you come in for a minute? Amelie would really like to see you."

Rachel shook her head. "Not yet, Michael," she said sadly. "Maybe in a little while."

"You're welcome any time," he said, jiggling the baby. "Bye kids, be good and I'll see you soon."

Alice got a kiss while Charlie grunted and hugged his father.

"Rach …"

She stopped and turned at the sound of Michael's voice. "Yes?"

"I hope you had a nice time with your friend. Last night, I mean."

She smiled back at him. "I had a very nice evening, thank you."

"Good," he said, a slight frown on his face. "I'm glad."

And she had had a nice evening, she thought, watching her son kicking leaves along the pavement as the three of them walked back to the car. If she was going to have an affair, she might have done better to choose a man who was actually staying around for a while, but she had come out of it unscathed. It was definitely a very promising first attempt at a new relationship.

\* \* \*

The following weekend, Rachel met Margot and Philippe in town for lunch. They talked about Margot's sons, Philippe's shop and their various plans for Christmas, but the conversation inevitably turned to Rachel's dinner date.

When she broke the news that the number one man on their hit list was leaving town, their faces fell.

"No! That is such a shame," said Philippe, distracted momentarily from his meal. "I thought Paul Callot would have been just right for you."

Rachel shrugged. "Who knows. It's been so long

since I've been out with anyone, I find it hard to judge."

"Really? Surely you felt some sort of ..." Philippe twirled his glass in the air, searching for the right word. "Chemistry?"

"To jump into bed with someone I barely know, you mean?" said Rachel, laughing.

Philippe tutted and returned to his monkfish. "I'm trying to be discreet."

Rachel leant across and gave him a kiss. "You are super discreet and sensitive."

Margot paused from her mushroom risotto, patted her ruby red lips with a napkin and sat back in her chair. "So tell us how you feel. Are you terribly disappointed?"

Rachel took a sip of her wine. "I'm not going to mope about it, not that I feel like moping, anyway," she added with a smile, spearing a prawn with her fork. She chewed thoughtfully for a moment. "I'm a free woman and I can sleep with who I want when I want."

The young waiter who had come over to top up their wineglasses glanced at her curiously, clearly intrigued by the conversation. They waited until he had retreated to the bar before continuing.

"That's a very sensible attitude, my darling," said Margot, patting her hand. "We don't want you getting your heart broken again quite yet."

Rachel huffed. "Michael didn't exactly break my heart. He jumped all over it and wore it down to the point where I barely feel anything any more. But I'm okay now."

Her friends exchanged one of their glances. It was clear that Rachel's feelings towards Michael fluctuated wildly from day to day and they were concerned that he could still hurt her in his cavalier fashion.

# Chapter 13: Open for Business!

Rachel was kept busy over the next couple of weeks with final preparations for her first guests. She had asked some of her neighbours over for a practice run at breakfast, serving eggs in various forms with bacon and all the trimmings to Monsieur Bertrand, Monsieur Seurat and the Lamberts. Monsieur Bertrand turned up with his little dog Fifi who quivered in terror at the cats and had to be soothed with slices of top-of-the-range English sausage.

Rachel was hoping that her paying guests would go for the easy option and choose fresh local pastries and cereal, but at least now she was prepared for visitors who opted for the "full English".

The day before the first visitors were due, Michael turned up unannounced to wish her luck. Against her better judgement and in breach of Margot's strict rules on the subject, Rachel invited him to stay for lunch. Despite everything, she was fond of the man – when she didn't want to break his neck.

Her brief encounter with Paul had left her feeling sexy, strong and less dependent on Michael for approval. Being with Paul had shown her she was attractive to other men and she was beginning to see that she could have a future which didn't involve her ex-husband.

"I'm very proud of you," said Michael, raising a glass to her. "You're going to make a great landlady."

"Let's hope so, for the poor innocent souls coming to stay here," said Rachel, laughing. "Anyway, here's to new babies and new businesses."

"And to old friendships, Rach."

She smiled back at him. "I'll drink to that."

\* \* \*

The day had finally come: the Tournesol Guesthouse was opening for business! Rachel squinted at Madame Piquot's description of the first guests: "M. & Mme Karlsen, 15–23 November, 2nd visit. Monsieur can't manage stairs." The notes had led Rachel to expect a fairly doddery couple, but Mr and Mrs Karlsen turned out to be a very sprightly Swedish pair in their mid-seventies.

When they turned up in their hire car, the Karlsens were welcomed by quite an impressive receiving line: Irina was there, plus both children and Rachel herself in a dress that was entirely free of paint. She had decided there was no point pretending to be an old hand at the B&B game: Madame Piquot had been typically frank with her guests, advising them that they were being handed over to someone new to the business but who was "quite charming".

Rachel put them into what had become Bedroom 3, overlooking the big courtyard. Thanks to Philippe's tender ministrations (and the judicious use of chicken wire), the terrace was now edged with colourful glazed pots filled with variegated shrubs and looked quite attractive.

Alice and Charlie had been bribed with the promise of a trip to the cinema if they managed to be polite to the guests and not fight with each other while they had visitors.

After the Karlsens had been there for a couple of days, the next guests arrived. First came two women from the Netherlands who were walking and painting their way around the region. Finally, they were joined by a young Japanese couple who looked perpetually baffled and giggled a lot.

On the evening of day seven, Jilly called round with a bottle of wine to see how Rachel was managing.

"So far, so good – I think," she said, collapsing onto a chair with her drink. "But I am exhausted."

"Already?"

"Yes! Having to be cheerful all the time doesn't come naturally to everyone, you know. And I have to remember not to swear at the cats and shout at the kids." She blew out her cheeks. "I mean, don't get me wrong: it is fun and they are lovely people, but being the 'hostess with the mostest' isn't really my forte."

Jilly tipped her head to one side, thoughtfully. "Perhaps I could help out now and then."

"Could you? I've got Irina on chambermaid duty but if you could cover for me in an emergency that would be great."

"Happy to," said Jilly, with a grin.

Rachel jumped up and gave her a kiss. "You're fabulous! It's such a relief knowing I can go into town without leaving my guests alone and unloved."

"I thought you were just doing bed and breakfast?"

"So did I, but I seem to be laying on entertainment, too."

"How so?"

"Well, the other evening the Dutch ladies and the

Swedes arrived back from some huge long walk, so I expected them to be tired. But then the Japanese pair turned up with a load of wine and they all had a boozy picnic in the Karlsens' room then started playing charades," said Rachel, pausing to savour a mouthful of Jilly's delicious rosé wine. "Anyway, I had to dig out a fur rug and a mop head so Mr Karlsen could impersonate some famous troll or other."

"That sounds fun!"

"There you are, you see," said Rachel, patting her hand. "You're the ideal person for the hospitality business."

"So, changing the subject," said Jilly, after a moment. "Have you had any news from Paul?"

Rachel sighed. "No, but then I didn't expect to."

"Really? I'm surprised after ... well, everything."

"It's okay, Jilly," said Rachel, with a shrug.

"If you say so."

"I do say so. Look, it was fun while it lasted but Paul wouldn't have been right for me."

Her friend looked at her doubtfully. "It seemed to me that you had quite a lot in common."

Rachel snorted. "Yes, like both being married. As Margot would say, it was just a practice run, so don't you worry about me." She looked at her half-empty glass. "Would you like to practise your hospitality skills and top me up?"

Jilly laughed and tipped some more of the pale pink liquid into their glasses. "Cheers Rachel."

"Cheers Jilly. And thanks for your support."

"Any time. So long as I don't have to dress like a troll."

# Part Two: December–January

# Chapter 14: A Surprise Visitor

Rachel was looking forward to a peaceful night in with no guests to worry about. The Japanese couple, the Karlsens and Els and Sara from Utrecht had gone, leaving warm words in the Visitors' Book and promising to tell all their friends what a charming place it was to stay.

Wonder of wonders, some brand new guests had arrived from Italy, having found the B&B thanks to the website. After a few days at the Tournesol, they had done a deal – brokered by Claude le Taxi – to hire a minibus and driver so they could do a wine-tasting tour of the area. The four of them were due back at the weekend, but Rachel had a whole two nights free.

On Monday, she had taken the kids into town to see the latest blockbuster as promised, but this evening she planned to do absolutely nothing.

After supper with the kids, she had enjoyed a blissful couple of hours reading a brand-new paperback that had been on her "to-read" pile for at least three months. Lying on the sofa, the warmth from the wood-burning stove made her sleepy and she must have nodded off.

She was startled by a knock at the door. Glancing at the clock she saw that it was well past 11pm. Alice and Charlie had disappeared to bed hours before and the guests had gone off on their jaunt, so she couldn't imagine who it might be.

Padding over to the door in her socks, she switched on the outside light and peered through the spyhole to see Michael standing there on his own.

Alarmed, she flung back the door. "Michael! Come in. What's happened? Is everything okay with the baby?" Michael staggered into the room – his face grey and drawn – and collapsed onto the sofa. "God, you look like you haven't slept for a week."

He leant forward with his head in his hands. "That's just it," he said, throwing his arms out across the back of the couch. "I haven't! Not for days, weeks, months." He groaned dramatically and rolled over, hitching his feet up onto the sofa.

Relief that nothing was seriously wrong made Rachel furious. She sprang over, grabbed Michael's feet and swung them back onto the floor.

"Ouch, mind my back!"

"Never mind your ruddy back. What about my sofa? And your wife?"

"Girlfriend. She's fine. She can sleep through anything."

Michael had risen to his feet again and was leaning lopsidedly against the wall, eyeing up the drinks' cupboard.

"Can I have a whisky, Rach? And half an hour of peace and quiet? Then I'll go back and face the music."

He looked at her with his big sad eyes and she wanted to thump him.

"No, Michael. You cannot have a whisky and a lie down. What on earth are you thinking of, turning up in the dead of night and giving me such a fright?" As he turned, she noticed a sticking plaster covered in fluff dangling down over his ear. "And what have you done to your ear?"

"Can't sleep. Horrible noise. Cotton wool." He clutched his ear and, as he spoke, slowly sank back down onto the sofa like one of those Duracell bunnies running out of steam.

Rachel went over and hauled him roughly back upright. "Come on. I'm making you tea then I'll damn well drive you home myself, if I have to."

"But I need to slee ..."

"You're not sleeping here! Call Amelie now. She'll be worried sick."

As she waited for the kettle to boil, she could hear Michael's soft murmur into the phone. When he came into the kitchen, she stirred the tea and plonked it down in front of him.

"Thanks, sweet ... Sorry. Look, you don't need to drive me home." The word hung heavy between them. "I'll be fine when I've had this. Nice cuppa, by the way."

If looks could kill, Michael would have been dead that instant. How Rachel stopped herself throwing a mug at him, she didn't know. She sat down at the table and they sipped their drinks together.

"You go to bed, Rach. I can let myself out."

"No chance! I don't want the kids to come down here in the morning and find you crashed out on the sofa."

A wistful half-smile came over Michael's haggard face and she almost felt sorry for him. She stood and released the empty mug from his hands. "Now go. Go home."

He pulled himself heavily to his feet and rubbed his scalp, nodding. "Thanks Rachel. Goodnight."

She watched him lumber down the drive and into Di-Di, not closing the door until she was sure he had left. The encounter had totally shattered the peace, she thought, as she washed the tea things. It was nearly midnight, but there was no way she could settle after Michael's ridiculous performance. She decided to read for a while, hoping that would calm her down before going to bed.

She was stretched out on the sofa, flicking crossly through one of the TV magazines – who were all these so-called celebs anyway? – when there was the unmistakeable sound of a car on the drive followed by a timid knock at the door. She raised her head and listened for a moment.

"No, it can't be … " The knock came again, more insistently this time. "I'm going to kill him," she muttered under her breath, chucking the magazine down on the sofa and stomping over to the door just as the knock came again.

"For heaven's sake," she said, pulling back the heavy latch and throwing the door open. "Bloody well go home!"

"Sorry. I mean, er, *pardonez moi*. I was looking for the Tournesol Guesthouse."

The dark bearded man on the doorstep, who was obviously not Michael, held out a piece of paper in front of him like a medieval beggar asking for alms. Behind him, Claude le Taxi gave Rachel a cheery wave, turned and crunched back down the road at speed.

"Oh! Sorry. No, I mean, yes. That's us." She racked

her brains for who this person could be, but nothing came. "I'm sorry, but you are?"

"I'm Josh Perry. I have a reservation," he peered over his glasses at the paper. "Or at least, I thought I had a reservation."

"Perry?" The cogs whirred and clicked into place in Rachel's brain. "Professor Perry? Yes! Please come in." Rachel saw the register in her mind's eye and stepped back to let him in. "I'm sorry, I thought you were someone else. I mean, we were expecting you, of course, but not until tomorrow. And you're so young, for a professor I mean."

Professor Perry looked longingly over his shoulder at the empty space left by the taxi, then at his watch, which showed just after midnight. "Well, I guess it is tomorrow. Kind of," he added doubtfully. "If it's a problem, I can always stay somewhere else tonight."

Rachel couldn't help a snort escaping from her mouth. "I'm afraid this is your only option in Pelette!" Realising that she was not making the best of impressions on her new guest, she pulled herself together. "Look, let's start again. I'm Rachel," she shook his hand. "Welcome to the Tournesol Guesthouse. Let me show you to your room."

She offered to take the smaller of her guest's two bags, but as this was still slung over his shoulder it proved rather impractical, so she led the way as he banged along the narrow staircase to the top bedroom.

She switched on the standard lamp just inside the door. "*Et voilà*, as they say in these parts." She wafted a hand around the room, indicating the rough stone wall, the heavy armoire, the armchair and the bed with its ornate headboard. "There's no en suite, but you have your own private bathroom at the end of the corridor."

Josh Perry frowned slightly, but was evidently too tired to argue about the absence of facilities. He grunted – favourably Rachel hoped – as he saw the big bath and the pile of fresh towels and caught the scent of the locally made lavender soap in its brown paper wrapper.

"Well, if there's nothing else, I'll bid you goodnight." Rachel backed out of the bedroom with a grin frozen on her face. In her own room, she collapsed onto the bed and groaned.

"I'll bid you goodnight?" Why had she started speaking like a Dickensian landlady? And how could she forget a booking? She got up to brush her teeth and looked at herself in the mirror: she was wearing one of Michael's old cardigans over a yellow sundress and jeans, with her hair tied back with a rubber band.

She groaned again as she loosened her hair and attempted to yank a comb through it. "I'm really not sure we're in the right business," she said to the cat on the windowsill. The look she got was not encouraging. "Well, it can only get better, eh Mousey?"

# Chapter 15: A New Day

Josh had hardly taken in his surroundings on arrival: the furniture looked rather old-fashioned, but he had spent enough time in Europe not to expect shiny new fittings. Taking off his conference gear, he had just washed his face quickly and scrubbed his teeth before falling into bed.

Waking early the next morning, he slipped on the courtesy dressing gown – nice touch – and pattered over to the window. As he unlatched the shutters and folded them back, he was impressed by the view. From the window at the top of the house, what lay before him was the garden and, in the distance, the mound of St Martin's Church was backlit by the sun that was still low in the sky. Somewhere close by he could smell coffee brewing. He felt better. It was obviously going to be a beautiful day.

At the end of the garden, he could see the owner hanging out washing, the wooden pegs clamped in her teeth. He ducked back into the room, not ready to deal with Madame quite yet.

He opened the bedroom door, made sure the coast was clear and dashed into the bathroom, unwilling to encounter the other guests – assuming there were any – until he was decent. Washed, beard trimmed and freshly dressed in a pale blue shirt and chinos, Josh felt ready to face the world.

Downstairs, Rachel could hear the distant creak of floorboards and clank of plumbing that meant her guest was up. After the disaster of last night, she was determined to put her best foot forward.

When Josh came into the breakfast room, he found Rachel in a floral pinny with her hair brushed and lipstick on.

"Good morning Professor. Breakfast inside or on the terrace?"

"Call me Josh, please."

"It's lovely outside, if you have a sweater and don't mind the chickens, er, Josh," she added, even though it didn't feel right to call a professor by his first name.

"You keep chickens?"

Rachel smiled. "It's sort of an unwritten rule around here: if you're English and you live in rural France, you have to keep chickens or they kick you out."

He gave her a look that suggested he wasn't entirely sure whether she was joking or not. Maybe it was true and Americans really didn't do irony. This was not going well, but Rachel decided to keep calm and carry on with her impersonation of a competent hostess. "Would you like scrambled eggs and bacon?"

"Sure, that would be great."

"And help yourself to coffee and fresh pastries. The honey is produced by an elderly neighbour so that's local, too." She smiled nervously. "It's just like *The Little House on the Prairie* here!" Why was she talking nonsense to the poor man?

Rachel retreated to the kitchen as Josh went onto the patio. From the window she could see him open a serious-looking magazine.

"I can't see this one wanting to play Guess the Troll," she muttered under her breath as she whisked eggs for Josh's breakfast.

"Good morning Madame. We have new guest?" Irina had come into the kitchen with the post.

"Yes, we do. And he looks rather serious."

Irina shrugged. "Serious is good. I have to buy new head for mop because of other guests."

"Yes, I'm sorry about that. Mr Karlsen does seem to have taken it away with him." Rachel smiled. "But at least he left us the rug."

Irina made a noise that indicated she was not placated by this, then started to load the dishwasher.

A Bee Gees tune was on the radio, the sun was out and the smell of bacon wafted through the air. Rachel bopped along to "Stayin Alive" as she piled Josh's breakfast onto a warm plate.

"I take it for you, Madame."

"Oh thanks, Irina." This was good. Suddenly Rachel felt like a proper guesthouse owner as she prepared a lovely breakfast for her sophisticated visitor.

After a while she went out to check whether Josh needed anything else. He folded his paper and smiled at her. "No, that was just right, thanks."

Rachel picked up the plates, bread basket, coffee cup, jar of honey and cutlery, balancing everything precariously on a tray which, she now realised, was far too small. It was pretty obvious from Josh's expression that he had sussed that waitressing was not one of Rachel's skills.

"So how long have you had the guesthouse?" he asked.

Oops, this was going to be tricky. She really didn't

want to let on quite what a newbie she was. "Oh, we've had the house for about fifteen years."

"We?"

"Yes, my husband and I. Though we're not together any more."

"Oh, I'm sorry."

Rachel shrugged. "It's okay. We still see each other all the time. Unfortunately," she added, under her breath. "In fact, that's who I thought you were last night."

"I see." Josh remembered the greeting he had received and felt sorry for the poor guy. "So you set the guesthouse up all those years ago? You must have been very young. You and your husband, I mean," he added, in case she thought he was flirting.

"Oh no. I started the guesthouse on my own." Rachel picked up a fork that had slid onto the grass and wiped it on her pinny. "Since we split up."

Josh nodded, waiting for her to go on. "So … ?"

"Okay, actually, this is my first season. Which is why we're not quite on top of things yet."

"So, I'm your first guest, right?"

"Oh good heavens, no!" she said, nervously plucking at the tea towel that she had slung over her shoulder to look professional. She wafted a hand in the general direction of the Big End. "There are lots of other guests."

"Okay," said Josh, doubtfully. "It's just that, well," he looked over at the house, "there doesn't seem to be anyone else here."

"They're here but just not here at the moment. If you see what I mean."

Josh shook his head slowly. "No, I can't say that I do."

Rachel explained that her other guests were on a tour but that she had agreed to keep their rooms for them while they were away.

"You'll know when they're back, believe me."

Josh looked alarmed. "Are they noisy? I was hoping to get a little bit of work done while I was here."

"No, not particularly." How to describe her latest guests? She thought about the evening before they had gone off on their trip and had insisted on showing her and the children how to make proper pizzas. It had been great fun throwing dough into the air and twirling it around, but Irina was still finding flour and bits of anchovy on the walls three days later. "The guests are just rather, er, jolly."

Josh savoured the word. "Jolly? That's okay. I can cope with jolly."

Rachel smiled. Maybe he wasn't so dull after all.

# Chapter 16: The Great Outdoors

After breakfast on Josh's second day, Rachel cleared away the pans and went out onto the terrace where he was reading under a tree. She was still a little wary of him. Her other guests had all been so boisterous that she didn't really know how to deal with this rather quiet academic.

When Josh saw her standing there and nodded a greeting, Rachel decided that it would be rude to duck back inside, so she tried to make another attempt at small talk.

"Good morning Professor, er, I mean Josh. What brings you to Pelette? We are rather off the beaten track here."

"Partly this," he said, indicating the stack of papers on the table. "I've been doing research and attending a conference in Grenoble, so I thought I might as well take advantage of the trip to see a bit more of the country."

"What was the conference on?"

"Oh, it was called 'Mother Church: hegemony or harlot?'" Josh smiled. "Conference organisers like to have question marks in their titles. It adds an air of intrigue."

Rachel nodded and smiled, not quite sure what to say next. "And you were speaking about the hege-watsits or the harlots?"

"Both and neither," he answered, with a frown. "Sorry, that's the kind of answer you get from an academic." He took off his glasses and put them down on the table. "Sorry," he said again, rubbing his eyes with the flat of his hands. "I've been in the Bibliothèque nationale in Paris for weeks, then trapped in a conference centre for days. It's hard adjusting to normal life again."

"You've come to the right place then – we're a kind of halfway house between sanity and eccentricity."

"That's just what I need," said Josh, smiling.

Rachel looked thoughtful. "I can imagine it's hard to get those harlots out of your head."

He laughed outright now. "My work is not that exciting, believe me!"

She smiled, waiting in vain for him to explain what it was. "You haven't told me what you work on."

"Oh, I'm researching the Huguenot experience in the southern states of the US. That's where I'm from, if you hadn't guessed."

"Ah, that explains your accent. I mean, I wondered where you were from exactly," she added, hoping she hadn't sounded rude.

He leant back in his chair and smiled at her. "Yours is quite something, too – if you don't mind my saying so."

Rachel wrinkled her nose. "I know – my English friends say I sound like a cross between Pam Ayres and Maurice Chevalier."

"I've no idea who Pam Ayres is, but I'm sure she's charming."

"Thanks – I think?" She stood there for a minute longer as they smiled at each other, not knowing what to say next.

Eventually Josh turned and looked across the tops of the trees at the Alps in the distance, still misty in the morning sun. "Do you happen to have any walking guides for the area? I'd like to get out into the countryside while I'm here."

"Lots. Come into the house when you're ready and I'll dig them out for you."

Josh picked up his papers and his glasses. "I'll come now, if I may. I've done enough reading for the time being."

Rachel led him into the guest sitting room where there was a cupboard full of hiking guides, maps and photographic studies of the area.

"Wow, that's quite a library."

"Oh, it's stuff we've collected over the years. Some of it is rather old, I'm afraid," she said, as a thin piece of paper fluttered out from between the pages of a restaurant guide to Chevandier. "You won't get lunch at Chez Christophe for 10 francs any more, I can tell you," she said, peering at the receipt, its words faded with age.

Putting the book back on the shelf, she pulled out a couple of walking guides and handed them to Josh. "I think these are actually from this decade. Have a look and let me know if you need any help."

He smiled, taking them from her. "Thanks, I'll do that."

It was after breakfast the next day that Josh asked Rachel if she would like to join him for a hike at the weekend. "If you don't have other plans, obviously," he added. "And maybe the kids would like to come, too?"

Rachel was surprised and pleased to be asked. It

had been years since she had done any proper hiking. When they were first together, she and Michael would often pack up their rucksacks and go off exploring the Ardèche gorges and even the lower Alps. Having the kids had put an end to that, though the family had occasionally driven into the hills for short walks.

"My children don't walk, I'm afraid. I'm hoping that when they have got through adolescence and turned into proper human beings, they will want to come hiking with their old mum. But I'd love to come," she said, beaming at him. "Thanks for inviting me."

"Hey, you'll be doing me a favour. I'd probably get lost or eaten by bears or something if I went out on my own."

Rachel laughed, relieved to find that her guest did have a sense of humour after all.

When she woke on Saturday, she realised how much she was looking forward to her outing. She had checked the weather beforehand to make sure there were no storms on the way and had prepared a delicious picnic for them.

It was fun doing something different and she felt quite wicked "bunking off" from work. She realised that getting all her prints and cards out for Christmas on top of setting up the guesthouse had taken it out of her and hoped a day in the fresh air would clear her head.

The Italians had returned from their wine tour. She had given them breakfast and they were now out for the day. Irina had been put in charge of the house and Alice and Charlie were staying with Philippe and Albert in Dreste that evening. Albert's teenage children were sleeping over and he and Philippe liked to lay on some entertainment for them in the form of youngsters a bit closer to their own ages.

Josh had left the route planning to Rachel who suggested that they do a circular walk starting from a neighbouring hilltop village, crossing the valley and getting back in time for an aperitif before driving the short distance home.

Rachel couldn't remember the last time she'd gone for a walk with a strange man – or woman, for that matter. Her life was so focused on the house, her work and the children that she no longer explored the countryside around her.

She parked the car at a local beauty spot, they put on their boots and off they went. As they strode along in silence, the sky overhead looked vast and the crisp winter air was invigorating. Rachel felt as though the walk was washing all her tiredness away. She stopped and breathed in deeply. "It feels good to be up here."

"If I lived in Pelette, I'd be out all the time."

"You wouldn't want to walk in high summer. It's far too warm then."

Josh shrugged. "I'd get up early or wait till evening." He stood still and looked out at the view. "It really is beautiful here. You're very lucky."

Rachel gazed across the patchwork of fields – some of them fragrant with lavender in the summer – and nodded. "I know. This landscape and the buildings are what first inspired me to become an artist, if you can call me that."

"I would definitely call you that, and I want an original 'Rachel Thompson' to take back to Atlanta."

"That could be tricky."

Josh looked disappointed. "Really, why?"

She smiled. "I've started to use my maiden name on the new work, so you'd get a genuine Rachel Greaves."

"Even better."

"So, how come someone from the Deep South developed an interest in this bit of France?" she asked. "I mean, most of your compatriots visit Paris and some of them might even venture down to Arles or to Carcassonne in search of Cathars, but that's about it."

Josh looked thoughtful. "I guess I feel a connection because of the family history. This region is where the Perrys came from all those years ago."

"Would you ever consider moving back to the old country?"

"Sure. Actually, I'm hoping to get a teaching post in Grenoble next term."

"How exciting. And do you think you're in with a chance?"

Josh shrugged. "Maybe. I know virtually nothing about the subject area but I'm cheap and keen."

Rachel laughed. "Sounds hopeful, then."

"What about you? Do you plan to come over to the States sometime?"

"Oh, I've been once. My brother lives over there, so we spent a few days in Massachusetts some years ago."

"And were the natives friendly?"

"Very," said Rachel, glancing around. "This looks like a good picnic spot. Fancy lunch?"

* * *

Back at the house, Rachel left Josh in the guest sitting room in the Big End while she went into the garden to shut up the chickens. When she came back in, she was disappointed to find that her guest had disappeared up to his room. Over the course of the day she had definitely warmed to him. He was much younger than she had originally thought and entertaining company.

The Italians and her kids were all in Dreste, so the house was spookily quiet. It was strange being a mother/landlady – one minute you had a house jammed with people, then you were completely on your own again.

Rachel went into the kitchen to feed the cats, poured herself a glass of red wine then hobbled upstairs to change. Having walked all day she decided to have a soak in the lovely old roll-top bath instead of her usual hasty shower. She sank under the bubbles, enjoying the sensation of being enveloped by the hot water and wriggling her tired toes with pleasure. Mousey had crept in after her and was sitting on the edge of the bath, patting the mountains of froth with one delicate paw then licking it dry.

"Cheers cat."

After the bath, she pulled on some comfy jogging bottoms – not that she had ever jogged in her life – fluffy bedsocks and a warm woollen sweater and headed down to the kitchen. It looked like she'd be having a quiet night in. On her own.

Generally, she savoured those evenings alone and enjoyed her own company. But sometimes, when she was feeling particularly maudlin, she wondered what life would be like when Alice and Charlie had both left home. Would she end up a toothless old crone surrounded by cats, turning out ever more lugubrious prints?

"Quite possibly," she said to herself, taking a sip from her glass. She was about to call Margot to see if she wanted to come over for supper when Josh put his head around the door.

"Knock, knock. Sorry to bother you in your private quarters."

Rachel smiled, pleased to be interrupted. "No problem – *mi casa es tu casa* and all that."

"Hey, you speak Spanish. Great."

"No, that's pretty much it. Anyway, how can I help?"

"Well, I wondered if I could take you out for a meal tonight? To say thanks for a really great day." Josh paused in the doorway and looked her up and down, from her damp hair twisted up in a scrunchy to the pink spotty bedsocks. "But I guess you're planning a night in, right?"

"Actually I was heading out to my philosophy class."

"Oh, okay."

Rachel frowned. "That was a joke."

"Gee, shucks." Josh put his hands on his hips and shook his head. "I guess I'm not quite attuned to British humour yet."

"Sorry, I'm a very unprofessional landlady, tormenting my guests like that," said Rachel, feeling chastened by Josh's mocking tone. "Can I make it up to you with a glass of wine?" she asked, getting another glass from the dresser.

"Sure," said Josh, rubbing his stomach, which emitted a low gurgle. "But I do need to get some food."

Rachel handed him a glass of Pinot Noir. "This is great with Chinese food. I mean, if you fancy a takeaway meal."

"That would be perfect."

"Great. I'll give them a call and you can pay!"

"It's a deal," said Josh, clinking his glass against hers.

They ordered a huge meal and chomped their way through it, both ravenous after their day's walking.

Sitting at the kitchen table surrounded by dishes, Josh smiled. "I've had a lot of fun today, Rachel. Thank you."

"It's all part of the service."

"Really? And there I was feeling special."

Rachel laughed. "Okay. The hiking service is only available for our VIP guests."

Josh was looking at her intently now, his hazel eyes locked on hers. "I wish I was staying around here a little longer. So we could become friends."

"That would be nice," said Rachel quietly. He was attractive and single and there was no one in the house. She could feel the colour rise in her cheeks as, for several long seconds, she actually considered taking him upstairs. If it hadn't been for the aborted relationship with Paul, she might well have done it. However, she didn't feel ready to hop into bed with another passing stranger quite so soon.

To break the mood, she began clearing up the dishes. "So, were you serious about buying one of my prints?"

Josh nodded. "Yes. Absolutely."

"Right. Follow me."

Rachel grabbed her glass and led the way to the studio. There she showed Josh the stacker filled with unframed prints.

"That's some of my more recent work," she said, as Josh began flicking through the images. "I've got framed pieces too, of course, but they would be a little more difficult to take back to the USA."

"I'm sure I'll find something here," he said with a smile. "Hey, do you have any views of the spot where we had our lunch?"

"And nearly froze to death?" Rachel smiled, pulling out five or six landscapes. "These are all views of the valley."

Josh took them over to the work bench and studied them carefully. "They are really beautiful."

She watched his face as he studied the prints. He had, she now noticed, a very elegant profile. Her artist's eye took in his long eyelashes and perfectly straight nose. He had nice lips and the close-cropped beard gave his chin definition, she decided, and made him look older than he actually was. He looked like a handsome conquistador and she had an urge to whip out her sketch pad and draw him.

Josh caught her studying him and frowned. "Do I have noodles in my beard or something?"

Rachel laughed. "No, not at all. It's just ..." What was it exactly? Apart from the fact that she found him quite appealing, there was something more. "This is going to sound creepy, but I feel like we've met before."

Josh laughed. "Well, I have been here for five whole days now."

Rachel sat down on one of the work chairs and swivelled her body from side to side, frowning. "I know, but it's more than that."

"And we did spend some quality time together on our walk today."

"You're teasing me."

Josh shrugged. "It's something spooky, maybe? Perhaps I'm the reincarnation of a Pelette peasant who used to live in your house?"

"Now you're being silly," she said, hopping off the chair. "Let's go back downstairs. It's getting chilly in here. Bring those prints with you," she added, nodding at the two he had selected.

Back in the cosy sitting room, Josh held the landscapes up in front of him again as she topped up their glasses. "I love them both, but I think I'll take this one," he said, turning it over to look at the details on the back.

"Excellent choice, sir," said Rachel. "That's from my new collection. There are lots of Rachel Thompsons in circulation, but the Greaves work is pretty rare. At the moment, anyway."

"Oh my gosh," said Josh, sitting bolt upright and staring at her hard.

"It's not that exciting. I mean they're not valuable or anything." Rachel looked on amazed as Josh leapt to his feet and began to laugh.

"That's it," he said, pacing up and down and chuckling to himself. Rachel was looking at him strangely now.

"What's 'it'? Are you okay? What's wrong?" She was getting quite concerned.

"Nothing's wrong at all," he said, but still laughing and shaking his head.

"Josh, what is this? You're making me nervous. Will you please tell me what's got into you?"

"Okay." He stopped in front of her with his arms folded. "You said your maiden name was Greaves, right?"

She looked at him quizzically. "Yes. But it isn't that unusual a name."

"And you have a brother in the US?"

"Yes."

"And what's his name?"

"Henry Greaves, though I don't see what my brother has to do with anything."

"Ha! You were right." Josh laughed again and came to sit down beside her. "We have met before," he said, grabbing her hand.

Rachel looked at him as though he had taken leave of his senses. "You've lost me now."

"We met at your brother's wedding."

Rachel was dumbfounded for a moment. "What, how?"

"I was there. You were there. We met."

Rachel thought back to that manic day when Henry had married his American girlfriend in Boston six years before. Michael had paid for the family and her parents to fly over for a week's holiday. The wedding itself had been a whirlwind of faces. She was preoccupied with the children – and keeping an eye on Michael who was flirting outrageously and hamming up his English or French accent, depending on who it was he was trying to impress.

She tried to run the events of the day through her mind's eye, but she could not find Josh in her memory. "Are you sure? I mean, that you were there?"

He raised an eyebrow. "I don't get invited to that many fancy-schmancy weddings, you know. My girl-friend at the time was a friend of the bride and I went as her Plus One." He shrugged. "It was one of the last things we went to together, actually."

Rachel bit her lip. "I'm sorry."

"That's okay," he smiled. "It was no big thing."

"I meant that I'm sorry, but I really don't remember meeting you at all." She scrutinised his face, scrolling back in her memory through the people she had met on that day. "I mean, you're right – I feel it – but I don't remember seeing you."

"It's not that surprising  – I was six years younger, about twenty pounds heavier and I didn't have this," he said, stroking his beard. "But I remember you. And the family."

"Oh dear, were we that badly behaved?"

He laughed. "No, not at all. The kids were cute. And I think I spoke to your parents."

"Yes, that makes sense. My dad knows how to work a room." She jumped. "Oh, I've got it now! I do remember you." Rachel clapped her hands together, laughing. "My folks started a conga line at the reception and I grabbed you and pulled you in. At least I think that was you."

He nodded slowly, trying to remember the lost details. "Yup, that was me. And you were wearing an orange and purple dress."

"Oh God, yes," said Rachel, squirming. "Susan wanted us to wear 'Fall' colours – never again."

"It was very striking."

She snorted. "I think you mean bloody awful."

Josh shook his head from side to side. "You could

never look awful, Rachel." And when he leant over to kiss her she didn't resist him.

* * *

When she awoke the next morning, she was naked apart from the pink fluffy bedsocks. And she was not alone. She groaned inwardly as she looked at Josh and rolled over, hoping to creep out of bed before he woke. Too late.

"Well good morning, beautiful," he said, turning around and wrapping himself around her. She felt him nuzzle into her neck and gently kiss the tops of her shoulders, his beard tickling her in a not unpleasant manner.

She turned back to face him, pushing him away when he tried to kiss her breasts. "No, we musn't."

He pulled back and smiled at her. "I think you'll find that we already have. Or was it just a particularly vivid dream I had there?"

Rachel wriggled away from him and hopped out of bed, grabbing her robe from the armchair by her side.

"Nice socks." Josh lay propped up on his arm, smiling at her. "Come back to bed, Rachel," he said, throwing back the covers and patting the place beside him. "It's still early."

"Damn, bugger, bollocks," muttered Rachel, running around the room, collecting clothes and rejecting them again. "I've got to collect the kids at nine and it's already twenty-to."

Josh sat up, attentive now. "Is there anything I can do to help?"

"Make me tea!"

"I'm on it," he said, running towards the door.

Rachel looked back from the bathroom. "But maybe put your clothes on first?"

"Sure thing," he said, coming over to kiss her. "Last night was great Rachel."

"Milk no sugar. Go!"

* * *

Rachel and Josh had three more days together before he had to leave for Switzerland and another library before flying back to Atlanta. It was a strange time: because of Irina, the kids and the other guests, they didn't spend the night together again. Josh spent ages chatting with her in the studio as she worked and they walked around the village a couple of times, but that was it.

Rachel had feared that Josh had just jumped into bed with her because she happened to be there, was available and randy, but he seemed genuinely to like her. When he was leaving, they promised to keep in touch – especially, as he put it, since they were very nearly related.

When she told her friends what had happened, Jilly had looked pained. They were having tea in Rachel's kitchen, whispering in case Irina was nearby.

"I think all this …" Jilly wafted her hand in the air vaguely, "*activity* shows that you need a man in your life."

Rachel sighed. "It's all very well you telling me I need a man. Unfortunately, all I get are ships that pass in the night."

"And one or two that occasionally dock," said Margot, with a smile. She was far less sentimental than Jilly. "A little rumpy-pumpy with handsome strangers won't do you any harm, darling."

"There won't be any more rumpy-pumpy from now on. I can't cope with the stress."

Margot patted her hand. "Don't they say these things always come in threes?"

Rachel puffed out her cheeks. "Not for me. I'm not getting involved with anyone from now on unless they are one hundred per cent available."

# Chapter 17: Christmas Eve

The next ten days went by in a blur of Christmas preparations. Philippe and Albert had invited Rachel and the children to supper at their house before midnight mass on Christmas Eve. She was pleased to have the invitation: the house seemed rather empty without the guests. And Josh.

Christmas Eve at Philippe's place involved lots of eating and drinking, a stroll across town, then more delicious food, drink and conversation at their town house after the fairly short service. The priest was sanguine enough to turn a blind eye to Philippe and Albert's close "friendship" and would pop by for a drink. They had been together for several years, although Albert kept his own flat in another part of town. Until recently, his ex-wife had only ever allowed their children to visit him there. This was the first year that the youngsters were staying with their dad and Philippe for the holiday, and Albert was overjoyed.

The pair had a broad range of friends and Rachel was looking forward to the evening very much. On Christmas Day itself, she planned to drive back home with the kids for lunch and pressies. In the past, Michael would come to collect them for a sleepover at his flat, but this year he and Amelie were spending the holidays with her parents.

It was going to be a quiet time for the children and she hoped they wouldn't be too bored at home with her.

She was on her third glass of champagne and second helping of canapés when she heard laughter and raised voices from the kitchen. Albert came into the room with a grin on his face.

"Rachel, there is someone in the kitchen for you."

She put down her glass and followed him into the hallway from where she could see a flurry of greetings being exchanged and her children locked in a "team hug" with their grandfather and Connie.

"Happy Christmas, sweet pea!"

Rachel dashed over as Harold released Charlie and Alice and opened his arms to embrace her.

"Dad, Connie! What a surprise!"

"I hope you don't mind," said Connie, standing slightly to one side and looking sheepish. Rachel approached and gave her a kiss on both cheeks.

"Of course I don't mind," she said, surprised to find that she actually meant it. In the past she had found her father's lady friend rather overbearing, but she knew that Connie made Harold happy and the pair's arrival in Philippe's kitchen had completely transformed the children's prospects for Christmas.

"Your father was worried you'd be lonely this year," said Connie, adding in a whisper, "especially now that 'You Know Who' has got himself a new family and everything."

"We shan't stay long, love. Just a day or two," added Harold. "Just to make sure that you and the children are coping with the new guesthouse."

"I think you should stay forever, Grandy!" said Charlie, giving him a hug.

Harold smiled and kissed him on the forehead before Charlie could wriggle free and escape back to the TV.

"We won't take up any room, either," said Connie. "I persuaded my daughter, Eleanor, to lend us her campervan for the trip, didn't I love?"

"You did indeed."

Nowadays, Rachel was frequently surprised by her father's adventures. "Good heavens. Did you really drive all the way down here in that ancient vehicle?"

"We certainly did and it was tremendous fun."

Alice looked perplexed. "What's a campervan Granddad?"

"It's like a little house on wheels," said Harold.

"Yes, you can cook in it and sleep in it. Everything really," added Connie, giving Harold a coy look that was fortunately missed by Rachel.

"Wow, cool!" said Alice. "Can I see?"

"Of course, darling," said Harold, as the entire party trooped out of Philippe's kitchen to admire the lime-green vehicle under the pale orange glow of the streetlamp.

# Chapter 18: Christmas Day

Before setting off from Devon, Connie and Harold had packed the campervan with gifts and an array of goodies, including the makings of an entire English Christmas dinner. In the morning, everything was transferred from the van to Rachel's kitchen. Among the ingredients were sprouts, which her children had only ever encountered French style, i.e. boiled to oblivion and then canned.

They were recreating the genuine English experience by starting the day with mince pies, sherry and a brisk walk, despite the freezing weather.

By mid-afternoon, candles were lit, the dining room was draped in tinsel and everyone's thoughts were turning towards turkey with Paxo stuffing when the Ukrainians arrived. Irina had said she might drop by with the cousins for a drink, but Rachel had not expected them to sweep into the house with vodka and bear hugs all round.

After the introductions had been made, Irina – dressed in a figure-hugging white dress and silver ankle boots – ceremoniously presented Rachel with an enormous cooked carp, while Alexei and Gregor dished out bottles of wine and chocolates to Harold and Connie, as well as gifts for the children that included a rather lurid T-shirt for Alice – which she adored – and a football decorated in City Kiev colours for Charlie.

Having patted their stomachs and declined the offer of lunch, Irina and the cousins squeezed themselves into gaps around the table and joined them for the champagne, vodka, smoked salmon and blinis that now began the meal. This was accompanied by lots of toasts, laughter and backslapping.

Rachel had already prepared a *boeuf bourguignon* for their lunch, so that went on the table as well as the turkey. To finish, there was fruit and a French chocolate log, but the *pièce de résistance* was Harold's Christmas cake, which was decorated with lots of icing swept into extravagant snowdrifts.

As Rachel was distributing slices of cake at the end of the meal, Gregor began to sing in a warm, deep voice.

Irina sat humming to herself, swaying gently in time to the music.

"What is he singing about?" whispered Rachel.

"Ah, it is a very sad song, Madame," Irina looked suitably mournful despite the paper hat on her head. "It is about a man with an unhappy wife who goes fishing and sees a very large fish."

"Biggest fish in the Dnieper River," added Alexei.

Charlie, who had done some fishing with his father, perked up at this. "Does he catch it?"

"He follows it many times, but each time it swims further and further away, and the wife – she gets sadder and sadder."

Rachel nodded and tried to look serious.

"But shouldn't finding a big fish make the fisherman happy?" asked Connie, who had taken rather a shine to Gregor with his soulful baritone.

Alexei shook his head vigorously. "No, Mrs Connie.

The fisherman tries and tries, but the fish escapes and is caught by another man from the village."

Irina put a finger to her lips, shushing them as Gregor arrived at the climax of the song, which ended with him clasping his hands to his chest and letting out what could only be described as a groan.

By this time, they were all quite gripped by the tragic story that was unfolding and applauded enthusiastically.

When silence had fallen, Harold leant over to Alexei. "So how does it end, old chap?"

He shrugged his shoulders mournfully then winked at Gregor who flashed them a grin. "Then the unhappy wife leaves her husband for the neighbour who has the big carp and the poor fisherman is a free man once more. Happy ending!"

After another burst of applause and shouts of "Bravo", Gregor stood and raised his glass in a toast to Rachel's hospitality.

"And now," he said, addressing Harold, "you sing us a beautiful English song, yes?"

"Well, goodness me," said Harold, looking bashful. "I really don't think that my ancient voice is any match for yours." He turned to his companion and squeezed her arm. "Connie's the singer here."

"Nonsense! You've got a lovely voice, darling," she said, pinching his cheek and chuckling.

Harold gave her a kiss on the lips as Charlie and Alice made pretend-vomiting faces behind their backs.

"Sorry Gregor. English people don't sing in public," Rachel explained.

"Well, we do, but only when we've had too much to drink," added Harold with a twinkle.

Irina raised an eyebrow at Alexei who passed the vodka down the table.

Rachel held up her hands in mock alarm. "I think today counts as having too much."

"I know a very good English song," said Alexei, getting to his feet and launching into "Waltzing Matilda". Everyone joined in, then Harold started them off on "On Ilkley Moor Bar T'at" and Connie led them through the alto part of Handel's "Hallelujah" chorus with everyone singing along as best they could. The grand finale was a medley from *Grease*, which even Alice joined in with.

After that, the adults staggered into the sitting room and collapsed on chairs and sofas while the kids studied their gifts. While it was quiet, Rachel decided to get some air and check on the animals.

When she came back into the house after shutting up the chickens – and tipsily apologising to them for eating the turkey – she found a scene of post-prandial bliss. Everyone had made themselves comfortable in front of the fire and the Ukrainians were chomping their way through the candied fruits, Brazil nuts and After Eights. Charlie was in a corner playing a computer game with Irina; Harold and Gregor were involved in a very intense game of chess; Connie was dozing in an armchair and snoring gently. Alice was curled up on the sofa listening to music and texting her friends.

Rachel decided tea was needed and went into the kitchen where she was pleased to see that her guests had made a start at clearing up while she was out. Listening to the low murmur of conversation in the next room she smiled to herself, feeling squiffy but quite content. As she waited for the kettle to boil, she fed the cats, adding morsels of turkey to their biscuits and making them purr with delight.

"Have you had a nice Christmas, too, pusskins?" she asked, as they concentrated on the contents of their bowls.

"Everyone has had a very nice Christmas, thanks to you, Rachel."

She turned to see Alexei leaning against the door-frame, grinning at her. With his one gold tooth and dark wavy hair, he looked like he should be on a pirate ship. I've had too much to drink, she thought. He was gorgeous and he filled the new "one hundred per cent local and available" criteria, but life was already too complicated. And she had a feeling that Irina would not approve.

Right on cue, Irina came in with Charlie. "Mum, Irina cheats," he grumbled.

Irina grabbed him and ruffled his hair. "Is not cheating. Is all about learning, remembering and being smart."

Alexei went over and stood by Charlie's side. "You never beat Irina. She is too clever here," he said, tapping the side of his head. "But she cannot play good football like you."

Charlie grinned. "Can we have a game?"

"Not now, love. It's pitch black outside," said Rachel, peering out into the gloom.

Alexei shrugged. "So, we put on the lights."

"Yeah! Can we, Mum?"

"If you're mad enough, that's fine by me."

"You play, too, Rachel," said Alexei, taking her hand as Charlie ran off to fetch his brand-new ball and choose his team-mates.

So that's how Christmas Day ended: three Ukrainians, two loved-up pensioners, Rachel and her children playing football in the moonlight with extra illumination provided by the Ukrainians' truck. Rachel and Irina acted as goalies with the teams split: Charlie, Alexei and Harold versus Alice, Connie and Gregor. No one was quite sure what the final score was, but everyone agreed that it was the best Christmas Day they'd had for a very long time.

# Chapter 19: New Year's Eve

After Christmas, Harold and Connie had been persuaded to stay for a little while longer, but Rachel could see they were restless. A couple of days later, they packed up the campervan and prepared to head back north.

Harold was raring to go. "We fancy seeing in the New Year from the Eiffel Tower, you see."

Rachel smiled. "Okay Dad. But take your time and drive safely."

"I will sweet pea, don't you worry."

"We've had such a lovely time," said Connie, giving Rachel and the children hugs. "Do come and see us in the spring, won't you? I've already invited Irina and the boys."

Rachel waved and the children ran after the van as it creaked down the drive. "See you next year!" Now all she had to sort out was entertainment for New Year's Eve.

\* \* \*

In France, New Year's Eve is a much bigger deal than Christmas although – being Brits – Rachel and Michael had always celebrated both. This year her friends were all having family dinners or romantic evenings at home. She was invited, of course, but wanted to do something fun with the kids.

Charlie claimed not to care what he did to

celebrate Saint-Sylvestre, but Rachel knew that all of Alice's friends were doing something exciting and she didn't want to let her children down. So when Madame Lambert told her there was going to be a shindig at the community hall, she said they would all love to go. There was going to be lots to eat and drink, fireworks at midnight and a band had been booked to play traditional music. It promised to be fun and presented the perfect opportunity for Rachel to wear the red velvet dress that Alice had frowned upon all those weeks before.

When Rachel turned up at the hall with the children, she saw plenty of familiar faces as well as new people who had come to live in Pelette during the year.

Looking around the room with its long tables laden with food, she felt as though she had slipped into a festive country scene by Pieter Bruegel. Monsieur Seurat was there in his best suit, his collar and tie painfully tight at the neck until his wife turned her back and he pulled them loose. Claude was wearing a rather natty pair of red trousers and a tartan waistcoat. Monsieur Bertrand had brought Fifi, who was specially dressed for the occasion with a gold ribbon around her neck.

The wives were also in their finery, which largely involved lots of black and diamanté. The children ran around the room, getting hyper on cola, impatient for the firework display to begin.

At 9pm, the taped music was turned off and the chairs were pushed back against the walls to make more space for the musicians who included an accordionist as well as people playing bagpipes, violins, guitars and a flute. The band struck up a traditional

tune and people rose to their feet and grabbed partners. Alice and Charlie had been taught French country dancing by their unofficial stepmum Amelie, and
Rachel had picked up a few steps over the years as
she and Michael had been drawn into village life.

Rachel was hoping to sit out the first couple of
dances, but Claude had other ideas and she was soon
whirling around the room in a vigorous jig. Alice
danced with boys from the village and Charlie tried
to hide but was swept up by Madame Seurat.

It is a feature of folk music around the world
that the tunes last a very long time, and Rachel was
pooped after two dances and had to excuse herself
and return to her champagne.

Retreating to a chair in a corner near the grannies,
she watched the dancers form a circle then snake
around the room, hand in hand. She was struck by
how graceful her daughter was and how tall Charlie
seemed to have become in the last couple of months.

She clapped enthusiastically as the dance ended,
the line broke up and everyone separated – some
standing and eagerly awaiting the next number,
others panting and reaching for their glasses of beer
or water.

Revellers were coming and going through the
heavy oak doors of the building. It was a clear night
with a full moon and the kids were dashing in and out,
checking on preparations for the firework display.

Rachel was chatting to Madame Lambert about
the guesthouse and didn't notice Paul Callot enter
the room until he was standing right in front of her.
His face broke into a smile as he bowed and extended
his hand. "Would you care to dance, Madame?"

Before she could answer or ask him what on earth he was doing there, he had grabbed her by both hands and pulled her to her feet as the band struck up a lively *bourrée*. As they joined the group dancing forwards and back, swirling and stamping, she didn't have the breath to speak.

Paul was a good dancer, light on his feet and vigorous. Rachel enjoyed herself although she was also perplexed by his sudden appearance. At the end of the dance, Paul took her hand and led her to a quiet corner.

Rachel was desperate to touch him, but she wanted to clear up a few things first. "What are you doing in Pelette? I thought you were gone for good."

Paul smiled. "So did I, Rachel. I wasn't lying to you when I said I wouldn't be coming back."

"So what has changed?"

He looked pensive for a moment. "Meeting you and seeing how you were embarking on a new life made me think seriously about my own situation."

"Really?"

"Yes, really." A look of sadness passed across his face. "I've realised that Paris has nothing to offer me any more. My marriage is over so the city has only bad memories for me. Unlike here." He lightly caressed Rachel's cheek, making her catch her breath.

She took his hand away, but held it on her lap. "I still don't understand, Paul." Was he saying that he was coming back because of her?

He leant back in his chair. "Before coming to Dreste, I thought that I might move north, perhaps to St Malo where my mother lives." He smiled, squeezing both of her hands in his. "But since leaving here

I've had time to think and I've made a decision." He looked at her, serious for a moment. "While my uncle was resting his shoulder at home, he discovered that he really liked the idea of being retired. So, after I left, he called me in Paris to ask if I'd like to take over his picture-framing business. He can still make frames now and again, but he won't have the burden of running a shop." Paul's eyes had lit up with excitement and he had a big grin on his face. "It won't happen for a while yet, because I have to find someone to take over the shop in Paris, but I've decided that that is what I'm going to do: I'm coming back to Dreste."

Rachel was quiet. Paul looked at her, his face questioning. "I hoped you might be pleased, but I can see that you're not."

"I don't know what to think." Knowing now that Paul had planned to come back, Rachel was offended that he hadn't called to speak to her about it. "I'm just surprised that you haven't been in touch at all since …" Rachel looked around and saw some of her neighbours smiling across at her. "Since, you know what," she whispered.

Paul squeezed her hands again, looking serious. "I didn't want to say anything until I was sure about my decision. And I wanted to be sure I was coming back for the right reasons."

"You mean, for business reasons?"

"Purely business, of course!" The musicians had finished their break and had struck up another lively tune. "Let's dance. There'll be plenty of time to talk later."

She took his hand and they danced again, then swopped partners and danced with her children.

All of the kids were keeping a keen eye on the clock. "Mum, it's nearly midnight," said Charlie, rushing outside. Rachel grabbed their coats, hats and scarves and went out to join the group.

She smiled as Paul took her hand and they stood counting down the minutes to midnight. When the church bells rang out and the fireworks blasted off, they kissed and hugged each other tightly until they were pulled apart and embraced by Rachel's children, her friends and neighbours and everyone else who was there to celebrate the sheer joy of welcoming in a brand-new year.

# Chapter 20: Best of Three

After the dance, Paul went back down to the house with Rachel and the children for a cup of tea before heading into Dreste. Rachel had agreed to call him later in the week; the party had been fun, but she needed time to get accustomed to the fact that he was coming back and to decide what to do. Was he the man for her? Would she have fallen for Josh if her time with Paul really had meant something? Post-party she wasn't in the right state to make any kind of decision. Yawning, she climbed into bed and turned off the light.

She hoped to get a few hours' sleep before it was time to let the chickens out and feed the cats. If they weren't fed promptly, the cats took turns to sit on her head and chew her hair. There was only so much purring and dribbling that Rachel could take, so she batted Fudge away and went into the kitchen to feed him and Mousey.

It was another bright clear morning and despite her woolly head she found she was smiling as she measured out grit and pellets for the chickens. Paul or not Paul? It was quite a nice dilemma to have.

Back in the kitchen, she gazed vaguely at the phone while waiting for the kettle to boil. The light was flashing, indicating that she had messages. Yawning, she made tea then sat down to check the phone.

"It's probably Dad and Connie calling from a casino. Or jail," she chuckled to herself as she stroked the cats. She pressed the button and listened to slightly drunken New Year messages from Irina and the cousins, Philippe, Jilly, Margot and other friends. Then there was one from Michael sounding drunk and sentimental, and a cheery one from Harold and Connie. She smiled as she listened to the fireworks whizzing in the background as they shouted their New Year's greetings from the capital.

The last message caught her completely by surprise: "Hi Rachel. It's me, Josh. Hey, guess what? I got that teaching job in Grenoble, so I'm coming back! Yes, and I'm arriving tomorrow. Warm the bed up for me! See you soon, beautiful."

Rachel played the message through again then sat staring at the phone. "Damn and blast it." Things were getting very complicated indeed. She staggered back to bed and fell asleep.

Waking two hours later and feeling blurry, she showered and woke the kids. After lunch, she called Margot and told her about Paul turning up out of the blue the night before and the phone call from Josh.

"This sounds like an emergency, darling. I shall be right over."

"Come for supper and bring some of your special herbal remedy."

"Don't worry, you can count on me."

By the time her friend turned up that evening, Rachel was in a bit of a state. "Christ, Margot. I've got myself into quite a pickle. What am I going to do?"

Margot sat down at the table, pulled out a notepad,

a pen and an enormous spliff from her bag and waggled an empty glass at her hostess.

Rachel grabbed the bottle and topped them both up.

"Lists, my darling," she said, lighting the spliff and inhaling deeply. "I would say spreadsheet, but a list will do for now."

Rachel curled up on the sofa with her feet tucked underneath her. "Okay. Where do we start?"

"Come and sit at the table. You need to concentrate – this is your future happiness we're talking about."

Rachel pulled a face but uncurled herself and sat down opposite her friend at the big wooden table and took a puff from the joint.

"Right," said Margot. "Headings. Number 1: Michael ..."

"Michael!" screeched Rachel. "We don't need him in the equation."

Margot narrowed her eyes as the smoke swirled up and coughed lightly. "*Au contraire*, darling. He needs to be on there because he may be a cheating, lying little toerag ..."

"I couldn't have put it better myself."

"But, despite all my words of wisdom, you're still in love with him ..."

Rachel snorted and nearly choked on her wine. "Rubbish! I hate him."

"And he'd be back in a flash – baby or no new baby – if you'd have him."

"Ha! No chance."

Ignoring her, Margot wrote "Michael" firmly at the top of the page.

"Then there's Paul," she said, adding his name in the next column. "And last but not least, The Professor."

"Okay, now what?"

"Down the left-hand side we list things that are important to you, then we give them a score out of five."

Rachel tried and failed to stifle a laugh.

Margot carried on. "Then you can add and deduct points for other things."

"Like?"

Margot twirled the pen between her fingers and gazed up at the ceiling.

"Oh, I don't know." She watched as Fudge sashayed across the table and rubbed his head against Rachel's cheek. "Maybe they get points if they're nice to the cats."

"Okay," said Rachel. "So that's *nul points* for Michael who always claimed to be allergic to them and made them sleep outside, didn't he pusskins?"

"Cats are more of a tie-breaker, if you will," said Margot, clearly keen to get down to the nitty-gritty. "Let's start with the basics."

"Okay – I'm ready!"

"Points for who's actually available?"

Rachel frowned. "Two for Michael, three for Paul – because he still has a wife – and five for Josh."

Margot marked the scores. "Right. Attraction?"

"Michael zero, Paul five, Josh four."

"I thought you said Josh was cute?"

Rachel shrugged. "Beard."

"Okay. Intellectual stimulation?"

Rachel guffawed.

"We'll get on to the other kind of stimulation in a

minute," said Margot, trying to stay serious. "Who would be your best match when it comes to things of the mind?"

Rachel relit the spliff and took a long puff. "That's a hard one," she said, blowing the smoke over her shoulder and trying not to cough. "I guess Michael gets a five because he knows me so well, the bastard."

"Yes, but does that count as 'stimulation'? Rachel, try and be serious."

Rachel had her hand over her mouth and was giggling again. "Sorry, sorry! Okay, right. Well, I suppose top points for intellectual stimulation should go to The Prof because he tells me things I never knew about."

Margot marked a five under Michael and Josh. "What about Paul?"

"Who cares! He's just sex on a stick."

Margot sighed and took what was left of the spliff back from her friend. "I really don't know why I bother sometimes."

Rachel stood up and came round to the other side of the table to give her friend a hug. "Because," she said, making a big effort to sound serious, "it's fun, but it's only men and they don't really matter. So what's the score so far?"

Margot sniffed. "Can't say because you haven't scored Paul on 'intellectual stimulation'."

"Okay," said Rachel, perching on the table top. "Let's say four, because he appreciates my art but his skills lie elsewhere."

Margot gave her a sideways look before totting up the scores. "Woo," she said, in a whistle. "This is interesting."

Rachel slid down off the table and leant over the notepad. "And?"

"The scores are in, *Mesdames et Messieurs*. In reverse order: third is Michael the Love Rat. Second is Sex on a Stick Paul, but our winner this evening is ..." Margot beat a drum roll on the table, "The Professor, with an unbeatable fourteen points."

"Wow," said Rachel, retreating to the sofa.

"Wow, indeed."

The women were silent for a moment, each lost in thought. "Is there any of that cheese left, Rachel? I feel a bit peckish."

"Sure, I'll bring some out. Crackers?"

"Yes please."

Rachel mulled over the results as she fetched the goat's cheese and biscuits. Who would have thought that Josh would come out the winner?

The women were sitting deep in contemplation in front of the fire with mugs of coffee and empty plates when Alice came in.

Kissing her mother, she sniffed suspiciously. "It smells funny in here."

"Really, love?" said Rachel, trying to look innocent.

"I hope you're not smoking dope again. I could be taken into care, you know."

"Don't worry, darling, it's only a little herbal relief for my bad back," said Margot. "The doctor said it was good for me and the occasional puff won't do your mother any harm either."

Alice looked unconvinced but gave Margot a New Year's hug, kissed her mother and went off to bed leaving the women to ponder the results of their highly scientific survey.

"Well," said Rachel, when her daughter had gone, "I need to think about our research a little bit more."

"And I need to go home," said Margot, rising a little unsteadily to her feet and looking at her watch. "Claude will be here to whisk me off any moment."

At the sound of Claude pulling up outside the house, Rachel hugged her friend and smiled. "Thanks Margot. This has been a very interesting and informative evening," she said, giggling again.

"Any time, my darling," said Margot, as she tottered off towards the taxi and home.

# Chapter 21: Decision Time

The next day, Rachel kept taking the sheet of paper with Margot's lists out of her pocket and looking at it. She knew it was silly, but the exercise had got her thinking about what she wanted – and what she could and couldn't have.

Margot was right. Until baby Olivier had arrived, Rachel had secretly hoped that she and Michael might one day get back together. Now Michael had the baby, Rachel knew he wouldn't desert Amelie. At least not for a while, she thought sourly.

She was back in the studio, leafing through some of her reference books in search of inspiration for a new range of birthday cards. She looked up as the alarm clock clanked: Claude would be depositing Josh at her door very soon and she had no idea what to say to him.

At the sound of an engine, she sank to her knees and crawled over to the window. Peeking out over the sill, she could just see the taxi snaking its way up the road towards the house. There was nothing for it: she was going to have to hide.

"Oh buggeration," she muttered, running down the stairs and into the laundry room where her housekeeper was extracting sheets from the tumble dryer. "Irina," she hissed, "tell him he can't stay and that I'm not here, will you?"

Irina drew herself up to her full height and looked fierce. "I make Mr Claude take him away, Madame."

"Thank you," said Rachel, dashing into the pantry and closing the door. Although she referred to the place as a pantry, it was actually more like a large broom cupboard. Once inside, Rachel managed to wriggle in between the Hoover and the ironing board, resting her bum on a shelf.

She sat there for what seemed like ages, unable to hear what was going on because of the noise from the washing machine. Eventually, the cupboard door was pulled open and Irina stood there triumphantly.

"All safe now, Rachel. I tell him to 'bugger off' – no room here. He looked very sad, but I make him go back to town." Irina actually chuckled. "Mr Claude is happy because he has double taxi fare!"

"Thank you."

Poor Josh. Rachel did feel guilty as she dusted herself off and thanked Irina. She knew that hiding in a cupboard was a cowardly thing to do, but she really couldn't face him. Sitting in the dark surrounded by spiders and tins of cat food she had made a decision: she wanted to be with Paul Callot.

Irina tried to look cool but had clearly enjoyed her role as defender. "Not a problem, Rachel."

"Could you feed the kids later?" asked Rachel. "I have to finish off some work then I need to go into town for a couple of hours. There's someone I have to see." With that, she bounded back upstairs to her studio.

After an hour or so, she decided she couldn't wait any longer. Having made her decision, she wanted to see Paul right away. She was going to go into town just as she was but, catching sight of herself in a mirror, decided that the cobwebs in her hair were not attractive.

"Okay. Shower, clean clothes, then I'm off."

She was in a bathrobe drying her hair when her son came into the bedroom. "Hi love. What is it?"

"There's a man downstairs asking for a room."

"Damn, is there?" Rachel was hoping not to have any guests until later in the week. "Can you tell him I'll be right down?"

"Okay."

"Oh, and did he say where he was from?"

Charlie shrugged. "America, I think he said last time."

Rachel put down her hairdryer. "What do you mean by 'last time', love?"

Her son rolled his eyes. "What I said – when he was here last time. You know, just before Christmas."

Rachel's heart sank like a stone. "You don't mean it's Josh, do you?"

"Oh yeah. That was his name." Charlie grinned. "Forgot."

The sympathy she had felt for Josh when she was sitting in the pantry now turned into indignation: the cheek of the man coming back when he had been told quite categorically that there was no room. Fuming, Rachel threw on her clothes and marched downstairs.

As she got to the last step, Josh scooped her up and swung her around. "Hey, I'm back. Isn't it great that I got the job? It means we can go on lots more hikes together!"

When she was down on the ground, Rachel

unpeeled herself from Josh's embrace and stepped back with her arms folded over her chest. "Well," she said, "I'm very surprised to see you here again when Irina made it quite clear there wasn't any room."

At this point, Irina came in from the kitchen. "Plenty of room, Madame," she said with a smile.

"That's my girl!" said Josh, with a wink at Irina who blushed girlishly.

Rachel stood there with her mouth open, thinking that everyone had gone mad. "No there isn't, Irina. Remember?"

Claude, who was standing in the doorway, cleared his throat. "Does it mean I have to take this one back as well?"

"As well as what?" asked Rachel crossly.

"As well as the gentleman from the picture shop."

Irina smiled. "The one I told to 'bugger off'."

Rachel put her hands to her face and whimpered. "Oh no. What have I done?"

Irina put on her fierce expression again. "Rachel, you ask me to tell Mr Claude to take the other man away."

Claude opened his hands in a gesture of defeat. "What Irina tells me to do, I do."

Josh was sitting on the staircase looking perplexed. "I have no idea what is going on here, but can I have a room or not?"

Rachel went over to him and took his hands. "Okay Josh, you can have a room," she said gently. "But you can't have *me*."

"Not even as a friend?"

"Friends yes, of course. But not …" she could see Irina, Claude and her son straining to hear what she said. "Not in a bedsock kind of way, if you get my drift."

"Sure thing," said Josh. "That's fine by me."

She kissed him on the cheek. "Thank you. I'll let Irina sort you out." Irina smiled and went to fetch a key.

Rachel went over to Claude. "I'm so sorry about the muddle."

The taxi man just shrugged. "That's okay. I've had some good fares today."

She gave him a kiss. "Can you take me back into town?"

"Of course."

"Hold on a minute," she said, dashing into the kitchen and returning with a bottle of champagne. "Right. Let's go!"

\* \* \*

There's nothing a cab driver likes more in the world than a chase, and this was a chase. As they left Tournesol, Claude told Rachel that Paul Callot was planning to catch a Paris train that evening.

They went first to the shop, only to find it locked and dark. They'd missed him. Jumping back into the taxi, Rachel felt desperate. What would she do if Paul changed his mind and decided not to settle in Dreste after all? Having decided that he was the man for her, she wasn't sure she could bear it.

Claude screeched across town, swung his taxi onto the station forecourt and slammed on his brakes. "Try Platform 6, Rachel," he advised, as she jumped out of the car. "I'll wait here."

"Thanks Claude. Wish me luck!" She dashed into the station, scanning the Departures board. It was only a small station, but Platform 6 was at the far end. Claude had been right: this was the place for the Paris trains. Rachel couldn't help a sob escaping from her throat as she dodged around the commuters, desperate to find Paul.

It wasn't long until she caught sight of him, sitting on a bench, gazing up at the board.

"Paul, don't go!" she cried, throwing herself at him.

Paul swept her up in his arms, laughing as he hugged her tightly against his chest. "My goodness, what's all this?"

Rachel was crying now. "I'm so sorry. I didn't mean to send you away. It was all a mistake." She stepped back, gulping. "Please don't go." She held up the bottle. "I brought champagne."

Paul laughed and kissed her. "Rachel, I'm not going anywhere."

"You're not?" She looked at him, surprised. "But Claude said you were going back to Paris. After Irina told you to, er, leave."

He caught her by the shoulders and kissed her firmly on the lips. "I think Claude misunderstood. What I meant was that I was *meeting* a Paris train." Just at that moment, the train slowly entered the station and slid towards them. "My uncle went to Paris for New Year and I said I'd meet him and carry his case back to the shop. He's not allowed to strain that shoulder of his."

"Oh." Rachel stood in silence, looking stunned. "Have I just made a complete fool of myself?"

Paul smiled and brushed strands of hair away from her face. "No, but you have made me very happy."

"Have I?"

"Yes," he said, grabbing her hand. "Now let's find my uncle."

\* \* \*

Back at Tournesol, Rachel smiled as she held her glass of champagne up to the light and watched the bubbles ricochet through the pale amber liquid.

Next to her sat Paul. Around the table were Charlie, Alice, Monsieur Claude, Irina and Josh, all with their glasses raised in a toast.

"Let's drink to health, happiness, new and old friends," said Rachel.

Paul kissed her and smiled. "And to a very happy New Year."

## THE END

# A London Affair

# Chapter 1: Best-laid Plans

Kate's announcement that she didn't intend to take up her place at university was not well received. She decided to tell her parents after Sunday lunch when she hoped roast lamb and a glass of wine would have put everyone in a good mood, but it didn't go according to plan. Instead, her mother Annie reacted as though it was the end of the world and tempers were starting to fray.

"What do you mean, you don't want to go? Of course you're going to university. You have the grades you need and everything's planned."

"Your plans maybe, but not mine."

Her mother tried to laugh it off. "Sweetheart, you're being ridiculous."

"Thanks a bunch for that considered view." Why did no one take her seriously? "I've reconsidered and decided that uni is not for me after all."

"Is that so? And how, precisely, do you think you'll ever find a decent job without a degree?"

"Lots of people do well who've never been to university."

"Like who?"

"Loads of people, like er ..." Kate's mind went blank. "Oh, I don't know – Kim Kardashian."

"I don't think having a large derrière and wearing clothes counts as a job."

"Sarcasm is the lowest form of wit, Mother."

"You see – you're clever with words. You're exactly the type of girl who should be studying for an English degree."

"Maybe I am, but I've had enough of exams and school and homework and I don't want to go just for the sake of it."

"Okay, forget English. What about switching to Drama? Or – I don't know – what about Media Studies? I don't think it matters what you do so long as you're using that big brain of yours."

"No way, Mum." Kate laughed, slightly hysterically. "As if I would want to spend three years on Drama or Media Studies. I don't want to be an English teacher and I think my chances of landing a job with the BBC are minimal, so what would be the bloody point?"

"Don't you swear at me, young lady!"

"That's not exactly swearing. You and Dad say 'bloody' all the time."

"Yes, but that's different."

Her mother was infuriating. "Anyway, I'm not swearing at you. I'm swearing at the idea of university and boring, pointless courses that cost a fortune and leave you no better off. I want a job and money, not debts."

Annie paused from vigorously scrubbing the kitchen table and crossed her arms across her chest, looking flushed. "David, speak to your daughter, will you please?"

Kate's father was a peaceable man who had hoped to stay out of the debate until everyone had calmed down. He reluctantly turned away from stacking the dishwasher and straightened up, knowing that what he was about to say would not go down well with his wife. "I'm sorry, Annie, but I think Kitty might have a point. Is it really a sensible idea for her to load herself down with debts with no guarantee of a job at the end of the course? Especially when she has no firm idea of what she wants to do as a career? Perhaps it would be more sensible for her to put things on hold and take a little time to think about her future."

"Thanks, Dad." Kate grinned. Her father nearly always supported her against her mother, though there had been no guarantee he would back her this time. "I knew you'd understand."

David looked at her seriously, stressing his point with a gravy-covered spoon. "I may understand your reasoning, but that doesn't mean you can hang around the house doing nothing while your mother and I do all the work."

"I won't hang around the house. I'll find something in town while I'm looking for a proper job."

Her father frowned. "Nice idea, but there's not much work going in Wenyard at the moment."

"Oh, there's bound to be something. I only need a boring job to tide me over for a short while until I'm snapped up somewhere else."

"Who's going to snap you up with no experience and no degree?" Her mother could always be depended upon to ask the really tricky questions.

Kate gritted her teeth, knowing she didn't have a very convincing answer. "I don't know. Somebody in London, perhaps."

"What do you know about London? We took you to London Zoo when you were eight and you went on a trip with the Girl Guides aged twelve. You don't know the place and we don't have any family there to keep an eye on you."

"I don't need looking after." Kate rolled her eyes. "And it's not the other side of the world. Perhaps you'd prefer it if I moved to Birmingham? Or how about Glasgow? Or darkest Peru? It doesn't matter to me. I just want to be somewhere that isn't full of losers, like this place."

"Well, thank you very much." Annie threw the dishcloth on the counter, startling the cat that was curled up on the windowsill. "What a nice thing to say to your parents."

Kate wanted to put an arm around her mother, but couldn't bring herself to do it. "I don't mean you and Dad are 'losers'. I only meant ..." What did she mean? "I mean people like Steve and all the other saddos hanging around town with nothing to do and no ambition. I want something more exciting and London might be the place to go."

"Steve's not a 'saddo'. He works very hard on his father's farm." Annie liked her daughter's boyfriend and wondered whether they might settle down together one day. "So, apart from ruining Steve's young life, what precisely do you intend to do in London?"

Kate looked at her feet, not wanting to confess that she and Steve had had one of their regular bust-ups. Kate was fond of him but she knew they had no future because she wanted more than to be a farmer's wife. Something better awaited her in life – she just didn't know what it was yet, which was why she needed to go out into the world.

"I don't know, Mum! That's actually the point – I don't know what I want to do. All I know is I don't want to be trapped in a university in some poxy town with a load of spotty youths doing yet more bloody essays just to get some half-baked degree."

"Don't shout at your mother."

"I'm not shouting," shouted Kate. And with that she stormed out of the kitchen in tears, feeling angry with her parents and furious at herself for losing her temper and behaving like a brat rather than the sensible young woman she knew herself to be.

After many more arguments and tense silences interrupted by sharp tears, Kate got her way and her mother reluctantly agreed that she didn't have to go to university immediately, so long as she promised to reconsider her options in the spring. In the meantime, she could stay at home provided she found herself a job and contributed to her living costs.

This suited her fine: despite her bravado, she was a little nervous about leaving her village to live in a "foreign" city, so she was happy to concentrate her efforts on finding work locally while she figured out what to do next.

Fortunately, she was smart and presentable and surprised them all by finding a job in the nearby county town helping a local cheese-maker, Geoff Green, to sell his wares. During the week, Kate worked at the factory shop, but what she enjoyed most was manning the stall at markets and food festivals. She particularly enjoyed helping to set up the stall and, once she overcame her initial nerves, she discovered she had a knack for charming customers into buying things.

* * *

Spring came and went and Kate was still living at home. By the end of summer, she and the disappointing Steve had split up for the final time. In their last few months together, things had changed between them. Somehow, Steve always managed to put her in a situation where she felt in the wrong. She shuddered at the memory of how he bullied her. The worst moment was when she learnt he was messing about with someone else. She was surprised by both the sadness and the relief she experienced when Steve eventually told her they were finished.

So here she was: nearly twenty years old, still single and smelling of sour milk. She hadn't entirely given up on her ambition to move to London and she did occasionally apply for jobs there, but it was beginning to feel like a distant dream. It pained her to admit it, but her parents had been right: without even a Media Studies degree, it was difficult to land an interview, let alone a serious job. Fortunately, her boss appreciated her skills and gave her more and more responsibilities, so she was content most of the time.

She wasn't surprised when Geoff Green called her into his office one Tuesday morning.

"I've got a meeting to go to in Gloucester later, so can you deal with the deli order for me?"

"Of course. I'd be happy to."

"Great. We always land a good-sized order when you deal with the shops," he said with a grin. "You're a damn good sales person."

Kate smiled shyly. She always enjoyed selling to the shops and hoped one day Geoff might let her do more of it.

The cheeses were bought by one or two specialist places, including a smart London deli. Once or twice a month, Ned the buyer would drive up in his van and take as much of Green's cheese as they could supply him with.

Kate always looked forward to Ned's visits because it gave her a chance to show off her knowledge of the produce. He was also by far the most intriguing man she had ever met. Tall and gangly with a throaty laugh and a louche charm, he had the look of a man who would be most at home on a beach in Goa where, in fact, he had spent two years at some mysterious period in his past.

"I'm a rolling stone," was all he would say when she asked him where he lived. Travelling the country in an old transit van, visiting small traders and collecting their produce, suited him because it didn't seem too much like work and it brought in enough money to pay the bills. Kate had a terrible crush on Ned for a while, despite his being nearly as old as her father.

After her boss had left, she busied herself tidying the stock until 11am when she heard Ned's van crunch across the gravel into the yard. She watched him as he emerged, looked around with a smile, then strolled across to the tasting room where she was waiting.

"So what's good today?" he asked after greeting her with a peck on the cheek. "The punters couldn't get enough of the Old Welly you recommended to me last time."

"It's actually called Old Willow, but I know what you mean." Kate made a note to pass that on to the cheese-maker. "I'll tell Geoff. He'll be really pleased the new products are going down so well."

Ned ambled to and fro, carefully loading up the van with his regular order. When he came back in for the final time, Kate put down her pad and pen and picked up a small packet, wrapped in wax paper.

"Before you go, I think you should try this. It goes really well with the homemade elderflower cordial we're now producing."

Ned sat down opposite Kate at the room's scrubbed oak table, unwrapped the parcel and smoothed a lump of chalky white cheese onto a chunk of crusty white bread. Closing his eyes, he chewed thought-fully. Eyes still closed behind the shades he wore even in winter, he stretched out his palm, indicating that Kate should place a tumbler of cordial into it. Having finished the cheese, he sniffed and sipped the pale yellow fluid.

"The elderflower blossoms were all gathered from the local woodlands and we use spring water, unwaxed lemons and a hint of fresh ginger. It's all natural and really good for you," she added, crossing her fingers and deciding not to mention the ton of sugar that went into each batch.

"This is lush," he said, at last opening his eyes and wiping his mouth with a spotted hanky. "I'll take as much as you can spare of this goat's cheese and six crates of cordial." He popped another morsel of cheese into his mouth, nodding contentedly. "I'll be back for more of this as soon as you can make a new batch." He smiled. "I hope you're on commission."

"I wish!"

"You should be. You have a gift for knowing what

our customers will like, even though you've never been to the deli."

"Oh, it's not so difficult," she said, modestly. "Who doesn't love artisan cheese and homemade cordial?"

Ned looked thoughtful. "You should pay us a visit and see where your produce ends up. There's more to it than the shop, you know. There's a very nice bistro area at the front where 'ladies who lunch' fight over themselves to enjoy your cheeses on tiny salads."

Over the months, Kate had heard a lot about Delish Organics and its customers from Ned, who made it sound very glamorous. "That would be fabulous, but I'm not sure I could afford the trip on my wages. And I don't have anywhere to stay."

"Look, if you want to come for a few days, I can find you somewhere to stay. In fact, I've got an even better idea." He grinned. "Christmas is coming and the shop is mad busy in the run up to the holidays. It would kill me to be indoors all day with no sunlight, but I reckon you should apply for a temporary job there. You'd enjoy it. And it would do you good to get away from all this and experience a bit of the big, bad world for a few months. Unless you have anything else planned?"

"No, nothing special." It was over a year since she'd started her job with Geoff and she still had nothing else lined up. She hadn't said much to Ned about her rather vague ambitions, but it wasn't the first time he'd asked what her plans were. She frowned as she looked at the trees covered in rich green growth. "But isn't it a bit early to think about Christmas? I mean, it's not even autumn yet."

"No, man. In the shop, Christmas prep starts in

June. Anyway, why not think about it?" He extracted a dog-eared card from the pocket of his cargo pants and handed it over. "Email Joseph at this address – tell him who you are and that 'Cheese Ned' recommended you. They don't expect junior staff to trek down to the shop for face-to-face interviews, so don't worry about that. Meanwhile, I'll put in a good word with the boss," he added with a wink. "I've got connections."

"Thank you." She took the card and smiled, not sure whether he was serious or not. "I might give it a try." Maybe it was time for a change. She had grown comfortable at the shop and was no further forward in discovering what it was she actually wanted to do. Her parents were great and didn't put any pressure on her, but she sometimes caught her mother studying her with an intense frown. Annie seemed to be resigned to the fact their daughter would never go to university, but that didn't stop the pair of them worrying about her.

When Ned left, Kate went back to arranging chutney in straw-filled baskets ready for the next day's market, but thoughts of the deli wouldn't leave her. Okay, so she'd probably still be selling the same cheese, but at least she would be doing it somewhere else.

After supper, she visited the website where there was a brief description of the West London café and shop and a short notice stating they were always on the lookout for "people passionate about great food, especially local, organic produce". She couldn't believe there wouldn't be hundreds of young people wanting to work in Chelsea, but she had two distinct advantages: she was good with customers and she could tell her Yarg from her Stinking Bishop. That would give her the edge, surely?

Deciding to act before she changed her mind, she quickly filled in the online application form and pressed "Send". Now all she had to do was wait.

# Chapter 2: A New Start

It was a bright autumn morning when Kate flew into the kitchen with the news. "I got it!"

"You got what, sweetheart?"

"The London job I really wanted." She hadn't realised how much being accepted meant to her until the letter came through confirming she'd been chosen to join the team.

"Well, that's great," said her father. "Er, remind me which job that was."

Kate sighed. "It's to work at Delish Organics, the place Ned put me on to." She did a twirl.

"Did you nip down there for an interview without telling us?"

"No, Dad. We did the whole thing by phone and on Skype. It was pretty amazing actually – me in my bedroom and these scary people in their swish offices."

"So it's another cheese shop?" asked Annie, nervously.

"It's more than that: they say it's the foremost café, gallery and organic shop in the entire country. Probably."

"That sounds very impressive. And what exactly will you be doing?"

Kate scrutinised the letter. "A bit of everything really. Helping in the shop, serving at tables, arranging the produce, keeping the place tidy. They were really impressed with my hands-on experience selling Geoff's cheeses and stuff."

"Can I see?" Her mother held out her hand for the letter and a frown formed as she read it. "This salary is next to nothing. How are you going to afford to rent anywhere?" She chewed her lip. "We'll help you as much as we can, but money's tight here at the moment."

Kate hugged her. "I know and I wouldn't expect you to subsidise me." She smiled happily. "Accommodation is part of the deal."

Her parents exchanged nervous glances. "It is? Really?"

"Yup. There's a flat over the shop and the owner keeps rooms there for junior staff doing work experience or on short-term contracts."

Annie wrinkled her nose. "A room over a shop doesn't sound very nice." Judging by the looks passing between her parents, Kate suspected they were imagining a sweatshop with overworked staff hot-bedding on thin straw mattresses.

"It does seem odd, expecting your staff to live over the shop in this day and age."

"Don't worry, Dad. It's part of the company ethos, which is 'To provide training and a nurturing environment for all the staff, from managers to baristas'. You see? It says it here."

David looked at the mission statement at the bottom of the letter. "It sounds bogus, but I expect it means they receive a government grant or something."

"You're so suspicious, the pair of you." Kate pointed to the address on the letter. "There, look. It's in a super-smart part of town." She took out her phone and Googled the address. "See?" She showed the photos to her mother who peered at the soft-focus images of perfect fruit and veg and smiling young people in long aprons lined up outside a handsome white building.

"It does look nice."

"And I'll have my own room just there," she said, pointing at one of the upstairs windows. "So what do you think?"

Her mother looked across at David, who smiled and nodded. "Sounds like a good opportunity for you to spend time in London and get a feel for the place. Go for it."

"Thanks so much," she said, throwing her arms around her parents before dashing off to email the shop with her acceptance.

* * *

A fortnight later, Kate was in London. By the time she had trundled her case through the station, fought her way up and down escalators and slogged round to the high street, she felt hot, sweaty and in need of a shower. There had been a thick layer of frost that morning when her parents tearfully waved her off at the station, so she'd chosen a heavy coat and wrapped herself up in a scarf and stripy hat with ear flaps knitted by her granny. Now she was far too hot and amazed at the number of people bundled up in Norwegian-style hats and woolly boots more appropriate to the fiords than the overheated streets of the capital.

She ducked into a doorway to drag a comb through her light-brown curls and smear on some lipstick before approaching her new workplace and home. As she turned the corner and saw Delish Organics on the opposite side of the road, she could feel her heart thumping with excitement and a smidgen of fear.

The pavement seating area was packed with customers corralled behind a thick rope, a yellow and white candy-striped canopy protecting them from the elements. Above the elegant row of shops, the sky was a smoky blue, crisscrossed with vapour trails made by planes that seemed almost as numerous as the taxis clogging up the road.

Kate stood and watched for a while, waiting for the pounding of her heart to subside. She smiled to herself as she watched waiters flit to and fro with coffees and pastries, thinking soon she might be doing the same. Once her breathing was back to normal and she had cooled down, she dashed across the road, dodging double-decker buses.

The glass front of the shop glided open as she wheeled her slightly battered suitcase past a gentleman reading *Le Monde* and feeding a plain croissant to his Dalmatian.

Inside, the shop was surprisingly noisy and busy with customers and staff milling around. Along the left-hand side, people were queuing to buy savouries – including Green's cheeses. Waiters appeared from the back of the room with plates of toasted sandwiches and bowls of soup. Kate stepped aside to allow a slender boy to whirl past with a tray piled with coffees. It seemed like chaos, but organised chaos. Eventually Kate approached a table laden with bread rolls in extravagant shapes and introduced herself to a man whose badge identified him as Joseph.

"Welcome, welcome!" he said with a broad grin. "I'm pretty busy at the moment, as you can see. Why don't you go upstairs and leave your suitcase, then I'll brief you properly after lunch when things have calmed down?" He looked around for someone to help. "Imogen here will take you up there, won't you?"

A tall blonde girl carrying a tray of dirty glasses stopped at the mention of her name and looked Kate up and down. "Sure. Let me get rid of these, then I'll show you around."

Kate followed the waitress to the back of the shop, past the kitchen and into the lift.

"Welcome to the madhouse." Seeing Kate's worried expression she smiled. "Only joking! Vitaly only employs people with decent social skills."

"Vitaly? I thought Joseph was the boss."

"No, he's the manager. Vitaly Polzin. He owns this place and most of the street, actually. Not to mention other chunks of London. He's Russian," she said, as though that explained everything.

The deli was in two large Victorian terraced houses that Vitaly had combined into one and the lift doors opened onto a wide landing with marble floors and high ceilings. As Imogen opened the door to the apartment, Kate could see the decoration echoed the minimalist look of the shop and café beneath with its clean, white walls, stone floor and simple lines. Vitaly had spent a year doing up the property, including digging down two floors to create space for another flat.

Imogen pointed out all the features in the style of a bored estate agent. "South-facing balcony. Handy for local amenities. Notice the high ceilings and big windows, blah, blah."

Kate was aware of her mouth hanging open as she gaped at her surroundings. The only time she had seen white leather sofas and black marble surfaces was in gangster films. She had grown up surrounded by furniture her mum and dad had inherited from their parents or picked up over the years from auction houses and car-boot sales. The height of sophistication at home was a set of birch-effect bookcases from Ikea that Kate had received for her sixteenth birthday.

"This is just, just …"

"Big? Expensive? Bland?"

She shook her head wordlessly. "It's lovely," she said, eventually. "And Mr Vitality lets us live here?"

Kate winced – how could she have got Vitaly's name wrong? Her new colleague would think she was an idiot.

"'Mr Vitality'! I like it." Imogen grinned. "Yep. I think it's some kind of tax dodge. Either that or he has so much money he doesn't care. Your bedroom is over here."

The room wasn't large, but it was light and bright, like the rest of the flat. It had a huge bed, masses of floor-to-ceiling cupboard space and a grey velvet armchair that looked perfect for curling up in with a good book. Kate walked over to the window, which looked out onto a small courtyard two floors below. Straight ahead was a garden and beyond it the back of another row of terraces, but these were red brick and handsome in an institutional kind of way.

"I'm afraid you get the smallest room and the worst

view because you're the most recent addition to the team. Sorry about that."

"Not at all," said Kate, with a smile. "It's perfect."

"Really?" Imogen gave her a doubtful look. "It doesn't even have a telly – you have to watch the one in the main room."

Kate had noticed the enormous TV covering half a wall and didn't think this was much of a hardship.

"It's fine. I don't mind sharing."

"If you say so. Come on, I'll show you the rest."

They went back out, past the living area to the kitchen, another massive room with a long table and high chairs in pastel colours and a fridge the size of a small caravan. Imogen tugged open the door. "We get loads of free food from downstairs that we shove in here and there's plenty of space for your own stuff down this side."

Looking around, Kate spotted what she recognised as telltale signs of male occupation.

"So, apart from you and me, who else lives here?"

Imogen saw her looking at the large muddy trainers and smiled in what seemed to Kate to be a slightly smug manner.

"As well as you and me, there's Clare and Freddy – she's training to be a chef and works in the kitchen and Freddy's my boyfriend."

"That's nice – did you both find jobs here together?"

"Nope. He's been at Delish for ages. I guess you could say Freddy was one of the perks of the job. We met here. You know how it is: you start off sharing a kitchen and end up sharing a bed. You'll meet him later."

Kate nodded and smiled in an effort to seem

worldly and sophisticated. She'd met her last short-term boyfriend, Pete, at a disco in the village hall, but she was not about to share that piece of information. She was determined to cast off her embarrassing rustic background and develop an entirely new personality oozing urban chic.

"The other person you'll meet is Valentina, Vitaly's niece, or at least that's what he calls her."

"You mean she's really his girlfriend?"

"No, I'm teasing. She's part of his huge, extended family. I think he moved her into the building because she's pretty old – like at least thirty-five – and hoped she would keep an eye on us. Actually, she's super nice and never interferes."

Kate nodded. "I look forward to meeting her later on, then."

"Oh, you might not meet her for a while. We don't see much of each other because she has her own massive apartment upstairs. She used to be a model and has one of those faces that make her seem quite fierce, but she's okay once you get to know her."

"Does she work in the shop, too?"

Imogen sighed wistfully. "Nope, she's got my dream job – she works in the most divine shoe shop in Covent Garden. Sometimes, when they have events, she sneaks me in and I'm allowed to wear Louboutins all evening. My feet hurt like hell all the next day, but it's worth it."

"Are we the only deli people who live here?"

"No, there's another flat below us where Megan, Jules, Ted and Paul live."

Kate frowned. "I don't think I'll ever remember all the names."

177

"Don't worry about it. We all wear name badges in the shop, so you'll figure out who's who soon enough." She smiled. "I'll make us a cup of tea and a sandwich while you unpack, then we'll go down and join the fray. How does that sound?"

"Sounds good. Thanks, Imogen."

"You're welcome. And call me Immy."

# Chapter 3: Deli Delight

It was Kate's first day on the job and she didn't have much of a clue what to expect. Joseph had given her a tour of the premises the previous afternoon, showing her the kitchen, the deli counter and the array of gifts. If someone wanted to buy any of the abstract canvases that adorned the walls, she was to tell him. She'd also been shown how the coffee machine worked and how to place and collect orders for diners. It had been a lot to take in, but she was determined not to show herself up. Would she be busy? Would she drop anything? Would the customers like her? Why shouldn't they like me, she thought. If I can sell green tomato chutney to Herefordshire pensioners, I can sell posh buns to Londoners.

It was still dark when she pulled on her white shirt and tied the long black pinafore over her skirt. Her hair was just long enough to twist into a sort of bun at the nape of her neck and she pushed stray curls behind her ears. Standing in front of the mirror, she smiled at the smart vision that stood before her. She looked far neater and more businesslike than she usually did in the jeans and old sweatshirt she wore on the chilly market square at home.

She knew she could do the job – she was good at selling, after all – but she was still ridiculously nervous. "You can do this," she said to her reflection. "You can smile and sell cheese without making a mess of it. This isn't scary." But her tummy was in knots as she opened the door and left the safety of her bedroom.

"Good morning." A girl with spiky red hair and a nose ring brushed crumbs from her lips and smiled warmly at Kate as she came into the kitchen. "I'm Clare, by the way. So, how are you feeling about Day One?"

"A bit nervous, but I'll be okay once I get going – I think. Though I've no idea what I'm supposed to be doing."

"Ah, sure you'll be fine," said Clare, in a soft Irish lilt.

Just then, a tall young man came into the room, his dark hair slightly damp from the shower. He greeted Kate with a broad smile and a peck on the cheek. "I'm Freddy. Nice to meet you."

"Nice to meet you, too," she said, noticing his clean, fresh scent.

Freddy put an arm around Clare. "Are you planning on scrambling any eggs to go with that toast, by any chance?"

Clare shook her head as she popped the last piece of toast into her mouth and headed over to the dishwasher. "Nope. It's my day off and I have no intention of cooking anything, not even eggs. You can toast your own bread and scramble your own breakfast."

"That's a shame," Freddy winked at Kate. "I was hoping you'd show our new recruit what a brilliant cook you are. How she is going to survive her first day of deli madness on a bowl of Coco Pops I cannot imagine."

"I'm fine with cereal, honestly," said Kate, feeling slightly embarrassed by the attention.

Freddy threw up his hands in mock despair. "You can't say I didn't try, but she's a hard woman."

Clare cocked her head to one side. "Have you noticed the big white thing in the corner of the room there, Frederick? It's full of this stuff we call 'food'. And you can make it hot by using the metal thing over here."

"I know that, my little leprechaun, and I'm pretty handy with the frying pan. But you're so much better at making breakfast than anyone else in this place. Even my own sweet Immy."

Kate turned to see Imogen shuffling in wearing fluffy slippers and looking bleary but effortlessly gorgeous with her hair piled up in a casual heap on her head. Kate was aware of Freddy giving his girlfriend an approving glance as she plonked herself down at the table.

"Morning, people. Is there any coffee going?"

"I think your boyfriend can probably manage to pour you a cup. I'm off for a run." And with that, Clare left the room.

As she looked at her remaining housemates, Kate realised she was the only one dressed and ready for work. "Er, what time do we have to be downstairs?"

Imogen glanced up at the clock on the wall. "About eight o'clock. There's loads of time yet." She yawned and stretched.

"Twenty minutes, actually," said Kate, hoping not to sound either too keen or bossy.

Imogen picked up her mug, stood and shuffled off to the bathroom. "I'm nearly ready."

Half an hour later, the three of them ran down the elegant marble staircase, ready for action. Imogen looked wide awake and elegant and Kate thought the long apron made Freddy appear rather French and appealing. "Okay team?" he said, swinging open the door on the ground floor that led into the deli. "Let's go."

* * *

Joseph liked to gather his staff together at the start of each day to iron out any problems and remind them of Vitaly's vision for the business.

Everyone was seated around one of the stainless-steel tables at the back of the kitchen area when the trio came down.

"Good morning, ladies and gentleman, thank you for joining us." Joseph looked at his watch, making it plain that they were late. "The main thing on the agenda today is to extend a warm welcome to our new colleague." Everyone smiled and waved their greetings to Kate.

"Okay, Ted and Megan – I want you in the shop. Freddy, Paul and Jules – inside tables, please. Imogen – you're in charge of managing the outside tables and of showing Kate how things work. But first, help Jim with coffees. What do we want our customers to do?" Joseph looked at his crew expectantly as they chorused, "Eat well, drink well and be happy!"

"That's right, people." Joseph's face broke into a big grin as he stood and exchanged high-fives with everyone around the table. "Let's get London caffeinated!"

Back in the shop, Kate caught up with Imogen and whispered in her ear. "Does he do that every day?"

"Not the hand-slapping thing, no, but the pep talk,

yes. It's so cheesy and embarrassing – I do my best to miss it as often as possible."

"He seems like a very positive person. Where's he from?"

"Ghana, I think, then he went to college in the States. Can't you tell? At least he doesn't make us introduce ourselves to the punters and tell them to 'have a nice day'."

Despite everyone looking slightly self-conscious, it seemed to Kate that Joseph's enthusiasm worked and her colleagues were all chatting and smiling as they took up their positions.

Joseph threw open the doors and it wasn't long before the first wave of customers arrived and made their way to counters piled high with pastries that wouldn't have looked amiss in the best French *boulangerie*. Soon, the buzz of conversation and the scent of good coffee filled the shop.

After the early-morning commuters had thinned out, the mid-morning crowd arrived and the pavement tables began to fill up. Joseph indicated to the girls that it was time for them to head outside.

Imogen grabbed a pad and took the pencil from behind her ear: customers liked the old-fashioned style of service, and tablets and other electronic devices were banned front of house. "Are you ready for your first experience of pavement duty?"

"Ready for anything!" said Kate, with more confidence than she felt. "Er, what does it involve?"

"Taking orders, serving, tidying up the tables and keeping an eye out for kamikaze toddlers intent on throwing themselves under the wheels of passing juggernauts."

"I think I can do that."

"Great. It's certainly more entertaining than being stuck in the shop making flat whites all day. And we get tips."

"Don't they go into a pot for the staff to share?"

"In theory, yes, but everyone finds the odd 50p accidentally falling into their apron pocket from time to time." Imogen laughed as she saw Kate's expression. "Don't look so disapproving! Think of it as compensation for the damage London air does to your skin."

Kate hadn't realised her thoughts were so clearly etched on her face for everyone to see. She needed to work on that.

Following Imogen outside she sniffed the cold air, which had the sharp tang of diesel and dust kicked up by the taxis and buses. "Wouldn't everyone be more comfortable inside?"

"Probably, but they sit out here so they can see friends go by in their Chelsea tractors. And people like to be seen, as well, of course." She poked Kate lightly in the ribs with her pencil. "This is a very fashionable venue, I'll have you know."

"Oh, I know." Since being given the job, she had read all the online reviews and bought several of the glossy magazines that had featured the store. Secretly she hoped that one day a photographer would come by and snap her chatting to one of their famous customers. How she would enjoy sharing that back home!

Imogen patted her arm, interrupting the daydream. "Come on."

Even though it was November, the sun was out and the tables were soon busy with young mothers and bored-looking au pairs watching infants in buggies as large as small cars and probably costing almost as much.

Kate grew hotter and hotter as she dashed back and forth with trays carrying *croques monsieur*, chunks of Stollen and frothy coffees. She frowned at the overhead heaters, thinking they didn't fit too well with the 'good for the planet' message presented by the shop. The road was packed with traffic, and the noise from motorbikes and impatient minicab drivers leaning on their horns made her jump several times.

Among the customers that morning were young men with hipster beards, local residents with assorted small dogs, and women of indeterminate age with identical shoulder-length hair in 'bronde', a fashionable colour formerly known as dark blonde. Kate was quite fascinated by the women and intrigued by the way they oozed money. It was something to do with their discreet clothes in muted colours, their pink-gold watches and perfectly smooth skins.

The clientele made Kate feel even more like a country cousin, but her colleague looked perfectly at home as she wove her way through the tables, dishing out macarons and Earl Grey tea and chatting to regulars. Immy was wearing eyeliner and a dash of bright scarlet lipstick, and her hair was tied back in a sleek ponytail. Kate had slapped on too much foundation and her curls were springing loose from the scrunchy she had wrestled them into just a few hours before. She made a mental note to refresh her look from the very next day.

# Chapter 4: Dating Dos and Don'ts

Kate had survived a whole week at the deli, so Imogen made them lasagne and bought a couple of bottles of wine to celebrate. Now they had been working side by side for several days, Imogen felt it was time to grill Kate about her love life.

"So, have you left a handsome hunk back at home pining for you?"

"I wish! Actually, I've been single for a while and it suits me fine." Kate frowned. "I've decided men are more trouble than they're worth."

"They can get in the way, but you absolutely cannot be on your own in London. It's totes against the rules. You've got to go out there and snag someone immediately or you'll have nobody to spend weekends with."

"You make it sound so easy."

"That's because this town is awash with luscious men. It's really not difficult to find them."

Not for someone who looks like you, thought Kate, as she watched Imogen casually twist her hair into a knot on her head and flash her perfect teeth.

"I'm just fine as I am. Anyway, now I'm going to be working all the time and I've got no money. Oh, and I look like a poodle."

Imogen looked her up and down. "Actually, you look far more like one of those guinea pigs with mad fur."

"Thanks a bunch," said Kate, running a hand through her unruly locks.

"I mean that in a good way. It's cute and men like the sexy unkempt look. Anyway, all you need is a decent profile and guys will be flocking to your door."

"A profile?"

"For the dating site." She raised her eyebrows doubtfully. "I know you've come up from the country and everything, but you have heard of them, right?"

"Yes, of course. We have these magic things called smartphones as well."

"Okay, okay. Just checking." As she spoke, Imogen was tapping away at the screen. "This is the best app to use for hot guys." She scrolled through the pages. "Wow, look at this one. And him."

Kate reluctantly looked at the screen, frowning as she saw the rows of impossibly gorgeous men. How come men in the capital looked like fashion models, whereas the boys back in the countryside were so lumpen and unappealing?

"No one who looked like him would be interested in me. I'm too, well, ordinary."

Imogen rolled her eyes. "That doesn't matter. You can be whatever you want to be on here." She might have pretended to disagree, thought Kate. "The main thing is to grab someone and have fun. Then by the time they discover you're not quite what they thought, at least you've had a good time."

"I'm not sure I'd be any good at pretending to be something I'm not."

"In that case, we need to accentuate the positive."

"What are you two plotting?" Clare came in and

plonked herself down next to them with a bag of crisps.

"I'm setting up Kate online so she can snag herself a bloke in time for Crimbo."

"I can't believe you're encouraging her to do that, not after everything I've told you."

"Really?" Kate looked worried. "What happened to you, Clare?"

"Where to begin – I've got a list of bad dates as long as your arm."

"Kate doesn't want to hear your sad tales." Imogen stopped what she was doing and smiled. "But then again, some of your tragic dates were quite funny."

"Thanks so much for your sympathy, roomie."

"You have to share your gruesome tales now," said Kate, handing her new friend a glass of wine.

"Let me see. Okay – so this was one of my first experiences of internet dating and it's a cracker." Clare was a good storyteller and didn't need too much persuasion to tell her tales.

"I was living in the sticks and most of the guys online seemed to be in Dublin, so I took the train into town. My date was called Edward and we'd chatted quite a lot online before he suggested we meet up. I hesitated for a while because I was new to the whole thing, but then I thought, 'Why not?' From his photos he looked quite cute: dark hair, blue eyes, fit. And he seemed to have quite a few female friends, which is always a good sign." Kate and Immy nodded encouragingly. "So, that evening I make my way into town on the train and find the bistro where we've arranged to meet. And I sit there for five minutes, ten minutes, fifteen minutes. I'm getting seriously pissed off and ready to leave when this guy I've never seen

in my life before comes in and sits down at my table."
She paused to grab some crisps.

"I guess there was nowhere else to sit?"

"Nope, it's early evening and there are loads of free tables, but this bloke marches over, sits down right opposite and grins at me like we're old friends. It was a bit creepy, d'you know what I mean?"

"I can imagine," said Imogen, who hadn't heard this particular tale before. "So what did you do?"

"I told him I was waiting for someone, thinking this would make him leave, but he just sat there with this soppy look on his face."

"But was he fit?"

"No! He was podgy and pale." Clare cast her eyes to the ceiling, searching for the best description. "With skin the colour and texture of cold porridge."

"Yuck," said Kate. "Defo not worth dumping the no-show for, then. So Mr Pasty Face is sitting there eyeballing you – how did you get rid of him?"

"I said again I was waiting for someone, and yer man says, 'It'll be me you're waiting for.' So I ask him what he means and he says he's the guy I'd arranged to meet. This was starting to freak me out, so I say, 'So what's your name and where do you live?' The bastard gets it right. Lucky guess, I think. So, then I ask him, 'What's my cat's name?' and he gets that right too. It's him – the guy I've been emailing."

Imogen laughed. "Ah, you fell for the phoney profile pic – that's the oldest trick in the book."

"You're only half-right, Miss Know-it-All. Turns out, he was a non-identical twin who used his brother's persona and picture to get dates because he was so feckin' ugly and boring."

"Wow, that's a good story," said Kate.

"Oh, there's more. Top me up, will you?"

Imogen refilled all their glasses. "Go on."

"Okay, so I've finished my beer and he's showing no sign of offering me a drink – I'm thinking I've schlepped all the way over from home for a date with someone who's a phoney, so at least this guy will do the decent thing and buy me a beer. But no, so I wave over the waiter and buy us both a drink because I'm a nice person. Jesus, you'd think I'd turned water into wine. He starts going on about what a kind, genuine girl I am – just like I was in my profile – and how happy he is to have met me. Sure, the man was nearly in tears."

"Ah, he sounds quite sweet."

Clare snorted. "Not sweet – nuts. And it gets worse – the dude then offers me five euros to hold my hand because, he says, he rarely has any contact with people. Are we surprised?"

Imogen was on the edge of her seat by now. "Did you take it?"

"No, you dipstick. And when he follows this by asking how much it would cost to kiss me on the lips, I pretend to go to the loo then leg it out the back door."

A low whistle escaped from Kate's lips. "That's pretty freaky. I'm not sure how I would cope in a similar situation."

"Don't you worry," said Imogen, patting her friend's knee. "Clare's stalkers are all safely locked into their padded cells in Dublin. You'll only meet nice guys over here."

"Hah! I'll save my London dating traumas for another evening then, shall I?"

Kate shook her head. "Actually, Clare, I'd rather you didn't."

"Don't put her off. You'll be fine, really." Imogen picked up her phone, turning her attention back to the screen. "Your profile is set up, so all you need do now is contact some luscious chaps and see what happens."

After another glass of wine, Kate let Immy persuade her to take a look at the dating app and three days later she went off on her first blind date.

\* \* \*

At breakfast the morning after the big event, Immy was keen to hear all about it.

"So how did it go with the guy from Streatham?"

"Ugh. You don't want to know. I should never have let you talk me into this internet dating thing."

"It can't have been as bad as all that. Nothing matches Clare's stories."

"Oh this comes close, believe me."

"Goody!" said Imogen, gleefully. "Pass me the yoghurt and tell me what happened."

Kate handed over the plastic tub, pushed her breakfast bowl to one side and began. "It didn't start too badly. Graham did actually look quite like the photo, so I guess he was only five years older than he claimed to be. And he had a fascinating job managing the recycling schedules for his local council, which isn't as easy as it sounds because people will confuse their card with their cardboard."

"Oh dear."

"And I learnt a lot about Tetrapacks."

"Which may come in handy one day."

"You never know."

"And he didn't once ask me a thing about myself. So I sat and ate and smiled and waited for the evening to end so I could come home and rearrange my sock drawer."

"So it was dull, dull, dull?"

"It was completely, utterly dull until the end of the meal when he leant across the table and yanked out a strand of my hair." Kate frowned, rubbing her scalp at the memory of the sting.

"Pervert. What's he going to do with it? Keep it in a locket around his neck?"

"No, much worse. Or maybe not, depending on your view of weird versus mean and dishonest."

"Go on," said Imogen. "I'm agog now."

"He dunked it into what was left of my coffee mousse then made a big fuss of calling over the manager and saying I'd found it there, that it was disgraceful, especially as this was a special anniversary dinner …"

"No!"

"Yup. And he made such a hoo-ha about it, threatening to bring in the environmental health people, blah, blah, that the manager wouldn't let him pay, so we ended up with a free meal."

"Now that's impressive."

"It was awful. And to cap it all, he had the nerve to ask if I'd like to see him again!"

"And would you?"

"Duh! Of course not." They'd known each other for some weeks now, but Immy still managed to shock her. "Why do you think I'd want to see him again after he behaved like that?"

"More free meals?" Imogen shrugged. "And he was quite nice-looking."

"He was nowhere near as young and handsome as he looked in his profile, he had bad breath and he was a lying scumbag. So no, I will not be seeing him again. Not ever, never."

Freddy came in munching on a piece of cold toast and pulled up a chair to sit next to Imogen. "What's up, ladies?"

"Kate was just reporting back on her date."

"Any good?"

"I think he could have potential."

"Have you listened to a word I've said?"

"I have taken in every single word," said Imogen, laughing. "And I think this one is good for a few more stories."

"If you think he's such a laugh, you go out with him."

"I might consider it if I didn't already have Freddy here." She threw her arms around him and gave him a big kiss.

"Ugh – get a room, you two."

"No time," said Imogen, looking at the clock. "We're due in the shop in ten minutes." She scooped the last spoonful of muesli into her mouth. "Anyway, you need to see who else is out there in dating land. There were loads of other people on your wish list."

Kate sighed. "Do I really have to have another go?"

"Definitely. Just think of last night as a practice run. Things are bound to get better from now on."

# Chapter 5: More Man Trouble

Later that week, Kate and Imogen were on their break and sipping tea in the back of the shop when conversation turned to the Christmas hols. Clare took off her apron and joined them.

"What are your plans, Clare?"

She shrugged. "Back to the rural charms of County Wicklow for the usual holiday hell with all the aunties and cousins. I expect you'll be doing the family thing, too, Kate?"

"Actually no. My folks are abandoning me and going off to the Canaries to work on their tans."

"Well, it's all right for some. Do you mind?"

"No, not at all. I was invited, but spending a week on a beach listening to my parents banging on about my future would be hell. And I'm bored of all the family stuff anyway. I want to spend Christmas in the capital. I want to see a bit of life and join in the excitement."

"You'll be lucky," said Imogen as she wandered past. "London's like a ghost town over the Yuletide. I mean to say, everybody will be in the country from late December then off to Megève for New Year."

Kate and Clare did synchronised eye-rolling. "When you say 'everybody' you mean people who've had their houses featured in *Country Living*. And our yummy mummy customers, of course."

Immy laughed. "Of course. Who else is there?"

"So, what will you be doing this year?" asked Clare.

"Oh, we're being wildly unconventional and spending Christmas on the slopes with friends."

"Anyone we know?"

"I doubt it, darling, unless you went to a very smart boarding school in Sussex."

"Nope. I attended one of Eire's finest educational establishments followed by a stint at catering college in Leicester, neither of which had skiing on the curriculum."

"So is Freddy going with you?" asked Kate, through a mouthful of croissant.

"Nope. He says he can't afford it, but that's just an excuse. Daddy would pay for him to come out, of course, but it's really not Fred's thing. I've tried to persuade him that being away with me and my crew will be super fun, but he says he had a go on a dry slope once as a kid and was rubbish at it. Anyway, I don't want to force him to do something he hates, and I'll see him at New Year."

The girls exchanged looks. They both had the distinct impression that Immy was not terribly concerned about spending the holidays away from her boyfriend. Clare frowned. "So what's yer man going to be doing while you're hitting the slopes with the glitterati?"

"I've no idea. You'll have to ask him yourself. But never mind Freddy. How did it go last night with your latest date?"

"Jeremy?" Kate took a glug of tea and sighed. "It wasn't too bad once he'd stopped crying."

Clare laughed. "You made him cry?"

"Technically no. I didn't make him cry. His ex-girlfriend made him cry when she went off with his best mate."

"You should never get a man on the subject of exes unless you know for sure he was the dumper rather than the dumpee."

"It wasn't deliberate, Immy. I made the mistake of ordering 'penne al salmone', which was what 'She' always had, so I got the whole sad story about how he came home from work and found a note on the kitchen table from Emily saying she'd had the hots for his mate, Phil, for months. Turns out, she couldn't resist him any longer and they'd gone off to Manchester together. What seemed to upset Jeremy most was the thought of not seeing his friend any more."

"Ah, a bromance. That's cute. I think it's nice when a man has a sensitive side."

"I agree sensitivity is a good thing, but this was ridiculous. He cried again when he told me his African grey parrot had just croaked. Then I made the mistake of asking about his hobbies and interests to get him off the subject of ex-girlfriends and dead birds and discovered his team had been relegated, which set him off again." Kate shook her head sadly. "When I heard Clare's story I knew this dating business was a bad idea, but I'm amazed there are so many nutters around."

Clare patted her sympathetically on the arm, doing her best not to laugh. "You've had a run of bad luck, that's all. I'm sure even our glamorous friend here has had some stinkers in the past. It's just the way it goes."

"But now she has Freddy who adores her."

"Yes," said Immy, chewing a bright pink fingernail. "That is a problem."

"Okay, so tell us why that's a problem?" Clare laughed. "Sure, I'd love to have a man who adored me."

"Well, you say that, but being adored is a teeny bit boring. Sometimes I wish Fred was more – I don't know – fiery."

Kate thought back to the last few months with Steve and shivered. "There's nothing great about fiery, believe me." The temper tantrums alternating with extended periods of sulking had been exhausting.

Imogen turned to her with interest. "It sounds like you've had some experience of this, chica. Tell us more."

"I'd rather forget all about him."

"Oh come on," said Clare. "You can't just leave it at that."

"I'm thinking about my ex, Steve. We were together for quite a while before I discovered he was a bit of a bully."

"Did he hit you? Or are we talking *Fifty Shades* here?" There was alarm in Imogen's voice, but her eyes shone as though the idea of being hit was actually quite exciting.

Kate sighed. "No, it was nothing like that. He was an emotional bully who made me feel small." She cringed at the thought. "Can we talk about something else now, please?"

"Okay. Let's forget your disappointing past and concentrate on your exciting future." Imogen had a gleam in her eye that made Kate nervous. "I have a foolproof plan to find you the perfect man with the minimum of effort."

"Oh dear."

"Don't say 'oh dear'. You don't even know what it is yet."

"So tell me."

"You're going back to school."

Clare laughed. "Now that sounds interesting."

# Chapter 6: Back to School

As Kate trudged along in the dark, her face muffled by a thick scarf, she wondered how Immy had managed to talk her into trying a themed dating event. Christmas tree lights winked and sparkled in the windows of the terraced houses lining the South London roads and she wished she was warm and cosy indoors rather than heading off yet again into the dating unknown.

The bus had taken forever to get there – wherever she was – and she felt slightly unnerved to be out of the centre of town, which had grown familiar to her. Looking up from the map that illuminated her phone, she was therefore surprised but relieved to see a familiar figure outside the venue. "Immy! What are you doing here?" Kate looked around at the scattered groups of men hanging around on the pavement. "And where's Freddy?"

Imogen rolled her eyes dramatically. "Well, not here, obviously. He's no need to go looking for 'lurve' when he's got me."

"So explain this to me: you're an item – boyfriend and girlfriend. Why are you at a speed-dating event?"

"I've come out to have a laugh, the same as you."

"Yes, but I'm single and you're not."

"Freddy and I have an arrangement – it's not a life-long commitment."

"But you practically live together."

"We have rooms in the same apartment – that doesn't make us married. And actually he's a tad clingy."

"I think you're being unfair, Immy. You're lucky to have someone so kind and thoughtful who will do anything for you …"

Imogen narrowed her eyes. "It sounds like you've got the hots for my boyfriend."

"No, not at all. I think he's a good guy and you shouldn't be … well, unfaithful to him."

"Christ, you sound like my mother."

"Maybe I do, but think about it. How would you feel if you found out Freddy was trawling dating apps looking for other women?"

"That so isn't going to happen, but if it did I don't think I'd mind too much," she said with supreme confidence. "Anyway, I'm more than enough for any man." Imogen stuck out her meagre chest and wiggled her hips with a grin.

"Ugh."

"Look, just shut up and let's do this thing."

Kate looked up at the red-brick building with its high windows decorated with strands of tinsel.

"Isn't this all a bit last century?"

"The century before last, if you're being pedantic. It's retro chic, hon. You'll love it."

The venue was a Victorian primary school that was scheduled for transformation into "luxury" flats. Until that time, the developers were letting it out for occasional events like the school dating parties Imogen had found online.

She and Kate went through the gate marked "Girls"

and crossed the playground to where a group of women were huddled together. The men had gathered at the opposite side of the playground and were stamping their feet and blowing on their hands to keep warm. The groups were met at the door by the Headmistress – identified as Miss Pickles – a scrawny figure in a dark grey dress with a pince-nez and a prominent Adam's apple.

"Girls, in a moment I want you all to go into room 3A and collect your badges. Boys, follow Miss Whipper to the Tuck Shop where you can pick up refreshments. Then you boys go off to the Assembly Hall and sit down where you're told to. You'll find your badges there. Off you go. Chop, chop."

The men immediately stood up straighter at the sound of the Headmistress's booming voice and marched off down the corridor sniggering. At the Tuck Shop they collected bottles of beer and wine before heading into the main hall.

Miss Pickles turned back to the women. "Now girls, off you go. And no dawdling."

"This is seriously strange," said Kate, under her breath.

Imogen smiled, wickedly. "I know. Isn't it great? We were so lucky to be given places. It's the hottest dating event in town."

On their way to 3A, the women also stopped by the Tuck Shop where sombre-faced staff wearing school uniform, boaters and prefects' badges handed out wine and Report Cards.

"What are the cards for?" asked Kate.

"They're for us to make a note of who we like the look of and who we don't. The guys will do the same thing. The school will tell you if you have any matches, then it's up to you what happens. With any luck, you'll get an invitation from the boy of your dreams to the end of term disco."

"The what?"

"It's a follow-up event they put on. Not my scene at all."

After a few minutes, Miss Pickles marched over and herded them into 3A. Looking fierce, she stood in front of the class and rang a handbell. "Right, girls. Pin on your badges, line up in twos and off we go."

With that she opened the classroom door and the women all trotted out, giggling nervously as though they were genuinely back at school, despite the fact each of them was clutching a large glass of wine.

A male "teacher" in a dark suit opened the double doors to the Assembly Hall and the girls streamed in, high heels clacking on the polished wooden floor.

The hall was filled with lines and lines of school desks, each with a potential date sitting behind it clutching a Report Card and a pen.

Miss Whipper directed the women to the back of the class. "Move along the lines now. Find an empty seat and sit down. And be quiet!"

When all the women had sat down opposite a partner, Miss Pickles spoke again from a raised plinth at the front of the hall. "Right, then. Your dates will start when I blow this," she said, holding up a silver whistle. "When I blow it again, ladies you will stand up and move two places to your left. We will repeat this exercise five times, then it will be breaktime and your chance to repair to the Tuck Shop for Wagon Wheels or a cold beverage of your choice. After the break, we will come back in here and carry on from where we left off. Then it's back to the Tuck Shop for replenishments, after which you are free to mingle with members of the opposite sex or not, as the case may be – we're a free-thinking establishment – until the final bell goes. You must then drop off your Report Cards and the results will be sent to you at the end of term which, you'll be pleased to hear, is tomorrow." She picked up the watch dangling from a gold chain around her neck. "You may begin your dates … now! Good luck, everyone."

Despite herself, Kate actually enjoyed the speed dating. Because of the setup, it was impossible to take it seriously, despite the "teachers" making it feel spookily like an exam. It was entertaining and Kate spotted a couple of men she liked the look of. One of them was a real hotty and it was clear that every girl who sat opposite him thought so, too. He was two or three rows away and she tried to calculate whether she would end up at his table as she progressed around the room. He caught her eye and smiled as she moved two seats to her left, her heart sinking as she later leapfrogged him to sit opposite a pale, serious guy who sat tongue-tied for the next five minutes.

After the break, there was definitely a lot of cheating going on as the women manoeuvred themselves to be near the men they liked the look of. It was all good-humoured, but Kate was quite relieved when the second session came to an end and they all streamed back to the Tuck Shop for a much-needed drink.

"Wow, that was intense," said Imogen. "There are so many cute guys here." She looked down at her card, which was covered in scribbles. "A girl really is spoilt for choice."

"That's not fair because you've already got a bloke at home. I kept getting stuck with the boring ones. In fact, I haven't met anyone really nice."

"You're just being fussy, Kitty Kat. This isn't about finding the man of your dreams – it's about finding someone to have a few laughs with."

It wasn't long before the Headmistress rang the bell indicating that the break was over. "Okay boys and girls. Once your glasses are replenished, I invite you all to make your way back to the Assembly Hall where you are free to mingle and make any last-minute adjustments to your Report Cards."

The chatter in the room grew as the men made a beeline for the most attractive women who, in turn, tried to chat to the guys they hadn't had chance to speak to in the formal sessions. For a minute Kate lost sight of Imogen, but then spotted her in a corner with a man who was whispering in her ear, making her hoot with laughter. He was tall with masses of fair hair and a handsome, open face. Kate chewed her lip, feeling slightly put out that her friend – who was only supposed to be there for a laugh – had snagged someone while she, a genuine singleton, had had no luck at all.

Imogen looked across and winked at Kate, who was feeling more like a wallflower every second. Then she felt a tap on her shoulder and turned to meet the most beautiful green eyes. "Hi, we've not met. I'm Nick."

"Kate. Er, pleased to meet you." It was the man who had caught her eye earlier!

Nick raised his glass to hers and clinked. "I've been hoping to speak to you all evening, but I kept meeting these really dull women."

"How do you know I'm not dull?"

"I can tell." His eyes crinkled into a smile. "I have an instinct about these things."

Kate couldn't think of anything to say.

"So, are you free for a drink now?"

"Oh I can't, I'm afraid. I'm with my friend." Kate watched as Immy kissed her new man on the cheek then walked over to the exit. "But maybe another time?"

Nick laughed. "Okay. We don't want to be given detention."

As they spoke, Miss Pickles walked across the hall and climbed onto the stage. "Don't forget to hand your Report Cards to Miss Whipper or Mr Grim on your way out. You'll receive your results by text tomorrow morning, so don't make plans for the evening. And remember: there is to be strictly no fraternisation in the meantime!"

Nick bent down and whispered into Kate's ear. "I love the 'no fraternisation rule'. It makes it so exciting, don't you think?"

"Absolutely." Kate nodded, shyly. "Well, goodbye then."

"Bye beautiful. I hope you get the marks you need."

"I hope so, too." She was aware of blushing, for goodness' sake! It was as though being back at "school" had turned her into a shy, tongue-tied teenager all over again.

Kate jogged out of the hall and caught up with Imogen in the cloakroom where she was fiddling with her phone and a business card.

"I'm just keying in Ethan's number."

"Who's Ethan?"

"The hot guy I was talking to at the end. He's something in the City and seems a real hoot."

Kate frowned. "This was meant to be about me finding someone, not you, remember?"

"Well, it looked to me like you were getting on rather well in there. Loads of men talked to you and the dark one in the pink shirt looked very keen from where I was standing."

"Okay, he did seem quite interested, but we'll have to wait and see what the Report Cards say."

"Did you put him down on yours?"

"I did, actually."

"Good for you! And I put Ethan on mine."

"Oh Immy, you didn't. What about Freddy?"

"I'll worry about that tomorrow. I'm starved. Do you fancy a pizza?"

Kate nodded. "Okay, but promise me you won't contact Ethan."

"Cross my heart and hope to die," she said, crossing her fingers behind her back. "I'll leave the matchmaking to Miss Pickles."

"That's not exactly what I meant."

Imogen grabbed her by the arm and forced a kiss on her cheek. "Stop worrying about me and let's hope Mr Cutie puts a big tick in your box. Ooh, that sounds rude!"

"I think you need feeding."

"You could be right," said Imogen, giggling. "The wine is kicking in. What was your guy's name, anyway?"

"Nick."

# Chapter 7: First Dates

When Kate saw Imogen huddled over her phone at the back of the deli the next day, she smelled a rat. "You look like the cat that got the cream, as my nan would say."

Immy stopped tapping and looked up. "I'm the pussycat who got the whole dairy." She grinned. "Ethan has asked me out for dinner."

"Dinner?" Kate had seen this coming, but was still alarmed. Grabbing her friend, she pulled her into the kitchen where Freddy couldn't see them. "You're not going, are you?"

"Of course I'm going. He's an interesting man."

"Interesting? I thought you said he was an insurance salesman or something equally dull."

"Er, not exactly. The company he works for insures luxury yachts, private jets and that kind of thing. He's not selling policies door to door, Kate."

"So he earns a packet?"

"I expect he earns squillions, like most of my friends." Imogen looked thoughtful. "He's exactly the kind of person I should be going out with."

"Instead of slumming it with Freddy, you mean?"

"Precisely," said Immy, in a tone that suggested she was only half-joking. Seeing her friend's expression, she sighed. "I deserve pampering from time to time, don't I?"

Kate didn't have a chance to answer before they were interrupted by the kitchen door being swung open with vigour.

"Ah, there you are." Joseph had noticed their absence and come in to find them. "When you ladies have finished gossiping, there are customers to be served. Quickly now – move it, move it!"

As they followed Joseph out into the shop, Imogen caught Kate's arm. "What about you? Have you heard from anyone?"

"I have actually." A Report Card had come through from Miss Pickles in the morning with a gold star against two names, quickly followed by texts from both men asking Kate out for a drink.

"Let me guess: not Nick, by any chance?"

Kate nodded, shyly. "And a maths teacher I quite liked."

"So, which one will you see first?"

"I said I'd meet Nick."

"Good choice. But you should meet up with the teacher, too. It's good to have a second player on the subs' bench, just in case the first one turns out to be a disappointment."

"No way, Immy. I can't cope with more than one man in my life. Not that Nick is even in my life yet."

Joseph turned and stared at them, his hands on his hips. "Kate! Imogen! Pavement duty now, please."

"Yes boss." And with that the girls hurried back to work.

* * *

When they met in a West End pub later in the week, Kate asked Nick how come he'd been at the school dating event. He smiled. "I was there with a mate who convinced me it would be a good way to meet interesting women. He said anyone who's willing to go to that kind of thing is pretty much guaranteed to be a laugh and he was right."

Kate smiled broadly, hoping to convey the fact that she was a "laugh". She was on her second vodka and tonic and starting to feel nicely blurred around the edges when Nick suddenly leant across the table and kissed her. "So, what do you think? Shall we get out of here and go back to my place?"

Wow, that's a bit quick, she thought. "Now? Well, erm …" The invitation was so unexpected that she really didn't know what to say. "Actually, I don't think that's such a good idea. I'm bushed and I've got to be at work really early in the morning." She sucked on her straw and tried to convey disappointment.

Nick shrugged. "No worries," he said, finishing his glass of wine in one swallow. "I didn't think you would accept, but it's always worth asking." At the sight of Kate's alarmed expression, he laughed. "Joke! I only ask the pretty ones. If I can't tempt you with my body, what do you say to food? There's a great Thai place round the corner."

"I didn't say I don't find you attractive."

He leant back in his chair, grinning. "So you do fancy me?"

"Yes, of course I do, but …" How to explain without sounding like a prig and putting him off forever? It was impossible, so she decided not to try. "I am ravenous."

"Noodles it is, then."

Nick took her hand and led her through the busy streets to a small restaurant. The staff seemed to know him and a smiling waitress in a silky peacock-blue outfit showed them to an alcove in the back room.

Kate had only had Thai food once before, so she was happy to go along with Nick's recommendations.

The meal was delicious and Nick chatted away nonstop about his job, but also asked Kate about the deli and her life in Herefordshire. It was great and yet she didn't feel completely at ease. It was almost like being interviewed and she wasn't entirely sure she met all the criteria – whatever they were.

After an hour or so, Nick looked at his watch. "I'm going to be a bore and head off, if that's okay. I don't want to be on the last train out with the Christmas party drunks."

"Sure, no problem." Kate patted her lips with the heavy linen napkin and smiled. "I've had a nice time, thank you."

"You're welcome."

Despite his haste to get Kate into bed, Nick was very gentlemanly and waited with her at the bus stop, but she had the distinct impression he was keen to be somewhere else. He shuffled from foot to foot and checked his phone all the time.

As she saw her bus arrive, Kate decided she had to say something before they went their separate ways. She wanted him to know that, although she'd not been prepared to rush back to his flat immediately, she did like him and hoped it wouldn't be the end of their fledgling relationship. "Will I see you again?"

"Sure," he said. "I'll text you tomorrow."

I bet you won't, she thought sadly, as Nick turned to kiss her. Placing her hands on his shoulders she pressed her lips against his with feeling, hoping he would get the message she was keen, but not so keen that she would go back to a stranger's flat after a couple of drinks. At the very least, he could have waited until she'd polished off her Thai green curry.

From the top of the bus, she watched Nick turn and enter the Underground, sure that was the last she'd see of him. It was a shame because she did like him and he seemed comparatively normal, apart from trying to jump her after half a date. But maybe that was how things went in the capital? She made a mental note to ask Immy – if her friend was still awake – when she got home.

\* \* \*

Kate made sure Freddy was out of the way before joining Immy in the living room. She really wanted her friend's advice but knew Immy would expect to talk about her own evening first. "How did it go with Ethan?" she asked, kicking off her shoes and curling up in an armchair. Imogen was lying on the sofa opposite with a dreamy look in her eyes.

"It was fantabulous. We met at this cute pub on the river near where he rows with his club and we talked and talked." Her eyes were sparkling. "It turns out that he went to school in Dorset with a cousin of mine and we have loads of friends in common. And you'll never guess what?"

"He drives an Aston Martin?"

"A what? Actually, he's got a Porsche. But that's not it."

"He's a billionaire?"

"Not at the moment, but he intends to be a millionaire before he's thirty."

Kate was beginning to feel tired and disgruntled

after her less-than-satisfactory evening and was suddenly not in the mood to play. "In his spare time he's a brain surgeon."

Immy sighed. "You're not trying."

"There's no need to pout."

"I'm not pouting: these are my naturally delectable lips."

"Seriously, Immy, I have no idea what I'm supposed to be guessing."

"So, do you give up?"

"I give up."

"Okay, so the really cool thing about Ethan is, not only does he ski, but his folks are renting the chalet next to ours this Christmas!"

"Great – which means you can introduce him to Freddy."

"Very funny." Immy pulled a face. "Freddy's not coming. I told you that."

Kate swung around to look at her friend. "So, let me get this right: are you saying you'll be spending the holidays skiing with Ethan while Freddy stays at the flat with me and Clare?"

"Yup, but it's his own fault. He turned down my very generous invitation, after all."

"And are you sure you want to go on holiday with someone you barely know?"

"You haven't been paying attention," she said, huffily. "I'm not going *with* Ethan. We just happen to be staying in the same place at the same time. And I intend to get to know him much better before we go."

"You mean you're going on another date?"

"I sure am. Anyway, that's enough about me. How did it go with thingy – Mick?"

"Nick. It was okay …"

"Just okay?"

"We had a meal and he paid for everything, which was nice."

"So why do you look so glum?"

Kate sighed. "He wanted me to go back to his place straight away, which seemed a bit fast as we'd only spent a couple of hours together. I mean, we hadn't even had the meal by then. He said it like it was a joke, like it was no big thing, but I think he was serious."

Imogen laughed. "I'm sure he was absolutely serious. The question is, were you tempted?"

"No."

"No as in 'not at all'?"

"No as in 'maybe a tiny bit'." She wanted her friend to understand. "Immy, you'll probably think this is weird, but I actually like to know a few things about someone before I jump into bed with them. To make sure they're not an axe-murderer, that kind of thing." She chewed her lip thoughtfully. "But now I'm wondering whether I'll ever hear from him again."

"Of course you will. You're really pretty and turning him down will make him extra keen to see you."

Immy thought she was pretty? "I'm not sure about that."

"I can guarantee it." Imogen put a hand to her mouth to stifle a yawn. "Now, I need my beauty sleep."

Kate stood up. "See you in the morning, then."

"Sweet dreams – of Nick!"

"And Freddy."

Imogen blew her a kiss. "Goodnight."

Kate hesitated at her bedroom door, wanting to go back and ask Immy whether she would actually sleep with Ethan, but decided against it. They were obviously getting on really well, but would her friend cheat on Freddy? She refused to believe it.

# Chapter 8: Out on the Town

All through the next day and the day after, Kate kept sneaking a peak at her phone even though she didn't expect to hear from Nick ever again. She had pretty much resigned herself to spinsterhood when a message appeared asking if she was free that night. Woohoo! He did like her after all.

Nick's text told her to meet him in the Bogey Man, a new bar under the railway arches near Aldgate in the City, but Kate was too nervous to ask him for precise directions. Anyway, everything could be found online these days.

She was impatient for the day to end so she could go on her second date with someone she was fairly certain wouldn't cry or try to steal strands of her hair. And if she liked him enough and he asked her to go home with him this time … Maybe she would.

From what she could tell from reviews, the bar was achingly trendy and she was pretty sure there was nothing in her wardrobe that would be appropriate. Most of her best clothes were still in her bedroom at her parents' house so she wasn't exactly spoiled for choice. What should she wear? Opening the cupboards, she pulled everything out and threw it on the bed. She wanted to look attractive but not give Nick the impression she'd put too much effort into it. She tried and discarded a few outfits before deciding

on skinny black jeans with a strappy top and a pair of
red heels she'd picked up in the sales. They weren't
particularly comfortable, but she didn't expect they'd
be doing much walking that evening.

Eventually it was time to leave the flat and jam
herself onto the Tube train that would take her east.
From the station, it was a short walk to the bar.

The entrance was down an alleyway smelling of
pee – not the healthy farmyard smell she was used
to at home, but the sharp tang of fizzy lager passed
through the bladders of numerous City bankers. Nice,
she thought, as she pinched her nose between her fingers and pressed on. Ahead of her was an unmarked
door with peeling paintwork and a small viewing
hatch. She stood outside nervously for a few moments,
wondering what to do, then the hatch opened briefly
and a dark brown eye appeared and looked her up
and down. The hatch slammed shut, then the door
opened and an androgynous figure dressed in black
with an orange beehive beckoned her in.

"Hi. Er, where do I go?"

"Cloakroom there. Bar there."

"Thanks," said Kate, as she felt her way along a
narrow corridor towards the sound of music and low
voices. She did as instructed and left her coat with a
sour-faced attendant who looked pained as she took
the garment and handed her a token in return for a
two pound coin. She hoped Nick would be happy
to "go Dutch", otherwise her meagre salary would be
spent in no time. Turning around, she still couldn't
see any sign of a bar.

"Thanks. Er, where's the bar?"

The cloakroom attendant sighed wearily, as though

handing out directional information was not part of her job description. "End. Right. Through curtain."

Kate gave her a beaming smile. "Thanks you old crone," she muttered under her breath.

Where had they picked up all this cheesy old stuff, she wondered, as she pulled aside the heavy velvet curtain and entered the holy grail: the über-cool Bogey Man bar.

She was anxious about seeing Nick again and having to meet him in such a trendy place only made things worse. Biting her lip, she scanned the dark, crowded room for her date. The banquettes lining the walls were filled with people huddled over tiny cocktail glasses, heads close together as they struggled to be heard over the chatter. She ran her eye over every table, but Nick wasn't sitting at any of them. She moved towards the bar, trying to spot him amongst the men clutching beers and mojitos. No sign of him there, either.

It was time to retreat. She slipped into the ladies and reapplied her lipstick. She'd done a reasonable job with the eyeliner pencil, but her face looked pale against the ruby red flocked wallpaper. She wasn't sure that Immy's scarlet lipstick really suited her pale freckled complexion and wished she'd stuck to the pink she'd worn since she was thirteen.

She washed her hands and brushed her hair, trying to waste as much time as possible before going back into the bar. Digging the phone from her bag, she checked the time. She was five minutes late – was that too early? There was no message from Nick yet, so he must be on his way. Maybe he'd be out there waiting for her.

She put the phone away, gave herself a stern look in the mirror and went back out. There was still no sign of him, but there was an empty seat at the end of the bar, so she made a beeline for it. She decided to get a drink, but what should she choose? Would a fruit juice make her look like a goody-goody? Probably. A waiter handed her a cocktail menu, but she didn't recognise any of the names and they all cost £18. In Hereford, she and her mates would go to the Laughing Frog and order half pints of pina colada for £5; here the drinks were almost four times the price and half the size.

After reading through the list twice, she decided to play it safe. "I'll have a glass of Chardonnay, please."

If the waiter was disappointed that she was choosing white wine over his famous bramble and rum concoction, he was too professional to comment. "Large?"

She hesitated for a nanosecond then nodded. She knew she should say "small" but somehow the word wouldn't form itself in her mouth. If she drank wine on an empty stomach, would she be pissed by the time Nick arrived? Probably, but what the hell. He'd be there soon, anyway, so she might as well relax and enjoy the surroundings.

The waiter brought over her wine in a glass almost big enough to fit her entire head into and so cold it burned under her touch.

"Thank you."

"You're welcome. Enjoy."

She took a sip, enjoying the sensation of the cold liquid on her lips. The room was hot, so the wine was pleasantly cooling as it caressed her throat. There were some crackers on the bar that everyone else was ignoring so she dug in, nibbling delicately.

"Delish," she said to herself as the wine kicked in and she began to unwind. One of several advantages of having a glass the size of a goldfish bowl was that it gave her something to hide behind as she looked around at the clientele.

There were groups of women about her own age with big hair and shrill voices who were studiously ignoring the young men with equally big hair gathered around the bar and moving half-heartedly to the music.

In between were a few much older men who looked as though they were in town on business, although it was a strange place to wash up in. Kate noticed there were also a number of suspiciously glam women draped across the old geezers. Either this was a knocking shop or the dumpy blokes were millionaires, which you would have to be to enjoy more than one drink in this place. She chuckled to herself at the thought. This was a fun venue, but it would be more enjoyable if she had someone to share it with.

She glanced at her watch – Nick was now twenty minutes late and she was beginning to worry. She took out her phone and reread his message. *Bogey Man, 8.30pm? Nick x*. It was close to 9pm and what was left of her wine was getting warm as she swished it around in her glass.

She decided to send him a well-crafted message. *You okay? Wine getting warm. Hungry. Kate x* She hesitated before sending. Did "Hungry" sound greedy? Would he think she was expecting him to buy her dinner again? Delete. She tapped in a new message.

*Bogey Man cool. Wine warm. You on your way?* No, that wasn't right either. It made her seem needy. *Loving the Bogey Man. See you soon? Kx.* Was that better? It sounded casual, like she was fine on her own but would be happy if he could join her. She pressed "Send", then took a last sip of wine, eyeing the empty glass gloomily.

The waiter appeared as if by magic across the bar. "One more Chardonnay for you, madam?"

"Just a glass of water, please."

"Still or sparkling?"

"Plain old Thames water will do me fine," she answered wittily, or so she thought.

The waiter – who Kate suspected was French – looked perplexed. "Still? Sparkling?"

"Tap."

He shrugged, unwilling to concede defeat. "Tap is not so good because of the rats in the pipes, but if you insist …"

Kate wrinkled her nose. "Okay, sparkling then." Christ. There went another £5, she thought grumpily, scooping up the last of the crackers. It was as she was licking salt off her fingertips that she became aware of someone grinning at her from along the bar. Looking over, she caught the eye of a middle-aged man with a droopy grey moustache who lifted his beer glass as he took a place two seats away.

"You'll never catch me drinking tap water – fish pee in it, you know?" He laughed at his own joke. "Let me buy you another glass of wine. It looks like you're ready for one. And some more crackers? You seem to have enjoyed those," he said, indicating the empty bowl.

All her mother's warnings about not talking to strange men kicked in together with a sense of irritation that a man who was patently overweight and ancient could imagine he stood a chance with someone like her! However, being a well brought-up young lady, she gave him a tight smile and declined before turning away and making a show of studying the array of bottles behind the bar.

"Suit yourself. Oh, and I'm not trying to chat you up, if that's what you're thinking. I've got Y-fronts older than you, sweetheart. Anyway, I like my women with more meat on their bones, don't I, Anna?"

"I tell you before – I am Elena," said the buxom woman who had appeared by his side. "But you can call me Anna if it makes you happy."

The man swallowed the last of his beer in one go and manoeuvred his sizeable buttocks off the bar stool, slapping Anna-Elena on the rear as he steered her towards the door.

"Don't worry about being stood up," he said to Kate with a wink. "It happens to the best of us."

"I haven't been 'stood up'. My friend has been delayed by work. Not that it's any of your business." Cheeky bugger! Kate's cheeks were blazing with a combination of wine, heat and fury.

"Well, that's all right then. I wouldn't want you to starve." He called to the waiter. "A portion of nuts for the young lady, when you're ready, pal. Oh, and make it the green ones."

"I don't want your nuts, thank you very much."

He shrugged. "The way you polished off my crackers, I thought you might need more to eat. Oh, and Merry Christmas."

Embarrassment and hunger fought in Kate as she watched her benefactor leave the bar. His crackers? Had she really eaten someone else's snacks?

The waiter silently placed a small bowl of what looked like dried peas in front of her.

"I don't want them, thank you."

He shrugged. "They're good and they are free – why not try?"

She stared angrily at the bowl before hunger got the better of her and she shoved a handful of the snacks into her mouth. The bloody man had paid for them, after all. Kate had never had wasabi peas before and the heat from the horseradish rushed up her nose, making her eyes water and her head burn.

She took a big swig of water, which caught in her throat making her cough and splutter. She gulped and wheezed, trying to ignore the amused glances of people around her. The waiter handed her a napkin, then came around the bar to pat her smartly on the back. "Better now?"

No, she was not better. It was 9.30pm, she was starving, half-choked by trick nuts and on the verge of tears.

Enough was enough. She paid the ridiculous bill, collected her sensible BHS coat from the sniffy cloakroom attendant and headed out into the pee-scented streets of East London. Checking her phone for one last time she found her inbox empty. Earlier, she had feared something bad had happened to Nick; now, she sincerely hoped he had gone under a bus.

Head down, she stomped towards the Tube station as best she could in the red stilettos only to find the gate pulled across the entrance. Several men in high-visibility jackets were trying to explain the bus system to confused tourists who, like Kate, had failed to read the signs advertising last-minute strike action that evening.

By now, the drizzle that had been falling all evening had worked itself up into proper rain with drops the size of plump tadpoles. Kate walked past Liverpool Street station, where commuters in party clothes formed long queues and huddled in doorways as overfilled buses trundled by. After waiting for twenty minutes and getting soaked and splashed with filthy water from the street, Kate decided to walk the four miles home in her best shoes. Could her evening get any worse? Yes, it could.

# Chapter 9: Home, Sweet Home

The sat nav on Kate's phone took her right across the City, which was deserted apart from men in grey suits leaping into the road, trying to flag down taxis. The beauty of St Paul's Cathedral was marred by a couple of drunken women arguing over a broken umbrella.

Kate kept her head down, trying to avoid the rain that blew into her eyes, making them sting. She was really grumpy and her feet were killing her by the time she reached the Strand, where the pavement was packed with office workers in soggy party hats whose Christmas cheer Kate found especially annoying. All she wanted was a hot bath, but the wasabi peas and bucket of wine had left her feeling slightly bilious and in need of food. She could have nipped in to any number of takeaways lining the route, but she couldn't bear the thought of eating in the street in the rain. No, she would hold out for tea and toast at the flat.

At Trafalgar Square, tourists in plastic capes and hoodies were taking selfies by the fountain, seemingly oblivious of the weather. As Kate tottered along the streets, being elbowed by revellers on pre-Christmas jollies, she clung to the vision of a warm bed and tea.

Given her luck that evening, she decided it probably wasn't a sensible idea to cut across St James's Park in the dead of night, so she went down the

Mall – waving at Buckingham Palace as she passed – before tottering along the side of Victoria Station for the final trek towards the deli and home.

Home! It took Kate an hour and a half to get back, ducking and weaving to avoid being speared by umbrellas or pushed under a bus or a lycra-clad cyclist. She was freezing cold, miserable and her shoes were ruined by the time she finally stumbled upstairs and opened the door to the apartment. Turning the handle and entering the hallway, she was so relieved to be indoors again she almost wept.

As she flung her bag on the floor, she heard a trill as her phone sprang into life. Digging around the soggy interior of her bag, she found it and, despite everything, her mood lifted at the sight of Nick's name glowing on the screen. At last, she would find out what had happened to him. It must have been an accident or maybe he'd been stranded somewhere because of the strike. The message was not what she had hoped for: *Sorry Babe. Drinks with mates after work. Couldn't get away.*

"Babe"? No one had ever called her "babe". Then another message: *Tube cocked up. Bogey Man tomoz?*

She felt like throwing her phone against the wall, then jumping up and down on it until it was smashed into smithereens. How dare Nick stand her up for drinks with the lads! "Bogey Man tomoz?" As if she would ever consider seeing him again after tonight.

She was furious and began composing a suitably caustic reply in her head, but first she needed to get warm and dry.

Her hopes of having the place to herself were dashed by the sound of music coming from the living room. She had expected everyone to be out and really wasn't in the mood for a cosy chat with her flatmates.

She slipped off her sodden shoes and squelched across the hallway in blistered feet, hoping to tiptoe into her room unnoticed. Yes, she was hungry, but she didn't feel strong enough to withstand the third degree from Imogen. All she wanted was a shower and bed – she'd even given up the idea of tea. She was nearly at her bedroom, when the living-room door opened and Freddy was there.

"Hi, oh it's you. I thought it might have been Immy coming back. She had a call from a mate who really needed to chat so she had to dash out. I could have gone, but I'm not great at girl talk." He grinned his lopsided grin as Kate bit her tongue. Bloody Imogen. Why did Freddy worry about her when she was such a slapper? "She said she might stay out, but wasn't sure."

"Nope. I'm afraid it's not your beloved. It's only me." Kate was stung by the obvious disappointment in Freddy's voice.

"I didn't mean it like that. I'm surprised, that's all." He scratched his head. "I thought you were out on a date with an old school friend or something."

Kate turned and gave him a tight smile. "I was, but I decided to come home early. It's no big deal." At that moment, she couldn't bear to talk about her grim evening.

Freddy leant against the doorframe and looked her up and down, as if only then noticing the bedraggled curls and black streaks down her cheeks. "Is there something wrong?"

"No, everything is absolutely fine," she said brightly, pushing a strand of wet hair behind her ear and shivering as a drop of cold water dislodged itself and slid down the back of her neck.

"You sure you're okay? You look a bit, er …"

"Crap?"

"Well, I wouldn't say that exactly."

Kate caught sight of herself in the hall mirror and wasn't sure whether she felt like laughing or crying. A grey puddle was forming around her sore feet as rain dripped from her coat and the shoes in her hand looked like they belonged in a skip. "I think 'crap' would be a pretty accurate description, actually."

"You're completely soaked. Is it raining? I mean, how did you get so wet coming back from the Tube?"

"Well, duh!" She didn't mean to be unkind, but anger at Nick and her frustration at the situation boiled over and she couldn't hold back any longer. "Yes, it's bloody raining and I'm soaked because I had to walk all the way back from East London because nobody told me there was a bloody Tube strike and all the buses and taxis were full of people dressed like Santa's elves. And I got bashed about by idiot commuters and half-drowned by speeding cars." She stopped and dragged a hand across her face, feeling salt tears warm on her skin.

"I can see why you're hacked off." Freddy nodded sympathetically. "So there's a strike, is there? I guess Immy might stay at her mate's, then," he said, peering down at his phone hoping for a message. Looking up, he caught Kate's strained expression and smiled encouragingly. Kate bit her tongue, expecting that Imogen would take advantage of the situation to stay out with Ethan or whoever it was she had slunk off to be with.

"But before it all went tits up, did you have a nice time, with what's-his-name?"

"Nick."

"Oh yeah, Nick."

Seeing Freddy's friendly face, Kate couldn't be bothered to pretend any more. Leaning against the wall, she sank down onto the floor, sighing. "No, I didn't have a nice time with Nick because actually the bastard didn't bother to turn up. Instead, I sat in an overpriced bar for an hour surrounded by hookers and One Direction rejects, ate someone else's crackers, had an argument with an old git who looked like a walrus and compared me to his underpants. And all I want to do now is eat toast and go to bed."

"That's a bummer." Freddy looked guilty. "I finished the last of the bread when I got in from work."

This was the final straw. Kate let out a howl and burst into tears.

"Christ, sorry Kate. I can nip out to the Co-op if you're desperate." At that, she cried even harder, rivulets of snot now joining the grime under her nose.

"No? Okay. Forget the Co-op." Freddy fished into the back pocket of his jeans and pulled out a pack of tissues that had clearly been through the wash a couple of times. "Here, have one of these." He knelt down to offer her the packet then stood up, eyeing her cautiously. "Listen. To make it up to you about the crap date and the absence of toast, why don't I get us a takeaway?"

Kate had finished blowing her nose on the slab of tissue and was now dabbing at the pools of mascara under her eyes. "Oh, I don't know. I should probably go to bed."

"Nah, don't let that wanker Nick spoil your evening," he said, helping her up from the floor then grabbing his jacket. "You jump in the bath while I nip out to Maharani's and get us a deluxe dinner for two. It'll be quicker than waiting for them to deliver."

Kate smiled, the thought of chicken tikka and all the trimmings making her feel hungry again. "Thanks, Freddy. That sounds perfect."

"Great. We're both Billy No-Mates tonight, so we might as well make the best of it." He turned as he reached the door. "Rice or naan bread?"

"Can we have both?"

"We certainly can." He grinned, then pulled open the flat door and ran down the stairs, two at a time.

# Chapter 10: Freddy's Story

Although they'd shared the same flat for months, this was the first time Kate and Freddy had sat down alone together over a meal. Freddy had always been friendly towards her, but everyone was always busy and grabbed meals on the run. Clare often stayed at her boyfriend's or ate at the deli with her colleagues from the kitchen.

As Kate watched Freddy open up the foil containers and hand out plates and cutlery, she realised she knew virtually nothing about him.

"How did you end up working here, then?"

"I walked in off the street and Vitaly gave me a job – simples!"

Kate looked at him doubtfully. She knew Freddy often helped Joseph in the office and did much more than waiting at tables and making cappuccinos. "I can't believe it was as easy-peasy as that."

"So, you want my life story?"

"I don't suppose it will take too long to tell."

"Hey, maybe I'm older than you think."

"Tell all."

"Well, I was born at an early age, then as a baby I mastered the art of crawling ..."

"Very funny," said Kate, piling mango chutney onto her plate. "Can we cut to the interesting part?"

"I'm not sure I've got to the interesting part of my

life yet," said Freddy, sounding serious for a moment. "But if you want to know my path to Delish Organics, here it is."

And so he explained how he had finished a course in hospitality and tourism with no clear idea what to do next. "I'd done pretty well and my tutors tried to encourage me to go on and do a master's degree in business studies with tourism on the side, but I'd had enough of studying by then."

"A master's? Wow, I'm impressed."

"Yep, I'm not as dumb as I look."

Kate smiled guiltily. She'd always assumed Freddy was like her and she was definitely not master's degree material. "Did you do a placement for the tourism bit of the course?"

"Yeah, and it was a quite an eye-opener. I ended up at this sailing club down in Cornwall that was like Fawlty Towers on acid. The manager was hopeless and it had a completely mad maître d' who hated people, which isn't great when you're running a restaurant. He had a terrible habit of hovering by a table and tapping his watch when he reckoned guests had sat over their meals for too long. The club was open to the public – not just members – but we didn't have a lot of repeat custom and the tips were virtually zero."

Kate laughed. "I can imagine an experience like that might put you off the hospitality industry for good."

"Do you know what? It had the opposite effect." Freddy stuffed the last piece of naan bread into his mouth. "It gave me loads of ideas of how I'd run a place – if anyone ever let me loose on their hotel."

"How come you didn't try for another hotel job?"

He frowned. "I suppose I fancied a change. And I missed London – it's where I grew up."

"So then you applied for the deli job?"

"Kind of."

\* \* \*

Freddy remembered being back in London and at a loose end. The sailing club had been fun, but he knew he needed to gain more experience before anyone would employ him in a managerial role, however junior. He was wandering around town pretty aimlessly when a new venue caught his eye.

The Delish Organics sign was up and workmen were assembling the deli's trademark yellow and white canopy. In the window was a large notice calling for "enthusiastic staff with sales or catering experience to work in the shop and café". The doors were wide open, so Freddy went in, hoping to pick up the name of the manager. He approached a slim, grey-haired man with piercing blue eyes who seemed to be in charge of the labourers. The man was friendly but distracted and gave Freddy a business card printed in English on one side and what looked like Russian on the other. "Today everyone is very busy, but call this number. Maybe we will be able to help you."

"Cheers mate," said Freddy, pocketing the card with a smile.

The following day, he rang up and spoke for about fifteen minutes to a nameless person with an eastern European accent. Somehow the conversation also moved on to Freddy's ambition to run his own place within the next ten years.

When he had finished speaking, there was a moment of silence on the phone when he feared he'd talked far too much and bored the guy rigid. "So, do you think I have a chance? I'm a hard worker and I'm willing to do anything: waiting at tables, food preparation – whatever you need, really." Freddy realised he was gabbling again, shut up and waited.

"Send in your CV and come back in two weeks when the shop fitting is completely finished. Then we'll see what we can find for you."

"Thanks – I'll do that."

A fortnight later, Freddy turned up at the premises at 8am to find people busily stocking shelves and setting out tables and chairs. He let out a low whistle: this place was impressive. The plain white walls were now hung with huge abstract paintings, making the room look like the restaurant of a swanky art gallery.

Looking around, Freddy was pleased to spot the foreman he had met a fortnight earlier and waved in recognition. "Thanks for giving me the contact number," he said, going up to him. "I had a long conversation with someone on the management side and I think I might get an interview."

"Ah, yes. You must be Frederick."

"That's right – well, Freddy really."

The man frowned, stroking his beard. "You have a job, if you'd like it."

Freddy looked puzzled. "I have? Really? But I haven't even met the manager yet."

The man extended his hand and smiled. "Allow me to introduce myself: Vitaly Polzin, owner of the Delish deli."

"Wow, great. But don't you want to interview me?"

"I am a very busy man," said Vitaly, his eyes darting around the room. "Let us say you had your interview." He liked young people to have enthusiasm and listening to Freddy on the phone he could tell the boy had it in spades.

"That's great. Sorry, I didn't realise you were the boss."

Turning towards him, Vitaly smiled. "Precisely. You thought I was a simple builder, but you were polite – this is important. We must treat everyone with respect." He tapped the side of his nose, lowering his voice. "You can never be sure who is who in this world."

"Well, yes. You're probably right. So, er, what exactly is the job?"

Vitaly shrugged, surveying his new premises. "Your job is to make my customers feel welcome, to sell lots of food and drink, and to learn something new every day." He wagged his finger at Freddy. "Each small thing you do here will be useful to you in the future when you set up your business."

Freddy felt himself flush with embarrassment and something akin to pride that this person he had just met believed he would one day run his own place.

"Now, Frederick, you can begin by helping Joseph over there to set out more tables and chairs. And I believe Ted in the kitchen needs help unpacking the tins of tomatoes and boxes of coffee beans. If you are still here at the end of the day, come and find me in the office and I will give you money."

\* \* \*

"And did he pay you?" asked Kate.

"Yup – in cash, as well. I did wonder whether Vitaly would get a day's work out of me for nothing, but the boss was as good as his word. Then he completely freaked me out by casually mentioning that accommodation would be provided for a few of the junior staff and asking if I'd like to apply for one of the rooms. Free accommodation sounded a bit dodgy and I wondered whether I was being set up as a rent boy." Freddy took a swig of his beer. "Anyway, I decided to risk my virtue and moved in a fortnight later."

Kate had been focused on Freddy's animated face but now she looked down, concentrating instead on the label of her beer bottle. "And that's when you met Immy?"

"Nope. She didn't arrive until a few months later. Anyway, never mind her." He looked at his empty bottle. "Shall I fetch us another couple of these while you choose a film?"

"Sure, why not."

# Chapter 11: And Then There Were Three

It was gone midnight and Kate's stomach was pleasantly stuffed with spicy food. They had moved from the kitchen and were lounging at opposite ends of the sofa drinking tea when they heard the unmistakable tap of Imogen's six-inch heels crossing the hall. As she came into the room it was clear from her glossy appearance and perfect make-up that she hadn't walked home in a downpour.

Immy's eyes flicked rapidly from Kate to Freddy, as though weighing up the situation. "Well, isn't this cosy?"

Freddy uncurled his long legs and went towards Imogen to give her a hug, which she ducked away from. "Ugh, curry breath. Stay away." She sniffed the air. "It smells like a souk in here."

"I don't think they have souks in Delhi." Freddy laughed, grabbing her around the shoulders and pulling her down onto the sofa between him and Kate who moved across to the armchair to make space. "It's a good job you don't like Indian food because we've scoffed the lot," he said, rubbing his belly and letting out a soft burp.

"Charming," said Immy, pushing him away. "Is there any white wine or have you finished it off?"

"Nope, you're in luck. We were on beer tonight."

Imogen kicked off her shoes and headed for the kitchen. She came back into the room with her glass filled and lay back on the sofa with her legs stretched across Freddy's lap. "What have you two been up to?"

A flicker of something passed between Kate and Freddy before he spoke.

"Nothing much. We got something to eat then watched a trashy film on Netflix."

Immy narrowed her eyes at Kate. "Weren't you going out for a meal with Nick?"

"No, not a meal. Just a quick drink." She studied the fabric of the armchair intently, unwilling to look her interrogator in the eye. "I've decided he's not for me." Kate didn't dare look at Freddy, praying he wouldn't tell Imogen what had really happened. Why did it matter so much? There was no reason for Immy not to know – after all, they had laughed together about plenty of bad dates. The problem was that the non-date with Nick had been humiliating, but Kate had enjoyed her night in with Freddy far more than any of her recent outings. It had been special and this – she realised – was what she didn't want to share with Imogen.

She needn't have worried because her friend wasn't terribly interested in their evening. Imogen grabbed the remote from Freddy and scanned the hundreds of channels.

"How was your friend? Is *she* okay? I gather you had to do a mercy dash to Balham." Kate couldn't stop herself from putting a teeny bit of emphasis on the word *she*. It was only intuition, but the way Immy was dressed and something indefinable in her expression made Kate sure she'd been with Ethan.

"Yup, fine," said Imogen, displaying a coolness Kate found impressive. "We had a few drinks and a chat and that sorted her out."

"How did you get home?"

Immy looked puzzled, making Kate suspect she'd had a lift in Ethan's Porsche. "Night bus." Yawning, Imogen pulled her legs from across Freddy's lap and stood up. "I've had it. I'm off to bed."

"I'll be there in a minute," said Freddy.

"Not tonight, bhaji boy." Imogen drank the last of her wine then kissed Freddy chastely on the forehead as she went by. "Not until you've got the vindaloo out of your system. You pong."

Imogen tottered off to her room and Kate and Freddy sat in silence for a moment. It wasn't until the sound of a shower running could be heard that Kate spoke.

"Thanks for not saying anything about Nick standing me up."

"No problem." He turned towards her and smiled. "I'm sure Immy has plenty of secrets, too."

If you only knew the half of it, thought Kate. How could Imogen take advantage of Freddy's trusting nature? The more she got to know him the more she liked him. He was a bit immature, but he was kind and thoughtful and really rather lovely in an older brother kind of way. Emboldened by the beer, she felt she had to say something. "I know it's none of my business, but I don't think you should let Immy boss you about the way she does."

"Like what?"

"Like not letting you join her because you've had a curry."

"Poor Immy." Freddy laughed. "Curry breath is not very appealing."

"Well, that's a matter of opinion." Kate leapt up, immediately regretting her words and hoping he wouldn't think she was flirting. "I'm off to bed, too. I'm knackered."

As she walked past, Freddy reached out to catch her gently by the hand. "If it's any compensation, I think Nick's a prick."

"Nick the Prick – that has a definite ring to it."

"Hey, I'm a poet and I didn't know it!"

Kate laughed. "Night, Freddy, and thanks for everything."

"Any time."

\* \* \*

Over the next few days, Imogen kept her distance from Kate and Freddy, claiming to be too tired to go to the pub or saying she had stomach cramps and had to sleep on her own. Kate also noticed Immy hurriedly stashing her phone in her work apron when Freddy was near and smiling at nothing in particular. Kate struggled to keep her mouth shut, but after a while she couldn't bear it any longer. One Sunday morning while Freddy was out playing football, she decided to ask her friend straight out if she was seeing Ethan. She knocked on Imogen's bedroom door then asked the question. The answer was what she had expected.

"Yes, I am."

"Seeing as in 'friend' or as in 'boyfriend'?"

"If you want to be precise, I guess you could say as in 'lover'."

"Oh Immy. What about Freddy?"

Immy patted the place next to her, but Kate stood at the end of the bed, her arms crossed over her chest.

"I can't talk to you over there. Come and sit down, for goodness' sake."

Reluctantly Kate sat down, tucking her legs beneath her. It's difficult to be fierce with somebody when you're lying on their bed.

"That's better," said Imogen, who was in confessional mood. "Okay – here's the deal. I am super fond of Fred, but I'm beginning to wonder how much we really have in common. We come from completely different backgrounds and we like different things."

"Is that reason enough to cheat on him?"

Immy ignored her. "On the other hand, we have been together for ages and I love him to bits."

"So dump Ethan."

"It's not that straightforward – I like them both."

"But if you care about Freddy, why risk losing him? I mean, what does Ethan have to offer?"

"Plenty." Imogen sat up, curling her arms around her knees. "He knows lots of the same people as me, he's good in the sack and he's filthy rich ..."

"Could there be a 'but' coming?"

"I have to admit he doesn't have much going on between the ears, but you can't have everything."

"I'm surprised you noticed."

"Ha, ha. We don't just bonk. I do like a decent conversation, too, you know?"

"So what's the plan? You can't keep pretending everything is normal when you're seeing someone else."

"Don't worry. I'm pretty sure that Ethan is

short-term entertainment not a keeper," said Imogen, examining her nails. "We're having a bit of fun, but Freddy's almost definitely the one for me."

"You don't sound too sure."

Imogen frowned in concentration, then nodded her head. "Nope, my choice is made."

Kate wasn't entirely convinced by this sudden conversion. "Does this mean you'll give up Ethan?"

"Yes Granny."

"Promise?"

"Totally."

Kate's sense of relief that Freddy was probably not going to have his heart broken was tempered by the teeniest sense of disappointment, which she pushed to the back of her mind. "I think it's the right thing to do – if you love Freddy."

"How could anyone not love him?" Immy smiled. "But I'm not dumping Ethan yet. He's taking me to a private view at the top of the Walkie Talkie next week and I don't intend to miss it. Damien Hirst's going to be there and it'll be awesome. And before you ask, I'll tell Fred I'm going with a girlfriend so you won't need to cover for me – not that you would anyway."

"You're right, I wouldn't."

"Thanks – I'll remember that the next time you need a favour doing."

Kate shrugged and got down from the bed. "Whatever." She was aware of sounding petulant, but she couldn't help the way she felt. She liked Imogen a lot, but found her attitude to friends hard to comprehend. Kate had never considered it before, but comparing herself to Immy she guessed she was probably quite old-fashioned. It was possibly down to having parents who'd stuck together over the years with no infidelities on either side, as far as she knew. She hadn't given it any thought until now, but perhaps she'd always expected to find a man to settle down with and have her own "happy-ever-after".

# Chapter 12: An Unwelcome Guest

The build-up to Christmas was reaching fever pitch. It was office party time and the shop was thronged daily with workers searching for small but expensive-looking gifts for their colleagues.

Each morning, Kate helped to arrange the goodies on the long table that dominated the centre of the shop. The table top was now covered in heaps of plum puddings in shiny red wrappers, enamel boxes containing amaretti biscuits, and gingerbread Santas with suits and beards in icing sugar. Everything had been given a touch of Christmas sparkle and Clare had been put in charge of making meringues the size of cabbages covered in edible glitter.

"I'm not sure how festive meringues are, but what Vitaly wants, Vitaly gets. Joseph said the idea was to give the place a kind of Nutcracker theme this year, whatever that means."

"I guess it means romantic and sparkly," said Kate, looking around. There were soft lights in every corner and classical music playing in the background. "It's all so beautiful." She was surprised to feel a tightening in her throat as nostalgia for childhood Christmases at home swept over her. Her parents had always made a huge effort to make it a special time for their only child.

"Ah, don't be welling up now. The customers don't want your tears in their Lapsang Souchong."

"I'm fine, Clare. Honest. In fact, I don't even like Christmas all that much."

"Shh – don't let Joseph hear you or he'll make it the subject of one of his early-morning pep talks."

"Ugh. Spare me." And with that Kate headed over to the counter to wrap up a family of white chocolate polar bears for a customer.

She was pleased to be busy because it took her mind off the situation with Immy and her own non-date. She hadn't bothered to reply to Nick's last message: *Bogey Man tomoz?* As if! But, despite herself, she kept sneaking a look at her phone, half-expecting some kind of apology, but nothing came. What a slimeball – had he ever liked her, she wondered? Why had he even suggested the Bogey Man? Had he stood her up as punishment for not ripping off his Calvin Klein's on Day One? And why was she even wasting time thinking about him? He wasn't worth it.

She had wondered about contacting the nice maths teacher who'd ticked her boxes at the dating event, but the Nick experience had made her wary of going out with strangers. She was going to remain single and celibate at least until the spring.

The rest of the day went by in a blur of goji berry muffins and commuters in shopping frenzies demanding chai lattes. By 6pm she was exhausted, but decided to make an attempt at Christmas shopping.

She quickly changed out of her waitressing gear, then headed out to the King's Road, hoping to pick up a couple of gifts and be stretched out on the sofa with the remains of one of Clare's tuna bakes before her favourite soap started.

An hour later, she'd had enough of the scrum and returned with two paperbacks for her mother, a DVD and a scarf for her father and a felt mouse for the cat. Climbing the stairs with her bundles, she was feeling pleased with her modest haul and looking forward to a nice cup of tea and some supper.

Her heart sank on opening the fridge to find an empty space where the milk should have been. Her flatmates were great, but only she and Clare ever seemed to notice when basics ran out. "Damn it," she muttered. Sighing, she put her coat and gloves back on, grabbed her purse and went downstairs once more to pick up supplies.

The last person Kate expected to see as she opened the door and stepped onto the pavement was her ex-boyfriend.

"Steve! What are you doing here?"

"Kitty Kat!" He grabbed her around the waist with both hands and kissed her before she could protest. "Aren't you pleased to see me?"

"Er, yes. Of course I am," she said, stepping away. "What I mean is, how did you know I was here?" If Elvis had turned up on the doorstep she wouldn't have been much more surprised.

"Duh, it's all over Facebook. And you told me you were coming here, thicko. Although you were probably too drunk to remember."

"Oh yes, I suppose I did."

She flinched at his words. "Thicko" was said jokingly, but in a tone that made her feel small and stupid – a way she used to feel all the time but had forgotten since she'd started work at the deli.

Now she remembered the last time she'd seen him.

Some of her girlfriends had arranged a going-away bash for her at a pub in town and Steve had been there with a few of his mates. It had been a shock because she hadn't seen him for months. At her leaving "do", he'd made it plain that the idea of her going to London was a big joke.

And here he was in Chelsea. "But why are you down here? I mean, it's great to see you, but why didn't you tell me you were coming?"

"I thought it would be a nice surprise, but obviously I was wrong," he said, sulking.

Kate bit her lip, her emotions torn between the ghost of an ancient fondness for her ex and annoyance that he had landed on her with no warning.

Steve's eyes wandered over the front of the shop and up towards the flats. "So aren't you going to show me around your pad and introduce me to your smart friends?"

She hesitated, her mind whirring. "Oh, the flat's in a mess and everyone's out," she said, pulling the door closed behind her.

"You don't want me showing you up – is that it? Your yokel ex-boyfriend?"

He'd got it in one: she didn't want to let Steve into the flat and she didn't want him to meet her friends either, but she wasn't going to tell him that. "Don't be daft! It's only that there's no one around. If you really want to meet them, I'll find out where they are."

If he had to meet the flatmates, she'd rather they met in a pub than at home. She took off her gloves and pinged off a message to Immy, hoping she wouldn't be anywhere close by. After a few seconds the reply came back: she and Freddy were at the cinema – not something that ever prevented Immy texting – and wouldn't be back until late.

"Everyone's busy," said Kate, hoping she sounded suitably disappointed.

Steve smirked. "So if the place is empty, how about you take me upstairs, cook me a meal and we get – what's the word? – reacquainted? For old times' sake?"

Getting "reacquainted" was absolutely the last thing Kate wanted to do and she couldn't help wrinkling her face in alarm. "I don't think so, Steve – I'm knackered after work, there's no food in the house and I'm a rubbish cook anyway."

"Your spaghetti carbonara was always edible, but I get the message. Why don't I get lost? Is that what you're saying?"

God, he was hard work. "No, not at all. I'm tired and the fridge is empty. How about we go for a meal instead? Just the two of us? There's a proper old-fashioned pub not far from here that does good burgers. Or we could go for a Chinese?"

"Yeah, all right. But I could do with a couple of pints first. You're the Londoner, so I'll let you lead the way. And if this pub of yours is crap, it'll be your fault."

Kate gritted her teeth, wondering how she had put up with this man for two whole years.

"Great." She slipped her arm through his, relieved to be getting him away from her new home and friends, both of which she knew he would hate on sight. They walked away from the busy high street and Kate led him through the back streets and across tree-lined squares the short distance to the pub.

It was the first time she could remember ever

taking the lead anywhere. Steve always had to be in front and she would follow meekly, her hand small and safe in his. It seemed strange being with someone she had once known so well in such an unfamiliar setting.

As they walked along, she struggled to find something to say that wouldn't provoke him. After a moment, she noticed the tatty sports bag slung over Steve's shoulder. "So, where are you staying?"

"I was hoping you'd invite me to stay at yours."

"Oh, I don't know, Steve. All the rooms are taken and the couch is really uncomfortable."

"I don't mind cosying up with you, Kitty. I bet you've got a massive double bed."

"I've got a weeny bed and, anyway, it wouldn't be right – since we're not together any more."

He shrugged, looking downcast. "Well, if I'm not staying at your place, I guess I'll find a warm doorway."

Kate felt a pang of guilt. "You're joking, right?"

He gave her one of his classic put-down stares. "God, you are so easy to wind up. Of course I'm not going to sleep on the ground like some loser. You're off the hook; I didn't want to stay in Chelsea with a load of nobs – I'll be kipping with my mate Dave in Norwood tonight. United are playing at Selhurst Park tomorrow, so we're going to the match then getting rat-arsed. But tonight, I'm all yours."

Tonight, she thought. I can just about manage one evening with this person I used to love.

At the pub, they found a quiet corner and Steve went to the bar to get the drinks. Kate watched him as he looked around at the dark wooden walls covered in prints and the flagstone floor and could tell he approved. The landlord had made a token effort at decorating the place for Christmas and there were sprigs of plastic holly tucked around the edges of the pictures and a lopsided Santa with a cotton-wool beard on the bar.

Steve smiled as she caught his eye and for a moment she felt a flash of the old attraction. He had no problems finding girlfriends: he was stocky and handsome, with the kind of physique needed by a farmer. Before they split up, he had enrolled at agricultural college but hated it and left. For a while he'd talked about giving it another try but after months of dithering he went back to helping on his father's dairy farm.

Kate thought about the different lives people led at home and was glad she had escaped, if only for a few months. A few of the people she'd been to school with had gone off to uni, but many were still working locally – like Steve's latest girlfriend. A buzz of something like happiness hit as she remembered that Steve now had another woman in his life. She'd met Liz once or twice and liked her a lot. She seemed to be the kind of girl who wouldn't put up with any nonsense, which was exactly what Steve needed. Looking back, Kate recognised she had been far too soft and amenable with him during their time together. She had learnt her lesson and would never make the same mistake again.

She relaxed, smiling as Steve came back to the table with their drinks. "Cheers."

"Cheers," she said, as they clinked glasses. "So, what have you been up to? And how's Liz?"

Steve's whole face changed and Kate could see the muscles tense around his jaw. "Silly cow went off with some Welsh arsehole. Good luck to the poor bastard, I say. She was a total pain. Always nagging at me for watching sport all the time or wanting to drag me around clothes shops. Not like you. You never messed me around." Now he smiled and tugged her towards him. "I was a complete dick letting you go."

She felt herself go rigid as Steve stretched his arm across her shoulders and she didn't know what to say. There was no way she would ever get back together with him, but she did her best to smile. It was true she'd never messed him about and she had loved him – but she was always wary of his temper, which could flare up in a moment.

She had been too young and naïve to recognise that behind Steve's hardman act was a vulnerability he was desperate to conceal. His mother had died when he was thirteen, leaving him unwilling to trust and then let go of someone he allowed under his carapace. As his first "proper" girlfriend, Kate had grown closer to him than anyone had done before.

"I bet Steve's a big softy underneath his tough exterior," her mother had said approvingly when Kate had first started going out with him.

"Don't let him hear you say that," her father had joked. "He'll wallop you."

Kate had laughed, not realising until a long time afterwards that her parents had summed up both sides of Steve's character perfectly. He never had "walloped" her, but there was something about him that made her feel increasingly edgy. It had been a relief to hear he had a new girlfriend and seemed to be calming down. Now she was sad to discover Liz had also bailed out. Maybe she, too, had found Steve's mood swings hard to deal with.

She grabbed her purse and stood, eager to change the subject. "I don't know about you, but I'm starving. How about a burger? My treat."

Steve examined his glass, which was already half-empty. "I don't mind if I do, and get me another pint while you're up there. It's not a bad drop."

At the bar, Kate sighed deeply, relieved to have got over the tricky subject of Liz so quickly and easily. After setting down the drinks, she grabbed a box from the pile of board games in the bookcase next to their table. "Fancy a game of something?"

"Sure. Though you know I'll massacre you."

"I'm willing to risk it," she said with a grin.

They played Connect and won two games each.

"Best of five?"

"Why not."

When Steve won the last game, he was triumphant and Kate was pleased to have given him something to brag about.

"I might only be a cow man but I'm not as dim as you like to think."

"I never said you were dim," she said. The fact he had ducked out of agricultural college after one term and never gone back still rankled with him, though he'd never openly admit it. "I know how complex farming is."

"Too bloody right." Steve laughed, bitterly. "And yet you're earning more than me for serving overpriced croissants to desperate housewives."

"That's not fair." Kate felt her cheeks flush. "I'm

hardly earning anything and some of the "house-wives" are really nice, interesting people." And almost before the next words were out of her mouth, she knew she'd made a mistake. "At least I'm not still hanging around at home in some dead-end job."

Steve slowly set down his pint glass and looked at her. "And what exactly is that supposed to mean? 'Hanging around at home?' Are you saying I'm a mummy's boy? Oh no. Wait a minute. I watched my mother die of cancer ten years ago. So you must mean I'm in a dead-end job. You're right – the dairy industry is totally screwed. While your dickhead customers are paying £3 for a frothy coffee, my dad is sending cattle to the abattoir because what he gets from the supermarkets isn't enough to feed the beasts who produce the milk." He drained his glass and stood up, almost knocking back his chair. "Let's go."

Kate grabbed her bag and hurried after him to the door, muttering a hasty thank you to the bar staff who had turned towards them at the sound of Steve's angry voice.

Outside he was walking so fast that Kate had to run to keep up with him. She tried to take his arm but he shook her off roughly. "Steve, look, I'm sorry. I didn't mean it the way you think." How was she going to get out of this? "I don't mean to criticise you. I'm talking about me and my job – selling cheese on a market stall for Geoff." Shut up, Kate, she said to herself. Don't say any more about cows, milk, cheese or anything related to farming.

At the end of the square, Steve stopped and looked around furiously.

"Where's the sodding Tube station?"

Kate pushed damp hair back from her face, panting. "You need to catch a train from Victoria. I'll walk you over there."

His face blazed with anger. "I don't need you to walk me anywhere, you patronising bitch. I'll find it myself."

Kate stood under a plane tree, her heart pounding, as Steve stomped off through the drizzle. She didn't dare tell him he was heading in completely the wrong direction.

# Chapter 13: A New Friend

Kate awoke late the next morning with a thumping headache and a feeling of dread that only made sense when she remembered the events of the previous evening. She sat up with a shock, her heart tight with anxiety until her brain accepted that Steve was not around.

She spent most of the day avoiding her housemates, curled up in her bedroom in pyjamas drinking tea and reading back copies of *Grazia* and *Hello!* magazines.

On Sunday, she rallied and agreed to join Imogen and Freddy for a trip to Battersea Park, taking in the zoo. It was a bright, crisp day and they had fun watching the baby meerkats chasing each other's tails and tumbling around in the dust.

"I'm starved," said Imogen after a couple of hours spent cooing over the chinchillas and shivering at the rat snakes and giant snails. "Is there somewhere we can grab coffee and a bun?"

"I think there's a caff by the lake," said Kate, who had done her homework.

"Great. Lead me to it."

They turned away from the Thames, strolled past the bandstand and walked around the lake, which the wildfowl had to themselves in the wintertime.

Freddy squinted into the low sun. "Shame we

can't go for a row, but the boats have been put away."

"I guess that means no paddling either?" Kate smiled as they watched the coots and moorhens squabbling over bits of bread and skidding over patches of ice to reach deeper water. It always soothed her to see wildlife in the middle of the city. "Let's sit outside. Can we?"

Imogen rubbed her gloved hands together and wrinkled her nose as she spied the damp benches. "If we must."

"I'll fetch the drinks."

Freddy put an arm around Kate. "No you won't – I'll get them."

"Last of the big spenders." Imogen watched him disappear into the cafeteria then turned to her companion. "You're very quiet, Kate. What's up? Are you still sulking about me and Ethan?"

"I'm not sulking about anything and not everything is about you, Immy."

"Okay, don't bite my head off."

"Sorry. I didn't mean to snap." Kate's good nature made it hard for her to be cross for very long. "I had a bit of a shock on Friday night, that's all."

"Tell me all about it, quick, before Fred comes out and we have to talk about meerkats and football again." They both looked at the glass front of the cafeteria through which Freddy could be seen studying a selection of cakes as he waited to be served.

Kate took a deep breath before speaking, amazed by how shaken she still was by the incident at the pub. "My ex from home, Steve, turned up on the doorstep and it didn't go well. He wanted to come into the flat and 'get reacquainted', even though we split up months ago and he's got a new girlfriend. Or at least I thought he did – it turns out she had the good sense to leave him. And he doesn't react well to being left." Frowning, she traced a circle of rainwater with her finger on the wooden trestle table. "We were in the pub by this point in the evening and he became quite angry with me and stomped off."

"Angry with you? Why? How is it your fault his girlfriend left him?"

"Oh, it wasn't just that. He has a massive chip on his shoulder about being a farmer and he thinks I don't take problems in the dairy industry seriously …"

"You're kidding me."

"It's a long story. Anyway, by now he'll be safely back in Herefordshire under a warm cow where he belongs and with any luck I'll never have to see him again."

Imogen patted Kate's hand, which was turning blue with cold. "Well, I'm glad he's gone and left you in peace."

"Me too." She smiled. "Goodness – what has our friend brought us?"

"Here you go, ladies." Freddy was carrying a formica tray with a selection of flapjacks and brownies plus three steaming mugs of hot chocolate adorned with cream and cinnamon sprinkles.

Imogen blew him a kiss. "You're the best, Fred."

"For you my lovelies, anything."

\* \* \*

By mid-afternoon, the sun had gone and they were starting to lose sensation in their toes, so they decided to head back to the flat and make a vat of chilli. Clare was at her boyfriend's as usual, but they discovered that Valentina was at a loose end and happy to join them for supper. To begin with, Kate had been nervous of their upstairs neighbour with her jet-black hair and perfect figure but she soon discovered that Valentina had a warm personality.

They were all gathered around the kitchen table, with nachos and sour cream at the ready, when the doorbell rang.

"I wonder who that can be?" said Imogen, wiping a morsel of avocado dip from her lips and showing no sign of going to find out.

When no one moved from their seat, Valentina unfolded her long limbs and stood up. "I will go and see." After a few moments, while Freddy filled their glasses with red wine, Valentina came back. "There's a man downstairs whose face I do not know. He won't tell me his name. All he says is he must see you, Kate."

"A man? I don't know any men apart from Freddy," she said, wiping her hands on a tea towel.

"It's probably one of your dodgy blind dates. Or maybe it's Nick."

"I doubt it." She frowned. She hadn't heard from him since the non-date. "He doesn't know where I live anyway." There was only one other person it could possibly be, but he was a hundred and fifty miles away, thank God.

Valentina was standing in the doorway, tapping her foot impatiently. "You can continue to guess or you could take a look at the video screen."

"You're right," said Imogen. "Let's go and see."

So the girls went out into the hallway and peered at the shadowy figure huddled on the pavement clutching a bunch of flowers.

Kate's heart sank. "Bugger. It's Steve. I was sure he'd be back home by now."

Imogen moved even closer and squinted at the small screen. "Hmm. Not bad looking, though his taste in flowers is pretty grim."

Down on the cold pavement, Steve pressed the buzzer again and peered angrily into the camera.

"I think you should invite him up so I can take a closer look."

"No way, Immy. I really can't face him tonight and I definitely don't want him in the flat."

"You might not want to see him, but I'd like to see the boy who stole your heart aged thirteen."

"I wasn't thirteen, I was seventeen and it was a big mistake. I told you what happened on Friday. It was grim."

Freddy saw the girls huddled around the video screen and came out to join them. "What's happening down there? It's not carol singers, is it?"

"No, it's much more exciting than that," said Imogen. "It's Kate's first love come to whisk her off to the sticks on his tractor."

"Ha, ha. Very funny."

The buzzer sounded again, more sharply this time.

"From what you've told us about him, if you don't respond he'll only come back again later or turn up at work and embarrass you."

Kate opened her mouth to protest at the same moment as Imogen pressed "Speak" and "Unlock" on the entry phone. "Hi, come on up. Second floor."

"Oh Imogen, no!" How could her friend be so thoughtless, especially when she knew about Steve's foul mood at the pub? Kate groaned. "You can see him if you want to, but I'm going to hide. Tell him I'm not in."

"Don't be ridiculous. And don't hide. I've got a much better idea – Freddy can pretend to be your boyfriend, which is guaranteed to get rid of lover boy."

Kate shot Freddy a look of alarm. "I can't ask him to do that. He's your boyfriend, after all."

Immy rolled her eyes. "It's only make-believe and you don't have to snog him or anything. Just look soppy. Fred, put your arm around her, will you?" They could hear the swish of the lift door opening then the sound of heavy boots echoed in the stairwell. "Quick, he's nearly here. Let's go back into the kitchen and you two try to look like a happy couple."

Freddy smiled at Kate as he raised his fists in a boxing stance. "I'm ready to leap to your defence if necessary."

"I really hope it won't come to that." She didn't know how Steve would react if he thought she had a new man in her life: would he want to fight him? Given how weedy Freddy was compared to Steve, she hoped not, but her ex was so unpredictable there was no way of knowing.

Valentina opened the door, but didn't invite Steve in. "Delivery for me?" she asked, stretching out a hand towards the forlorn bunch of supermarket flowers that Steve had been absent-mindedly whacking against his leg as he waited. "How delightful."

"Er, no. Sorry Miss. I was hoping to see Kate Hughes. I thought she lived here, but maybe I've come to the wrong flat?" He leant over, trying to peer past the elegant figure of Valentina into the expansive living room. In the distance there was the sound of chatter as the others tried to behave normally in the kitchen.

"No, this is the right place." Valentina's cool green eyes narrowed as she surveyed Steve. "Stay there," she said firmly, as though addressing a badly behaved poodle. "Kate," she called, "there is a visitor for you."

Valentina winked as she passed Kate in the hallway, the girl's shoulders hunched and her hands balled into fists and stuffed into the pocket of her apron.

Steve lumbered over, holding out the battered bouquet and looking embarrassed. "I'm sorry I lost my rag in the pub," he whispered, bending down so only Kate could hear. He nudged her with his elbow and grinned. "You know what I'm like – I don't mean anything by it."

Kate shrugged and looked at her feet. "That's okay," she muttered, knowing it wasn't in the least bit okay but wanting him to say whatever it was he had to say and leave her in peace.

"No, it's not. I behaved like a complete twat and I'm sorry." He held out the bruised carnations. "I've brought you some flowers as a peace offering."

Reluctantly, Kate took them. "Thanks. But how come you're still here? I thought you were heading home this morning."

"I got pissed and missed the train. So am I forgiven for Friday?"

She shook her head in exasperation. Getting drunk, missing the train, losing his rag about nothing. It was typical of Steve, but what could she do? If she didn't accept his apology he'd probably have another rant and refuse to leave. "Yes, you're forgiven."

Steve gave a sigh of relief and stood up straight.

"Good. Thanks, Kate. Great." He stayed there, expect-antly, a faint smile on his face. "Any chance of a beer? To bury the hatchet and wish me a happy Christmas?"

"Wait there a minute." She sighed and went into the kitchen to fetch a bottle.

"What's happening out there?" asked Imogen.

"He's said sorry for being a twat, so I'm going to give him a beer then throw him out."

When she went out again, Steve had moved fur-ther into the living room. His eyes were fixed on the enormous telly where adverts for sofas and perfume flashed across the screen. "Nice place you've got here."

"We like it, don't we darling?"

Steve's jaw actually dropped as Freddy came up behind Kate, grabbed her gently and kissed her cheek. She managed to subdue a squeal of alarm as she felt the unfamiliar hands on her waist. She'd been so focused on Steve she hadn't noticed her housemate creep up behind her.

"I'm Freddy, by the way," he said, holding out his hand. "I expect Kitty has told you all about me?"

Kate felt her cheeks flare with embarrassment and stared at her feet.

Steve's dark grey eyes narrowed with suspicion as he reluctantly took Freddy's hand. "No, mate. She didn't mention you at all."

Please God, don't let there be a fight, thought Kate, as she tried to interpret the emotions flickering across Steve's face.

At the same moment, Imogen approached glass in hand. "Oh, you must be Kate's childhood sweetheart. I've heard all about the fun you used to have down on the farm."

Steve was motionless for a moment, clearly not sure whether the pretty blonde was taking the piss or not. He relaxed when Imogen shot him one of her winning smiles and raised her glass. "There's plenty of chilli if you want to stay for supper."

Kate was frantically signalling "no!" with her eyes, but her so-called friend was studiously ignoring her.

"Oh, I don't know ..."

"Sit down, mate," said Freddy. "We've made far too much grub, haven't we, sweetheart?"

"I'm sure Steve wants to get back to his friend's place in Norwood."

"Actually, because Dave didn't know I was staying tonight, he'd already arranged to visit his mum, so I'm on my own until he gets back later."

"Well, that's settled then," said Freddy, patting Steve on the back. "Grab some chilli and you can tell me all about Kate." He laughed as Kate looked daggers at him. "Only joking. There's a good match on later if you want to stick around for it."

Steve nodded slowly. "You're on," he said, taking a swig of beer.

So they all ate chilli in the kitchen while Immy flirted outrageously with Steve. Freddy was very attentive, topping up Kate's glass and making sure she had enough of everything, and Valentina sat at the end of the table, not saying much but smiling enigmatically.

After the meal, the lads settled down to watch a game between a team in red versus a team in blue while the women escaped upstairs with a bottle of wine.

Kate was not exactly happy with the way things

had gone that evening so, as soon as they were in Valentina's flat, she felt she had to speak. "Why were you lot so bloody nice to Steve? I thought Fred was going to ask him to stay for Christmas at one point."

Imogen smiled. "Ask our clever friend. It was her idea."

"It's what they call reverse psychology," said Valentina, who was stretched out on a raspberry-red sofa looking more than ever like a very beautiful Siamese cat. "If you try very hard to make a bully leave, he will want to stay. But if you are nice to him, he feels in control. He does not feel threatened. Your Mr Steve now feels as though this is his place and that he can stay here. And so he is happy to leave."

"That sounds bonkers," said Kate, though feeling a little calmer, "but I really hope you're right."

"Definitely," said Valentina. "I read it many years ago on a psychology course."

"I didn't know you'd been to university," said Imogen.

"I have done many, many things in my life." She took a sip of wine and smiled. "Modelling can be very boring, so I liked to read between shoots. At one time, I did a little course at the Sorbonne."

"You speak French, as well as English and Russian?"

"*Mais oui*, Kate."

The younger girls exchanged glances, clearly impressed.

"Tell me more about your theory."

"It is clear – Steve will not try to woo you because he and Frederick have bonded like brothers and a man will not take his brother's woman." Imogen snorted with laughter, which Valentina ignored. "It is excellent that Freddy was so sweet and attentive to you, exactly as a lover should be."

Kate blushed. "He's a convincing actor."

"He was enjoying himself," said Imogen lightly. "You know what he's like – he's a big kid and it was all a joke to him." She picked up the bottle, emptying the last of the wine into their glasses. "Come on. We'd better go back downstairs and see how the boys are getting on. We don't want them fighting over Kate's favours."

"That's so not going to happen." Kate looked at her watch. "I hope the match has finished. I definitely do not want Steve staying here overnight."

Downstairs, they found the boys stretched out in front of the TV, shouting at the screen. Fortunately it was friendly shouting because they were both supporting the winning side.

At the end of the match, Steve stood and shook Freddy's hand and slapped him on the back in a man hug. "Good luck to you, mate. She's a great girl."

"Cheers bro."

As he was leaving, Steve gave Kate a chaste kiss on the cheek. "Freddy might look a bit gay, but he's a sound bloke."

"I'm glad you approve," the sarcasm in Kate's voice going right over Steve's head. It was only when the door shut and she heard him run down the steps that Kate let out a sigh of relief.

Freddy and Valentina stayed in the kitchen, but Kate went to the window to make sure Steve had left the building.

"Mission accomplished," said Imogen, as they watched Steve weave across the busy road. "He's convinced you two are an item but that he can pop back any time. I think my idea was brilliant, Valentina's nutty theory was spot on and your cowboy won't pester you any more. Job done."

Kate nodded thoughtfully. "I hope you're right. I couldn't go through any of this again."

"Oh, I don't know. You seemed to enjoy being Freddy's girlfriend for the night."

"I was being nice to him, nothing else."

"Yes …" Imogen narrowed her eyes. "Anyway, he's all mine again now."

"Good. And make sure you hang on to him." Maybe seeing Fred with his arms around Kate would remind Imogen what she had to lose.

# Chapter 14: Party Time

Every year, Vitaly Polzin threw a massive party to which he invited neighbours, friends, local politicians and all his employees from Delish Organics and other businesses. He liked to think of himself as a socialist at heart and it pleased and amused him to have the young people mix with old oligarchs like himself. He could tell that some of his more traditional friends were a little discomfited by the fact that the deli staff were difficult to tell apart from their own pampered offspring. In January, he held a second party to celebrate the Russian Orthodox Christmas with close friends and family.

Vitaly was born in a bleak, grey Siberian city called Irkutsk, a misfortune that made him determined to leave as soon as he could. His father had worked in the oil industry as a labourer and no one was quite sure where Vitaly's own immense fortune had come from. Whatever the source of his billions, he was happy to spend it on homes in Moscow, London and elsewhere. As well as several commercial premises and a mansion in Holland Park, he had an apartment on the Thames in an area that used to be busy with stevedores but now bustled with accountants and assorted penpushers.

It was an open secret that Vitaly was governed by his fearsome second wife, Martina, whom he married after his first wife had grown tired of their affair and thrown him out. Unlike some of his peers, he enjoyed sharing his money around, a trait of which Martina strongly disapproved.

Wife number one had known Vitaly since childhood, but number two was much younger than him and extremely high-maintenance. It was because of Martina that the Holland Park house had been completely gutted and had a three-storey extension with swimming pool and gym built beneath it, much to the alarm of the neighbours. Vitaly had spent millions turning the Victorian mansion into an ultra-modern dwelling while the brand-new riverside penthouse had been filled with false mouldings, Louis Quinze furniture and one or two nineteenth-century French masterpieces. It was here that he gathered his friends and associates for the party.

Kate had never seen anything like it and spent the first few seconds with her back glued to the wall and her mouth open. Valentina was chatting to her Uncle Vitaly and looked more stunning than ever in a Versace minidress. Kate watched in admiration as colleagues from the deli and other restaurants wandered around with their heads held high, clearly enjoying themselves.

"Let's get a drink," said Imogen, grabbing Kate's sleeve and intercepting one of the waiters. Having found herself a glass of bubbly, Immy crossed the room and stretched out on a chaise longue while Kate balanced on the edge, her bum only just on the plush apricot fabric and a champagne flute held out nervously in front of her in case she spilled it. She envied Imogen's obvious ease in such luxurious surroundings.

"You look at home here, Immy."

"I've been to these parties before," she shrugged, "and Dad and Vitaly are chums, of course."

"Oh, I didn't know that." Kate couldn't help marvelling – and not for the first time – at how different Immy's social circle was to her own.

She knew that Imogen's parents had separated when she was barely three. Her mother Maggie had insisted on staying in England while her father Frank kept their apartments in Monaco and Milan, where he did something worthy for an international charity when he wasn't playing with racing cars. This arrangement meant Imogen spent a lot of her childhood on planes visiting one or other of them.

Eventually, Maggie had decided to place her daughter in a smart boarding school in the depths of the English countryside where, for the first time, Imogen met other youngsters who had family lives as privileged but disrupted as her own. School was the closest thing to a regular family life she had ever known and her best friends were people she'd met there.

Frank had only visited the school twice and loathed it, finding the smug tone of both teachers and pupils hard to bear. He had gone to an ordinary secondary modern until the age of fifteen and strongly disapproved of his wife's choice of establishment for their only daughter, but he was outvoted.

Imogen's grandfather had made his money in the Midlands producing plates decorated with sentimental pictures of pink-cheeked peasants playing with kittens outside country cottages. When Frank took over the business, he banished the kittens and diversified into more tasteful pottery for stately homes and smart shops. Although he didn't exactly brag about the kitsch origins of his fortune, he was always aware of them and wanted his daughter to earn her own wage and be more grounded than some of her glossy friends.

He had met Vitaly in Monaco where one of the Russian's smaller yachts was moored alongside his for a couple of weeks. As well as a passion for sailing, vodka and Formula One cars, Frank discovered that he and Vitaly had a shared pride in their working-class backgrounds. It wasn't long before they became friends and Frank was delighted when Vitaly offered to give Imogen a job at the deli – but only if she was prepared to work as hard as everyone else. In exchange, Vitaly's son Pavel was sent to Frank's office in Milan to learn some business skills.

Now Immy and Kate were watching Pavel's step-mother Martina totter around the room in her killer heels, stretching her abnormally smooth face into a polite smile as she greeted her husband's mishmash of guests.

"I reckon Martina is planning to finish off hubby so she can get her hands on all his lovely lolly."

"And what do you base that bit of scandal on, Immy?"

"Women like her never have enough money."

"But hasn't she got enough loot as it is? I mean, Vitaly seems to be incredibly generous with his wealth."

"Yes, but it's not the same as having total control over the finances."

Kate frowned. How could anyone not be satisfied

with all this stuff? The gigantic mirrors with ornate frames? The pictures that looked remarkably like Impressionist paintings she'd seen in a school book? Valentina was in a corner talking to Freddy, whose hand was leaning casually on the head of a life-sized panther that appeared to be carved out of ebony. To an untrained eye, everything in the room looked as though it should be in a museum.

Freddy glanced across and waved. The girls waved back, then Kate took a sip of bubbly and whispered to her friend. "When are you going to ditch Ethan? Unless you've changed your mind, that is."

"Here we go again." Immy pulled her bored face, but Kate said nothing and waited. "Okay, okay – I haven't completely made up my mind. I do still love Freddy, but not the way I used to do. Since being with Ethan, things have changed."

"Well, that's a bit of an understatement."

Imogen looked at Kate sourly. "I've decided to think about it some more and talk to Freddy in the New Year, so as not to ruin his holidays."

"That's very thoughtful of you."

"I know."

"So, you don't think he suspects you're possibly about to break up with him?"

"No, why should he?" She looked at Kate suspiciously. "You haven't said anything, have you?"

"Of course not!" Kate felt guilty because she knew she should say something to Freddy, but she couldn't bring herself to do it. And anyway, it was Immy's responsibility. "I'm leaving it to you to break his heart."

"Good. And I will sort everything out with him. Just not yet."

At that moment, Freddy strolled over and sat opposite them on a flimsy chair whose delicate legs bent under his weight. "And what are you two gossiping about?"

"Why, you, of course," said Imogen with breathtaking nonchalance.

Kate couldn't bear it. How could Immy be so heartless? "I'm hungry. Did anyone see which way the canapés went?"

"Last seen heading into the riverside room," said Freddy, standing. "I'll come with you. Coming, Immy?"

She shook her head and sank lower down onto the chaise. "Nope. I'm too divinely comfortable here. But if you spot any seared scallops, grab me a couple, will you?"

"Certainly, my lady," he said, with a bow. "Right, Kate, I'll go and forage for food while you find us a spot on the balcony."

"Balcony? In December?"

"Wait till you see it," he said with a grin.

One whole side of the apartment was glass and the panels opened onto an enormous terrace. Underfloor heating and huge braziers ensured that even in December the place was warm enough to sit outside. For guests who were still cold, there were staff on hand with fur coats and cashmere blankets. Kate refused to wrap herself in a dead animal but did accept a blanket and went to sit in a high-backed chair overlooking the Thames. Fairy lights glowed in the apartments across the water and music could be heard from party boats ploughing the river far below.

After delivering canapés to Imogen, Freddy came

out to join Kate wearing a Cossack hat and what looked like a bearskin. In his hands, he held a bottle of champagne and a plate piled high with savoury nibbles. Kate couldn't help smiling. "Are you sure you've got enough to eat?"

He shrugged. "Nope. I'm not sure at all. I may need to go back for thirds. Here, have some."

Kate looked at the proffered plate and shook her head. She should have been happy to be at such an amazing party, but her stomach was twisted with anxiety at the thought of Freddy being deceived. And, what was worse, she was letting it happen. She smiled weakly and shook her head. "I'm not that hungry after all."

"I thought you said you were starving. Anyway, this isn't your average food. Look at this stuff – it's better than the turkey giblets and cod goujons you normally get at works' parties."

"You've been to lots of work dos, have you?"

"One or two. I had Saturday jobs in my local supermarket, where the party food was grim. All they ever gave us were paper plates covered with unidentified fried objects. Then there were the evenings practising our waiting skills at uni when we were obliged to eat any snacks left over at the end of the evening. It was like playing Russian roulette with salmonella instead of a bullet."

Freddy looked so appealing wrapped up in a floor-length fur coat, almost like a Russian prince, that Kate suddenly felt desperately sad. What was Immy thinking of, letting him go?

Freddy's laughter at his own joke faded and a worried expression crossed his face. "What's up? You're not ill, are you? That would be a bummer right before Christmas." His brown eyes studied her face intently.

"Oh, I'm fine, really. A bit overwhelmed by all this glitz and glamour, that's all. I'm a simple country girl and this is not quite what I'm used to." She smiled, pulling the blanket around her shoulders. Imogen had put her in a horrible position, but she decided then and there not to let it spoil her evening. "Actually, I wouldn't mind trying one of those mini blue cheese thingies."

"They're pretty good, especially with this chutney."

"Yum," she recognised the tangy sauce from the shop. "This is delicious."

"Mind if I join you?" Imogen appeared behind them dressed from head to toe in ocelot.

Kate shifted along so Immy could take the seat next to Freddy. "I hope all this fur is false," she said, eyeing up the garment.

"I think Martina would sue the shop if it was." Immy popped a salmon-topped blini in her mouth. "Yum. Vitaly's parties might be dull, but the food is always tiptop."

"Immy, you have no idea." Kate laughed. "If you think this is dull, you should try the New Year's Eve Disco at the Laughing Frog."

"I'm sure it's divine."

"Believe me, it's not."

"Speaking of excitement," said Freddy, "here comes Valentina."

They watched as their friend shimmied across, a fluffy shocking-pink coat now covering her gold dress.

"You look fabulous," said Immy, stroking the sleeve. "What animal is that?"

Valentina sniffed. "Nylon – real fur is so vulgar. Darlings, my uncle is about to begin the firework display so we must go up to the roof terrace."

"You mean this isn't it?"

"No, Kate. We must go up one more floor. It is a bore, I'm afraid, but at least there is a bar up there."

Freddy grinned. "I love fireworks!"

"Me too," said Immy. "Let's go and see."

# Chapter 15: An Adventure

The day after the party everyone was a little subdued – even Imogen, who refused Freddy's offer to accompany her to the airport. Kate knew her friend was meeting up with Ethan so they could travel together, so when she hugged Immy and wished her happy holidays it was with a sinking heart.

She hardly saw Freddy for the rest of the afternoon and in the evening he went out with friends while she stayed in and wrapped the last of the presents she'd bought for her parents but wouldn't exchange until the New Year. She sighed, thinking that perhaps she should have gone with them to the Canaries after all. The prospects for Christmas in London were not looking promising.

It was Christmas Eve and Vitaly had given the junior staff the day off, so Kate was surprised to hear someone knocking on the flat door at nine o'clock in the morning. She was even more surprised to see Cheese Ned in the hallway.

"Hello princess," he said, giving her a quick peck on the cheek then stepping back to look her over. "London suits you – you look great. Nice pyjamas, by the way."

Kate thought there was something different about Ned, then realised she'd never seen him without his dark glasses before. Laughter lines crinkled the corners of his eyes and there was just the right amount of stubble beneath his sharp cheekbones. As he walked past her into the living room, Kate became aware of the distinctive scent of roll-ups and joss sticks that always enveloped him. She smiled and gazed down at her bare toes, remembering the schoolgirl crush she'd once had on him. It seemed like a long time ago.

"Ned, hi!" Freddy came out of his bedroom, bleary-eyed. "Nice to see you."

"You two know each other?"

"Sure. Ned's been sourcing good stuff for the deli since it first opened. What are you doing here at Christmas, mate?"

"I've ventured into Babylon to spend a little down-time with my lady friend." He cocked his head sideways, indicating upstairs. Kate wondered who he meant for a moment. There wasn't anyone upstairs apart from ...

"You mean Valentina? Wow. I'd no idea you two were an item. You both kept that juicy gossip very quiet."

Ned put a finger to his lips. "Vitaly might like to think he's a man of the people, but I'm not sure how pleased he'd be if he knew his niece was hooked up with one of the delivery drivers."

"You're much more than a delivery driver."

"Cheese-wrangler, then." He winked. "Anyway, I like to be discreet about my liaisons."

"You're a legend," said Freddy, grinning. "So, you'll be spending the Christmas break down here?"

Ned creased his eyes as though avoiding smoke from an invisible cigarette. "No way, Frederico. It's

276

not good for me to stay in the city too long. I get bad vibes from the noise and the traffic on the road and under the ground."

Kate frowned, not sure whether he really was an old hippy and serious about the vibes or teasing them. "What are you going to do, then? Scoop up Valentina and jet off somewhere hot?"

He sucked his teeth and shook his head. "The sky should be for the birds, man. No, we're going to pack up the old jalopy and head out east."

"East as in … ?" For a moment, Kate thought he meant India, then realised it was rather a long way to drive in the deli van.

"East as in the coast. There's nothing to beat a bonfire on the beach: the magical combination of fire and water. It's powerful and elemental and the only place to spend Christmas." He smiled at them both. "And what have you chicks got planned?" He looked around the flat. "And where is everybody?"

"Clare's in Ireland and Immy left for the slopes yesterday, so there's only me and Freddy here now."

Ned rubbed his chin with his long fingers thoughtfully. "And are you okay with that? What will you do with yourselves?"

"I hadn't thought about it." Freddy shrugged. "I guess we'll eat takeaways and watch Netflix. Or we could roast a chicken and pull a few crackers. What d'you reckon, Kate?"

It came to her in a flash that this was the first time she had not spent Christmas with her family and had no idea how to cook a Christmas dinner. Of course, she'd been around when it had happened and had always helped out with the preparations, but she had never cooked a whole lunch from scratch on her own. "Whatever you suggest," she said, trying to sound unconcerned. "I don't mind. It's nice to be doing something different for a change."

Ned laughed. "Like eating takeaways and watching TV?"

Kate wrinkled her nose. "I guess we might go for a walk in the park …"

"Forget it, guys. Pack a bag and come to Suffolk with me and Valentina. There's an old house down there that we escape to when we want to get away for a few days. How about it?"

A broad grin crossed Freddy's face. "Sounds great. I'm definitely up for a road trip. What about you, Kate?"

Christmas over the deli watching action movies and eating Chinese or a mini-break at the seaside? There was no contest. "I'd love to come!"

"Great. Put some clothes on, chuck a few things in a bag and let's hit the road."

"What, now?"

"Yup – I want you both to see the place in daylight."

"Can I have a cup of tea first?"

"Of course." Ned smiled. "All the best adventures start with tea. Give me a call when you're both ready and we'll set sail for the mysterious east."

# Chapter 16: Christmas Eve

Kate had been a tad concerned about travelling all the way to Suffolk in the back of Ned's cheese-scented transit van, so was relieved when he led them to a car instead. It was an ancient BMW that creaked when you got in, but at least it had enough space for four people and all their kit.

"Everybody ready? Off we go."

Since Kate had been in London, she'd gone everywhere on foot or by public transport, so it felt quite decadent to be cruising along the river and around Parliament Square in a car. After leaving the city, the route took them through dingy suburbs and endless rows of grey houses with dreary squares of concrete where gardens used to be.

It was a relief to hit the countryside and, after a couple of hours, they stopped for tea and a bacon sandwich at one of the small towns along the way. There wasn't much time to hang around because Ned was keen to reach their destination by lunchtime. It reminded Kate of days out with her parents and she felt about ten years old again as Ned herded them back into the car after the briefest of pit stops.

As they travelled further east, Kate was amazed by the flatness of the country, the huge fields and isolated copses, all so different from the rolling landscape of her childhood home. They drove on for another half an hour before she asked, "Are we nearly there yet?" in a singsong voice.

"We are." Ned smiled, catching her eye in the mirror. "The house is at the other end of the next village."

They sat silently for a while longer, admiring the solid brick houses they passed on the way. Eventually, they saw a village sign and drove down a narrow high street past a pub and a church, then along a row of terraced cottages fronted by neat gardens. A little further on, Ned swung the car into a narrow lane that led to an imposing house set back from the road and fronted by a large lawn. "Here we are."

After a moment, they climbed stiffly out of the car and looked around.

"Wow, this is quite a place," said Freddy.

Kate gazed up at the end wall, which was patterned with brick interspersed by pearly white flint. "What a beautiful house."

"It used to be the vicarage. We drove past the church on the way in." Ned cast his eyes over the building and frowned. "It could do with some TLC, but these places are money pits." An ancient wisteria covered the front and a Virginia creeper had wound itself over the end wall, partly concealing the red and white pattern.

"Look, there's a walled garden. Could we take a peek inside, do you think?"

"Sure, Kate. Feel free."

She pushed open the intricate wrought-iron gate and stepped into the garden, followed by the others. Someone had trimmed the low box hedges and, although there wasn't much growing, Kate saw in her mind's eye the herbs and roses that would fill the place with colour and scent in the summer. An area of raised beds had plainly been used for vegetables in the recent past and in another corner were what she recognised as apple and pear trees. "It's lovely," she said, almost in a whisper.

Valentina smiled. "It is our special place, where we come to hide from everything."

Ned gave his girlfriend a squeeze. "Let's get unpacked and start to enjoy it." He strode back to the car and began unloading their stuff onto the path. "We've packed enough food to feed an army," he said with a smile. "Let's take everything inside and light a fire to warm the place up."

They all followed him around to the side of the house where he opened the door into a dark hallway leading on to a scullery that was cold and full of cobwebs. "You'd think the owners would have heated the place up for you," said Kate, frowning.

"You can't get the staff," said Ned, grinning. "Actually, someone should have been in this morning to get the oven going."

Valentina smiled and nodded. "This is better." Beyond the scullery was a massive kitchen with a range cooker and a scrubbed oak table and long benches. The range was on and Freddy went and stood with his bum against it. "Bliss," he said, rubbing his hands together.

"Don't get too comfortable young man, we need to fetch some logs to keep the wood burners topped up. Come on."

Valentina looked at her immaculate nails. "I will put the food in the fridge."

"Good idea, darling." Ned gave her a kiss then led

the others along a path that ran down the side of the building to the back of the house where there was a greenhouse and an outhouse piled up with logs. "Grab the wheelbarrow and we'll get started."

Kate wheeled the barrow over and she and Freddy started to pile wood into it.

Ned stroked his chin, thoughtfully. "I could do with chopping up some of these bigger logs to use on the bonfire."

"Are we really going to have a bonfire?"

"We certainly are, Kate. Now, where's the axe?"

Ned went over to the outhouse, took down an axe that was hanging from the wall and started splitting logs into smaller pieces. Freddy watched him for a while, seemingly fascinated. "That looks fun. Do you think I could have a go?"

Ned grinned and wiped a hand across his brow. "Be my guest," he said, handing Freddy the axe. "Okay, step back, get yourself balanced." Freddy concentrated and swung the axe violently. "Take it easy, man! Slow regular movements are what you need: the weight of the axe will do the rest."

Freddy nodded, shuffled back and straightened his arms. "I'll try again." He pulled the axe back over his head then let it fall onto the log, which split in half like butter. "Sweet!"

"You got it. Finish the pile while Kate and I take this lot to the kitchen."

In the house, Valentina had put away the ton of food they'd brought and dug out some bedding. "The house is still cold, Ned," she said, frowning.

"We can't heat the whole building but the kitchen and the bedrooms above it will soon be toasty and warm. You and Freddy are okay to share, I'm guessing?"

Kate looked startled. "Er, share a bed?"

"Well, that's up to you guys," said Ned with a wink, "but I meant share a room."

Valentina smiled. "You must not tease poor Kate."

"Oh, I misunderstood. Silly me!" Just then Freddy came in with an armful of logs, his face aglow. "That was awesome. Where do you want these?"

"Put them in the basket over there."

"What are you lot grinning at?"

"We were discussing sleeping arrangements," said Ned, "and I recommend sharing rooms if you want to keep warm in this place."

Freddy stood with his hands on his hips and nodded. "Fine by me. So long as Kate doesn't snore too loudly."

She stuck out her tongue at him. "You'll find out soon enough."

"Right, well that's settled." Ned looked at his watch. "Let's go down to the beach and prep the bonfire before it goes dark."

At the bottom of the garden was a gate leading onto a path that they followed for about five minutes until it reached a bank of dunes topped with rough grass. The four of them climbed over the dunes and dropped down onto a perfect sandy beach.

"Wow, I had no idea the village was so close to the sea!" Kate closed her eyes and breathed in deeply, savouring the fresh salty air.

"You can see the sea from the top of the house. I'll show you in the morning." Ned took Valentina's hand as they walked down to the beach. After a while, he stopped and looked around. The tide had gone out and the sea was pewter grey where it met the distant horizon. "This is a good spot. Okay guys, let's collect some driftwood to add to Freddy's logs."

They all headed off in different directions, eyes on the sand.

"Some of this wood is really beautiful." Kate stroked the blue-grey patina of the piece in her hands. "It's much too lovely to burn."

"Maybe you should make something with it," said Ned.

She laughed. "Like a sea sculpture, you mean?"

"Precisely. Here you go." Ned dug around in his pocket and pulled out a ball of thick twine and some pieces of wire. "Use this to tie the bits together."

So, while the others concentrated on building the fire, Kate wound string around pieces of wood, gradually transforming them into a rough star shape. Along the shoreline, she found opaque chunks of pale green sea glass and added them to the star with twists of wire cut with Ned's pocket knife.

Ned wandered over to see what she was doing and nodded approvingly. "If you tie the shape to a long piece of wood, it can be our Christmas star."

"I'll see what I can find," said Freddy. After poking around in the dunes, he returned with a fairly straight length of wood to which he and Kate attached the star and then planted the sculpture in the sand.

"What do you think?" asked Kate, as the others came over to admire their handiwork.

Valentina cocked her head to one side. "I think it is most beautiful, but it is missing something. More decoration, perhaps." Her dark hair blew across her face as she bent to pick up strands of dried-up seaweed that were skittering across the sand, then handed them to Kate who carefully wound them around the spokes of the star.

"Now, it is perfect."

Ned put an arm around each of the girls. "Just like you two."

"Hey, I'm feeling left out here," said Freddy, laughing as he ducked his head under Ned's arm and hugged his friends.

\* \* \*

Having set up the bonfire and their Christmas star, the group walked back to the house for supper. Valentina had prepared a spicy stew in London and put it in the oven to heat up while they were at the beach. Ned buttered thick slabs of crusty bread and asked Freddy to open some wine while Kate set the table and lit the candles.

The journey and the walk along the beach had given them all an appetite and they ate with gusto.

Kate thought they were set for an early night but, after the plates had been cleared away, Ned stood and made an announcement. "Friends, it is Christmas Eve. Therefore, we must head to the beach, build a great fire and drink to the health of our planet."

Valentina frowned. "You want us to go outside again in the cold and the dark?"

Ned grasped her gently by the shoulders and kissed her on the tip of her nose. "It will be magical, I promise." He rubbed his hands together. "However, it might be a little on the nippy side, so grab hats, scarves, boots and bring rugs to sit on."

Bundled up, the trio dutifully left the warmth of

the kitchen and followed Ned back along the path to the beach. He and Valentina carried paraffin lamps to light the way, but the moon was so bright they barely needed them. The landscape was quite different at night: the dunes could have been the edge of a desert range and the wind rustled through the coarse sea grass.

When they reached their Christmas star, Ned stopped and threw out his arms towards the sea. "Enjoy that fragrance, people. There's nothing like it." He breathed in deeply, then waved vigorously with both hands.

"Who are you waving at, darling?" asked Valentina. "I can't see anyone out there."

"We can't see them, but there will be people on beaches in Holland and Scandinavia waving back."

Kate and Freddy tried not to laugh at their eccentric companion.

"Have you done this kind of thing before then, Ned?"

He turned, his eyes crinkling into a smile. "Many times, Frederico."

"In England?"

"England, India, Thailand – the sea's the sea, my friend. Now, let's make fire." Ned knelt on the ground and lit the bonfire, which soon sprang into life. The others arranged themselves on the rugs and gazed into the flames. After a while, Valentina unpacked the champagne and glasses.

"Don't open that yet, darling," said Ned. "We need to dip our feet into the ocean first. Come on – get those boots off and roll up your trousers."

Groaning quietly, Kate pulled off her boots and

double layer of socks and stood on the cold sand, shivering. Freddy hopped over and took her hand. "Come on, Kate. Let's do it."

"I'm sorry about this. Ned is a bit bonkers."

Fred turned towards her and laughed. "Why are you apologising? This is brilliant."

The tide was in and Ned had already run the short way to the water's edge with Valentina, who had rolled up her skirt to her knees. "Hurry up, you two," she said, laughing. "We must do this together."

Freddy and Kate stepped gingerly across the sand, then the four of them walked hand in hand into the inky sea, squealing as icy water lapped over their ankles. Behind them the fire crackled, throwing a flickering red light over Kate's star, which stood like a beacon on the beach.

They dashed back and forth into the water shrieking and jumping over the waves, then separated so each of them could walk alone in silence. It was a spontaneous moment of contemplation under the moonlight: magical, as Ned had promised. Afterwards they dried their feet, put on their boots and lay on the rugs watching the stars and listening to the rhythmic whooshing of the waves. At midnight, they drank a toast to good times and wished each other happy Christmas.

The moon was high in the sky by the time the bonfire had burned down and all the champagne was drunk. Ned's body cast a dim shadow on the sand as he stretched and stood. "Friends, I think it's time for bed."

Valentina packed up the glasses while Freddy and Kate folded up the rugs. Ned pulled the star sculpture from the sand, balanced it on his shoulder and led them across the dunes to the vicarage.

Back at the house, Valentina filled four hot-water bottles and put them into the beds to take off the chill. Freddy had been sent into the scullery to find some whisky and Kate was seated at the kitchen table watching Ned heat milk for hot chocolate.

"This is such a beautiful place. How did you discover it?"

Ned turned towards her, smiling. "My father was the vicar here – it's where my brother and I grew up."

"Wow, how fabulous. So, do you actually own the house?"

"We do – every last brick and spider's web, but keep that to yourself. I don't like too many people to know that I own property," he winked. "It doesn't go with the image."

"Your secret's safe with me!"

When Freddy came back, Ned added a slug of whisky to each of the mugs and led the way to the bedrooms.

When Kate awoke many hours later it was daylight and Freddy was lying on his side in the twin bed a few inches away, smiling at her. "Merry Christmas."

"Merry Christmas to you, too."

"Nice hat you've got there."

"Thanks." She reached up, realising that she was still wearing the bobble hat she'd put on the night before to keep her ears warm.

Freddy rolled onto his back and stared at the ceiling. "I could murder a cup of tea."

"Me too," said Kate, poking a foot across the gap and prodding his leg.

"Okay, I can take a hint. If you lend me your hat, I'll go down and make us some."

"Deal," she said, taking it off her head and handing it to him with a grin. "You're a hero."

"I know," he said, pulling on jeans and a sweater then heading for the door. Passing the window, Freddy pulled back the curtains and laughed. "Kate, you've got to see this!"

She wriggled out from under the bedclothes, a blanket tightly wrapped around her shoulders, and padded over to join him. "Oh, isn't Ned brilliant?" she said, laughing.

In the middle of the front lawn was their Christmas star, now bedecked in tinsel.

# Chapter 17: Some Bad News

After a late start, Valentina rustled up a massive breakfast while the others helped Ned to prepare a goose and plenty of vegetables for their Christmas meal. Once the bird was in the oven, Ned led them on a walk through the marshes where he pointed out the various sea birds. Later that afternoon, their attention returned to a different type of fowl as they tucked into their goose with crispy roast potatoes and all the trimmings, washed down with copious quantities of wine.

By this time, the house had warmed up enough for them to move into the smaller of the reception rooms, where they began the evening playing charades and board games. Later on, Ned unearthed a guitar from somewhere and played a few tunes accompanied by Valentina who turned out to have a lovely voice – unlike Freddy, who didn't, and was banned from joining in.

The next two days went by in much the same fashion and the thought of returning to London and normal life made Kate feel a bit low. Ned and Valentina were kind, generous hosts and she hoped to be invited to the vicarage again one day.

On the long drive from Suffolk, she gazed out of the window at the thousands of cars speeding towards the city but her head was filled with visions of the special time she'd spent with her friends. It had been a Christmas break that combined the wacky with the traditional and she knew she'd remember it for a very long time.

On the back seat of the car, Freddy nudged her gently. "You're quiet, Kate. What are you thinking about?"

"I was thinking what a great Christmas we've had. And how much I enjoyed being by the sea." And being with you, she thought.

"Yes, it'll be a shock to get back to London grime, even though we've only been away a few days. But it'll be good to see the deli gang."

"And Immy."

He frowned. "If she ever returns."

"But she'll be home later today, won't she?"

"Not according to the text I got this morning."

Freddy held out the phone for Kate to see the message written there: *Still on the slopes. Will explain. Immy xx.*

"That's it? Nothing more?" This did not bode well. What was Imogen up to?

"Nope. She's probably bumped into some wealthy tossers from school and been invited to spend another week in their chalet."

Kate feared that Freddy's guess might not be too far from the truth.

\* \* \*

It took them a while to unload Ned's car and carry everyone's stuff into the building. He and Valentina embraced their young friends and disappeared upstairs, hand in hand.

As soon as Kate was in the flat and Freddy was

out of the way, she pinged off a message to Imogen asking what was going on. She was surprised when the phone rang a few minutes later.

"Hi, Kate! How's it going?"

"Everything's fine here, but what's up with you? Why aren't you home yet? Has something happened?"

"Everything's good. Well, apart from one teeny thing."

Kate had a sick feeling in the base of her stomach. "Have you had an accident? Lost your passport? Been arrested?"

"No, nothing like that, silly. But I do need a favour."

"Go on …"

"Well, the thing is, I've had the best time and Ethan and I got on so well and …"

The line fizzed so much that Kate could barely hear what was being said. "Say again, Immy. And?"

"And Ethan's company is sending him to Geneva and he's asked me to go with him and I've agreed."

All the calm, peaceful feelings built up over the last few days disappeared as Kate heard the words.

"Kate, are you still there? Say something."

"Like what? I'm literally speechless. Are you saying what I think you're saying? You're not coming back to the flat? Ever?"

"Nope, never. Well, not to live anyway. We're flying straight to Ethan's new place from here. You and Clare should help yourself to my stuff – there's nothing much there anyway."

Apart from some seriously expensive clothes and shoes. "But what about Freddy? I can't believe you're dumping him like that."

"'Dumping' is such an ugly word."

"It's an ugly thing to do." Kate's head was starting to throb. "Why are you calling me, anyway? It's your boyfriend you should be talking to."

"Actually, that's the favour I wanted to ask: can you tell him for me?"

"Me? No way. How could you even ask me to do such a thing?"

Imogen's word's came out in a torrent. "Because I don't know when I'll be back. And he really likes you and I thought it would be better coming from a friend because you're there and you can comfort him if he gets upset."

"Are you completely mad? That is the most ridiculous thing I've ever heard, not to mention horribly cruel." Kate's mind was in a spin. "In any case, I'm going to see my folks for New Year, so Freddy will be all on his own."

"You've got to do it for me, Kate. I mean, I can't finish with him by text message – it's way too uncool."

"Ring and tell him yourself, now."

"I can't – the phone's almost dead and I've lost the charger. I will talk to him when I'm back, honest, but that might not be for ages because I'm going to have so much to do in Switzerland sorting out the apartment and looking for a job."

"Never mind that." Kate was exasperated. "Borrow a phone from bloody Ethan or – I don't know – write Freddy a letter."

"A letter? What am I? Jane Austen? I wouldn't know what to say and, anyway, there isn't time because he's expecting me home today." Across the airways, Kate could detect a pout. "I'm pretty upset about this, too, you know. Look, I've got to go because my battery's about to die. Thanks a million." And with that the call crackled to an end leaving Kate with the sound of silence buzzing in her ear. Stunned, she sat for several seconds staring at the phone in her hand, trying to make sense of what she'd heard.

Freddy had gone out to the supermarket to pick up some supplies to make an evening meal for them all and she knew he'd be back soon. The sound of a key in the lock made her start.

"Hello, hello. Is there anybody there?"

"Clare! I'm so pleased you're back." Kate leapt to her feet and threw her arms around her friend.

"Jeez, I've only been gone ten days. Did you really miss me that much?" Clare stepped back and examined Kate more closely. "What's wrong? You look like you're about to cry. No, don't tell me – let's put the kettle on. I need to get the taste of vile airline tea out of my mouth first."

Once they were seated in the kitchen, Kate told Clare about the phone call.

"Imogen's a piece of work all right. What a nerve that girl has. So what are you going to do?"

"Do I have any choice?" Kate frowned as she crumbled a biscuit between her fingers and prodded the bits into a heap. "I'm going to have to tell him – and Joseph, too, I guess. Christ knows when Imogen will bother to grace us with her presence and Fred will fret like crazy if he doesn't hear anything from her. They were supposed to be spending New Year together."

"Joseph's going to be pretty pissed off, losing one of his crack team with no notice."

"Ah, she won't care about him."

"What a bitch."

Bang! They both jumped at the sound of Freddy kicking the door closed with his heel then thumping along the hall into the kitchen. A smile lit up his face as he dropped the heavy shopping on the floor and threw his arms around Clare.

"Hiya, mate. How were things in Ireland?"

"Grand, thanks."

"That's it? No stories to share about drunken aunties?" He frowned. It wasn't like Clare to be so taciturn. "Has Kate told you about the top time we had in Suffolk?"

"Er, no. We've not had chance to chat much about anything yet." She slipped off the chair and looked at her watch. "Right, well I'm going to hop in the shower if that's okay with you guys. Hot date." Clare turned away from Freddy, silently mouthing the words "good luck" to Kate as she fled the kitchen.

"Cup of tea, Fred?"

"Sure." He sat and watched as Kate wordlessly refilled the kettle and threw tea bags into two cups. After a minute or two of silence, he began unpacking the shopping and shoving it in the cupboards. "Have I done something wrong or have you and Clare had a bust up? There's a seriously weird atmosphere in here."

Kate turned towards him, her face a picture of sorrow. "Neither," she said, sniffing.

"Wow, are you crying? Come here and tell your Uncle Freddy all about it."

Kate tore off a strip of kitchen towel and angrily dabbed at the tears that were leaking from her eyes. "I'm fine, really." She blew her nose noisily. "Let's sit down."

"Follow me." Freddy grabbed the tea and led them into the living room. "It looks like you might need this," he said, throwing her the family-sized bar of chocolate he'd carried in clasped between his teeth.

Kate smiled weakly, snapped off a large piece and threw the pack back across the sofa. "I think you might need some of this, too."

\* \* \*

An hour later, the tea lay cold and abandoned and Kate felt sick from eating too much chocolate. After the initial shock, Freddy had listened to what Kate had to say almost in silence, his eyes fixed on the low table in front of them. She hated to see the pain on his face.

"Thanks for telling me – I guess. Though Imogen should have been grown-up enough to tell me herself. What am I saying?" He laughed, bitterly. "She was brought up to expect other people to do all her dirty work for her."

He stood and rubbed both hands across his hair, as though sweeping away the thoughts in his head. "I need to get out of here. I'll see you later."

Kate watched miserably as he walked across the room and out of the flat. After he'd gone, she tried to read for a while, but it was hopeless. She couldn't concentrate on the story and the words floated across the page, making no sense. Giving up, she collapsed on the bed, waking an hour or two later fully dressed. Putting her head around the door, she could see Freddy's room was empty. She undressed, brushed her teeth and tried to sleep but it was impossible: where was he and what was he doing?

Eventually she dozed off, then awoke with a start,

the blood thumping in her ears. What had woken her was the flat door opening and Freddy's heavy footsteps across the hall. Only when his light went out and all was quiet did she fall into an exhausted sleep.

# Chapter 18: New Year's Eve

Kate felt awful, leaving Freddy all alone for New Year's Eve, but Clare promised to keep an eye on him.

"Don't you worry about yer man. I can guarantee that after a few pints of Guinness he'll not be thinking about her ladyship, or anything else for that matter."

"Thanks, Clare. I know he seems fine, but he is pretty upset."

Over the days since Immy's phone call, Kate had tried to talk to Freddy about the break-up but each time he'd changed the subject or found a reason to walk away.

Now Clare looked at her oddly. "You're really concerned about him, aren't you? Is there something going on between you pair I should know about?"

"No! Of course not." Kate reddened slightly. "I feel bad because Immy asked me to keep an eye on Freddy and now I'm going away, that's all."

"He's not your responsibility and you don't owe Imogen a thing. Have yourself some fun and worry not."

* * *

When Kate arrived at the railway station, her parents were on the platform ready to welcome her. It was the longest she had ever been away from home and she felt quite emotional when she saw them waiting there with big smiles on their sun-tanned faces.

Annie had prepared a proper Christmas dinner to make up for the one that she and her husband had missed due to being in the Canaries. In the evening, they sat around in party hats watching DVDs of favourite comedy shows, drinking port and scoffing jellied fruit slices.

The next night was New Year's Eve and Kate had agreed to make the annual pilgrimage to the Laughing Frog with her best friends, Debby and Rose. They knew it would be awful, but complaining about the venue and its terrible music was part of the fun. It also had the advantage of being a place that Steve would never set foot in.

Kate had arranged to meet her friends there and she smiled when she spotted them in the doorway busily talking over each other, their breath forming clouds in the frosty air. The trio had known each other since they were eleven and moving away, as Kate had done, was not enough to break their friendship.

After hugs and greetings, Debby pushed open the heavy wooden door and the girls entered the club, which somehow always retained a faint whiff of tobacco. "I bet you don't have nights out in many establishments like this any more, Kitty."

"No, I only go to very smart places now!"

She looked around at the purple walls, authentic 1980s glitterball and sticky carpets and had to laugh – it reminded her of the Bogey Man. The owners of the London place must have spent a lot of money trying to recreate the slightly sleazy look that the Frog pulled off so effortlessly. She wondered idly what had happened to Nick the Prick. She'd never seen him again after the no-show and supposed that he was still haunting dating events looking for shaggable females.

Good riddance. What she really wanted was someone she could talk to and have fun with. Someone like …

"So tell us about all the shagtastic men in London. Actually, on second thoughts, don't bother. It'll depress me." Rose scanned the room and sighed. "It's the usual selection of drips and deadbeats in here tonight. Remind me why we come here year after year like lemmings heading for the same old cliff?"

"Sex on the Beach at £3.50 a pop," said Debby. "Get your purse out, we need to start a kitty, Kitty." Her friends laughed as they always did at the pun on her childhood nickname.

"Christ, it looks particularly grim in here tonight. I think you're mad coming back from the capital for this. You must have loads of parties to go to down there."

"Well, now you come to mention it, I did go to a millionaire's soirée at his penthouse apartment on the Thames with fireworks and champagne the other week. He had a Renoir on the wall and we travelled there and back in his private launch. Oh, and then at Christmas I went to a beach party at this amazing house out in the country with a Russian heiress, and there was a bonfire on the sand and more champagne, obviously."

"Obviously," said Rose, patting her hand. "And I bet Will and Kate were there, too."

Kate smiled. "Nah, they weren't invited." She knew the experiences she'd had since starting work at the deli sounded unbelievable, so she decided not to insist. "So, what shall we have: cocktails or wine?"

"Cocktails, definitely. And let's hit the bar before the Young Farmers turn up and the place gets too busy. Damn, we're too late. Look at the crowd."

"Blimey, who let in the silver surfers?"

Huddling around the bar was a sea of grey-haired people in party frocks and smart-casual suits laughing and waving tenners in the general direction of the one surly barman. It was a party of pensioners on a coach trip from the South West who, having found the entertainment at the hotel a bit dull, had necked a couple of free drinks then come next door to the club in search of some action.

Behind the bar, the manager looked around nervously, hoping that his young, hard-drinking customers wouldn't leave when they noticed the average age shift from twenty-five to seventy. Happily, the visitors were a lively bunch and soon had Kate, her friends and even the rough lads from the council estate on their feet doing the moves to "YMCA" and singing Abba classics.

It was like being at a wedding reception but without the expense and the inevitable tears, and everyone got along swimmingly.

Later in the evening, the DJ pulled out some slow tunes and the dance floor was soon covered with couples smooching to golden oldies.

When the time came, the manager turned on the TV and everyone counted down the seconds to midnight and watched the sky behind Big Ben explode with colour as the firework display began on the Thames. In the Frog, the girls pulled party poppers to send streamers across the room and there was much cross-generational hugging between the local youth and elderly visitors.

"Weird as it sounds, I think that was the best New Year's bash we've ever had at the Frog," said Debby in the taxi home afterwards. "Those wrinklies certainly know how to party. Did you have fun, Kitty? You've gone quiet."

"I had a great time – I always do with you girls."

"Ah, team hug."

And the three of them hugged tearfully and promised – not for the last time – to be best friends forever.

Back in her bedroom, surrounded by teddies and Spice Girls posters, Kate checked her phone. Among the messages was one from Freddy: *Happy New Year xx*. She was still smiling and clasping the phone to her chest when she fell asleep.

* * *

Spending time with her parents and school friends had been fun and Kate was a little forlorn to leave them all after just a few days, but when the train pulled into Paddington Station, the thought of seeing Clare and Freddy perked her up.

By the time she got over to the flat, she was quite excited. Opening the door wide, she shouted a greeting. When there was no answer, she dumped her bag in her bedroom and checked the kitchen. "Hello! Is there anybody home?" Empty. She didn't know why she'd expected her flatmates to be in, but she was surprisingly disappointed to come home to an empty flat.

She was drinking tea and reading one of the books her folks had given her for Christmas when the door slammed and Freddy walked in. He was grey-faced and unshaven and his clothes looked as though they'd been slept in. "Hi Fred. Are you okay? How was New Year with Clare? I've been worried about you."

"I'm fine. I've been walking about, hoping it would clear my head."

"Hangover?"

"Serious hangover and mild heartbreak."

"And did walking do the trick?"

"Not really." He shook his head, grimacing. "The headache will go and I guess I'll get over Immy, too. I always knew I was batting above my weight – she's posh and beautiful and I'm just an ordinary bloke with nothing to offer. I was an idiot ever to think it would last."

What could she say? Freddy had loads to offer but she knew that Imogen had been pretty uncommitted to the relationship. "Posh, beautiful and totally amoral."

He smiled sadly and sat down beside her. "I'm guessing you knew what was going on?" It was the question Kate knew must come and had been dreading most of all.

"I'm so sorry, Freddy. I tried to stop her seeing Ethan, but she wouldn't." Once she started to speak, all the emotions she'd been keeping down welled up. "And I told her she had to make a decision one way or the other and she kept promising she would." Kate stopped to wipe a tear from her eyes – she seemed to be perpetually in tears these days. "It was awful and I did want to tell you what was going on, but then I couldn't bear to either because I knew how upset you'd be."

"You were being loyal to a friend and I can't blame you for that." Freddy put out an arm and pulled her towards him in a rough hug. "She doesn't deserve a mate like you."

Kate looked at her feet, embarrassed by the praise she felt deep down she didn't merit.

# Chapter 19: Back To Work

The holidays were over and it was time to return to the shop. Clare went down early, so by the time Freddy and Kate arrived for Joseph's presentation about the year ahead everyone already knew what had happened. No one mentioned Imogen, though a couple of the male staff patted Freddy on the back and muttered sympathetically. Joseph had a face like thunder and was clearly not amused at having to rethink the shifts he'd spent hours arranging over the holidays.

Otherwise, the day went by much like any other, though sales of Delish Detox Juices and Raw Food Super Salads rocketed as the clientele put their New Year's resolutions into practice.

A day or so later, Kate found herself alone with Freddy at breaktime and decided to ask again how he was. Since New Year, they had skirted around each other at the flat, avoiding the topic of Imogen. Kate and Clare had discussed it endlessly, but always made sure to change the subject when Freddy came anywhere near.

"How are you getting on?"

"Oh, I'm fine." He smiled. "Thinking about it, I realise it's my pride that's hurt, more than my heart. So, in the words of Gloria Gaynor, 'I will survive'."

Seeing Kate raise her eyebrows at the unlikely

reference, he smiled ruefully. "Immy sang it a lot when she was pissed."

"I'm glad you're feeling a little more positive about things." She smiled, encouraged to think Freddy might soon be back to his cheerful self. And there was more: over the past few days she had dared to imagine he really liked her and even that they might become more than friends. Not straight away obviously because, whatever he said, it would take him a while to recover from the loss of his girlfriend. For all of Immy's infuriating traits, Kate recognised that her ex-housemate was quite fabulous – clever, charming and effervescent – unlike her own, unremarkable self.

She smoothed a stray strand of hair behind her ear. "Now you've embraced Gloria Gaynor, I know you're on the road to recovery." She looked at the antique clock on the wall and smiled. "It looks like breaktime's over, so I'd best get back to making ginger and alfalfa sludge."

Freddy caught her wrist as she stood up. "Sit down a minute, Kate. There's something I need to tell you."

Her heart leapt. Had Fred picked up on her new feelings for him? No, she told herself, don't be ridiculous.

"What is it? You're a fan of Adele as well?"

"I've got all her albums, obviously." He grinned, then looked around to make sure Joseph wasn't within earshot. "Don't tell the boss, but I've been here nearly two years now and I reckon it's time for a change."

"Joseph likes you. I'm sure he'd give you a better role here. Or a promotion."

"I mean a bigger change, Kate. One that involves leaving Delish."

"Right," she said, trying to ignore the anxious voice in her head. "Good idea. Vitaly has loads of other restaurants and bars in the area."

"Actually, I was thinking of moving away."

"Away? How far away? Like Clapham?"

He laughed. "No, a bit further. I told you about the Fawlty Towers place in Cornwall where I worked for a while during uni?"

Cornwall? "You mean the sailing club?" Kate nodded, trying to appear cool, as though the thought of Freddy leaving town was not the worst news she could imagine.

"Well, I've always kept in touch with the owner and now he's brought in a new manager who's shaking up the place, giving it a new look, appointing a maître d' who's not a sociopath, reorganising the kitchen – loads of good things." Kate couldn't take her eyes off Freddy's animated face. "Before Christmas they asked me if I'd like to join as assistant manager. Originally I said no because I didn't want to leave Immy and I knew she'd never cope outside the M25."

How ironic, thought Kate, that Imogen was now heading for the Swiss Alps.

"Anyway, I phoned them yesterday and, luckily for me, the job is still open. So I'm off."

Off? "How soon?"

"Well, officially, I only need give a couple of days' notice, but I'll stay till the end of next week so Joseph doesn't have a complete meltdown."

Ten days. He'd only be around for ten more days.

How could she bear it? Kate arranged her face into a grin, determined to hide the huge sadness washing over her as each detail was revealed. "Sounds exciting. Congratulations."

"Thanks." Beaming, he grasped her hands. "I knew you'd be pleased for me."

Cornwall. It was more than three hundred miles away, but he might as well have said America. She might never see him again.

"And what about you, Kate? Will you stay here or head back home?"

"Oh, I don't know. I guess under the circumstances Joseph will be keen for me to stay on for a while longer. And it's not as if I have many exciting options waiting for me in Herefordshire."

"I'm sure he'll be glad to have you." Freddy was so close that his legs knocked against hers under the table. "And there'll be loads of extra shifts to do when I'm gone."

"Yes, great." There's always a silver lining, she thought bitterly. I lose two friends, but I get to spend more time cleaning out the espresso machine.

# Chapter 20: Heading West

It was a dull, grey morning when Kate left London but, as she headed west, the clouds lifted and soon the sky was crystal clear overhead. It was, she thought, as though the journey was taking her from winter to spring and she smiled as she spotted pink and yellow primroses, tall daffodils and banks of snowdrops along the railway track.

Her gloom at Freddy's leaving had been tempered by an invitation to visit him as soon as he had settled into the new job. Now it was mid-February and she was on her way to Cornwall.

He had said he would meet her and Kate anxiously scanned the crowds as the train pulled into the station. Stepping from the train, she watched as a white-haired lady walked into the arms of an elderly gentleman, a pasty-faced boy with piercings submitted himself to the kisses of his mother, and lovers found each other and embraced. There was no sign of Freddy and she wondered for a moment whether he'd forgotten she was coming. Only when she'd left the platform and headed for the exit did she see him, leaning casually against a pillar.

He waved, then stepped towards her with his arms outstretched and a huge grin on his face.

"Great to see you, Kate," he said, picking her up and swinging her around.

"You look well! It obviously suits you down here." Kate tried not to stare at her friend, who looked more handsome than ever. "How did you manage to get a tan in the middle of winter?"

He rubbed his cheek, laughing. "Actually, my face is more weather-beaten than tanned. Some of the guys at the hotel are mad-keen surfers and they've been trying to teach me. No one has succeeded in the past, but they're determined to get me to stay upright for more than five seconds."

"Don't you freeze out there?"

"Nope, the water's surprisingly warm and I wear a dry suit. I'll take you for a swim later, so you can see."

She pulled a face and shivered. "I'm thinking that's not one of your better ideas."

"Shame. I guess it'll have to be Option 2 then."

"Which is?"

"Lunch at a very smart beachside restaurant, a walk and maybe a paddle later, if you're feeling brave."

She smiled up at him, wrapping her arm around his. "I can probably manage that – lead on."

Freddy picked up her bag and walked her over to the car park. "Your carriage awaits, Madame."

"Nice wheels."

"Why, thank you. I think I need to get one of those naff stickers saying 'My other car is something decent'."

The vehicle might have been an old banger but it went, and they were soon out of the town centre and heading along the coast road.

After about ten minutes, Freddy parked in a village a little way from the beach and smiled. "I think you'll find it's a bit wilder than Ned's coastline."

She smiled. "Coming from a landlocked county, every bit of coast is exciting to me."

"Come on. Let's get some lunch."

They left the car and walked through the village towards the "smart" lunch venue, which was actually a gourmet burger van. Soon they were settled outside, fingers sticky with ketchup.

"So how's it going? Are you happy at the new-improved sailing club?"

"It's great and I love the job. The new manager is almost as mad as the last one, but in a good way. He's happy for me to try out lots of ideas for events and stuff. The accommodation's not bad – as you'll discover later – and the other staff are friendly."

"Good," she said, nodding and doing her best to sound positive. "I can't wait to see it. And thanks for arranging for me to have a room at mates' rates."

"No probs," he said, smiling. "You are a mate, after all." The sun was in Freddy's eyes and Kate noticed a fleck of green she had never spotted before. For some reason it made her feel melancholy, discovering something in him and knowing they might not see each other again for months. "And how is the deli's cheese-wrangler-in-chief?"

"Oh, Ned's fine."

"Christmas was quite something this year."

"Yes, it was special," she said, softly. Scenes from their mad mini-break scrolled through her mind like a film, making her smile wistfully. It was the first time in her life that she'd gone paddling at midnight; the only time she'd lain down on the sand to watch falling stars, her hand clasped in Freddy's.

"And have you decided what to do about work yet?"

Kate popped the last chip into her mouth, chewing thoughtfully. "Oh, I guess I'll head back to the sticks and Geoff's market stall – my boss said there'd always be a job for me there. Working at the deli has been fun, and I'm really glad I've done it, but it's not the same without …"

"Immy? There's no need to apologise. You two were friends."

"Immy, yes. And you, too." She caught Freddy's eye then quickly glanced away, worried in case she'd revealed too much.

He smiled. "Thanks. It's nice to be missed."

They sat in silence for a moment, watching gulls skim over the sea.

"Have you seen her recently?"

"Only once." Kate pulled her jacket closer to her as the wind whipped up, throwing shingle against her shins. "Her father brought her over in an enormous car and they took away a load of stuff. You could tell her dad wasn't pleased at all, seeing as Vitaly had only given Immy a job in the first place as a favour to him. What about you? Have you heard from her?"

"Nope, but that's cool because it's completely over between us. For all her faults, she's a great girl and we had lots of good times together. But I've had time to think." He frowned. "I know I don't want to be with her any more so, in a way, she's done me a massive favour by going away."

"Really?"

"Sure. If she hadn't gone off with Mr City Wanker, I'd never have taken this job. And who knows what the future holds?" He smiled. "But, that's enough about Lady Imogen. What do you say to pudding?

I think they've got Mars Bar ice creams in the van."

"Yum, I'd love one. Thanks."

Freddy bought their ice creams, which they ate walking along the beach. At the end of the bay, they clambered over boulders then found a narrow path that wound its way up to the cliff top. There was a blustery wind and Freddy took Kate's hand. "I don't want you to be blown over the edge on your first visit!"

At the top, she was sorry when their hands fell apart as they paused to catch their breaths and take in the view.

"There's a bench over there. Shall we sit down?"

Kate nodded, wordlessly. Once she had her breath back, she smiled. "Wow. It really is beautiful here and so different from where I grew up. The scenery is endless vistas of fields, sheep and cows there. Oh no!"

As she spoke, a gust of wind caught the hat she'd rested on her lap and sent it tumbling along the path.

"I'll get it!"

Freddy leapt over the back of the bench, returning a few moments later with the hat safely in his hands.

"I'm glad you caught it – that's our Christmas hat," she said, stretching out a hand to take it from him.

"Here, let me." Sitting down beside her, he carefully tucked the crimson wool over her ears. She put her hands up to her head, her fingers interlocking with his. "You're cold," he said, putting his arm around her and pulling her towards him. She closed her eyes, enjoying the unfamiliar sensation of his body next to hers for all too short a time. "Come on," he said, jumping up and stamping his feet. "It's chilly up here. Let's get out of the wind."

They turned back from the cliff top and walked across fields that, in the summer, would be full of wheat. The pale winter sun was low on the horizon as they climbed over the last stile and dropped down into the village. Kate hesitated for a moment, wanting to imprint the image of the indigo sea and pink sky in her mind, so she could enjoy it again when she was back in London.

"Ready, Kate?"

She nodded. "Yup, let's go."

Soon they were huddled over hot drinks in the local teashop, their cheeks tingling after coming in from the cold.

Kate leant back, thinking how long Freddy's eyelashes were as he sat opposite her, stirring his coffee and frowning. "You look serious – is there something the matter?"

"I was wondering ..." He looked at Kate shyly. "This is probably going to sound completely mad, but if you're not sure about Herefordshire and you've had enough of the deli, why not come down here?"

"Me? Move to Cornwall?" Her heart leapt. "What as?" Girlfriend, colleague? "I mean, what would I do?"

"With your experience you could easily find a job in one of the local shops or restaurants – there's quite a tourist trade."

It was clear from the muddy boots that many of the café's customers were walkers. Looking around, Kate noticed maps and local guidebooks propped up on the shelves between the Valentine's gifts, Easter Bunnies and packets of fudge. "Right, yes." Now she understood: Freddy was being kind. He knew she needed a new job and why shouldn't it be here? It wasn't as if she had any ties. After all, there was no boyfriend waiting for her at home. And maybe he had a point – she couldn't stay at the deli forever.

"It was just a suggestion." Freddy drained the last of his coffee and smiled. "No pressure."

She nodded, determined not to show her disappointment that Freddy didn't have something more romantic in mind. "Thanks. I'll think about it."

Over the rest of the weekend, they went for more walks and Freddy persuaded her to go for a paddle that left her toes blue and aching with the cold. They went to the pub and he introduced her to his colleagues at the sailing club. When he was working, she wandered around the town, ate more ice cream and read romcoms in a comfy armchair at the club.

When the time came to catch the train back to London, she felt as though she'd had a proper holiday but her emotions were in turmoil. She'd been excited when Freddy suggested she should move to Cornwall, but sad that he only wanted her there as a friend. He liked her: this was good. But was it enough, given the way she now felt about him? Perhaps she should give up and go back to Herefordshire, she thought gloomily.

"Thanks for abandoning the big city and coming all this way to see me."

"That's okay – it's not the end of the earth."

"Er, actually it is," said Freddy, nodding his head. "If you carried on for a few miles in that direction, you would fall off this island altogether." He smiled. "I'll take you down there next time. If you come and visit again, that is."

"Of course I'll come again," she said, sniffing. "If you'd like me to."

"Are you welling up?" He laughed, dabbing at her face with the cuff of his sweater. "I've never known a girl cry as much as you do."

Kate laughed, tearfully. "I know, I'm hopeless. Mum said I used to cry at *Teletubbies*."

"Well, there was a lot of tension in that show."

She dug around in her bag for a tissue, hoping to hide the mixed emotions of hope and sadness building inside. This is ridiculous – Freddy's a friend, he doesn't fancy me: end of. He'd had a whole weekend to kiss her and it hadn't happened. He didn't find her attractive and that was that. "Here's my train."

"Let's find your carriage." Freddy took her hand and they walked together along the platform, Kate's heart doing a pitter-patter as the moment to leave came ever closer.

"Well, here we are," he said, stopping by her carriage and handing over the vast pink Michael Kor's tote bag Kate had inherited from Imogen. Freddy stood with his hands in his pockets, rocking back and forth on his heels and looking uncomfortable. "I think we need another deli team hug – come here."

With that he wrapped his arms around her shoulders and pulled her close to him, stroking her back. Was she imagining it or did Freddy hold her tighter and for longer than you would expect a friend to hold you? They'd shared plenty of hugs over the months but this one felt different. She closed her eyes wishing she could stay enfolded in his arms all day, pressing her cheek against his neck and breathing in his scent. All too soon he let her go and they stepped apart.

"Promise you'll keep in touch."

"Of course I will."

She reached up to the carriage door, then stopped and turned. Kate, she said to herself, you have to do something. If she walked away now, she knew that the next time she came to visit Freddy he would have been scooped up by one of the pretty waitresses at the sailing club and her chance would be lost.

"What's up, Kate? Have you forgotten something?"

"Yes, I think I have." Standing on tiptoes, she grabbed his collar and kissed him firmly on the lips. "It's the rule: you have to kiss someone on Valentine's Day."

There – I've done it! Whatever happened in the future, at least she'd had one kiss.

Before Freddy had a chance to say or do anything, Kate hopped onto the train. She was beaming with pride and amazed at her daring as she took her seat. On the platform, Freddy gazed up at her with a puzzled smile on his face. Then he kissed his fingertips and pressed them against the dusty window of the carriage as the train began to move, taking Kate away.

# Chapter 21: What Kate Did Next

Freddy stood glued to the platform until the train had disappeared out of the station and was no more than a green blip on the track. He wanted to laugh out loud and slap himself across the face at the same time. How could he have been such an idiot? It was obvious that he loved Kate and just as he realised this startling fact he had let her return to London. Okay, so she said she'd think about coming back, but why should she? He'd made it sound as though he really didn't care too much whether she moved west or not. He'd asked her to join him because she was a mate who needed a job. A mate? She was his best friend – the person he could talk to about anything. The person with the craziest hair and the sweetest smile he'd ever met. The only person he knew who could make a woolly hat look sexy. Now he wanted her to come back because he loved her and wanted to be with her. But she didn't know that.

Something had to be done. He looked at his watch, grabbed the car keys and sprinted to the car park.

* * *

Kate stared idly at the houses and gardens along the route wondering who they belonged to. Who lived there and were they happy? Happier than her? What should she do? She'd enjoyed her short time in Cornwall, but could she bear to live in the same town as Freddy if they weren't together? He was a friend and she knew she should be pleased for him when he moved in with the beautiful Polish waitress she had already conjured up in her mind's eye.

\* \* \*

Freddy banged the steering wheel and swore under his breath. It was sod's law that when you were in a rush, the traffic lights were always against you. "Come on, come on." The radio was on and a perky pop tune was playing. He pressed the buttons until he found something loud and Wagnerian – this was a mission that demanded serious music. He breathed deeply, trying not to lose his temper with a learner driver who was edging forward at a snail's pace.

\* \* \*

Kate closed her eyes and dozed. She was lucky to have both seats to herself so had stretched out, her head resting on her coat. She'd spent the last hour drawing up imaginary lists in her head noting the various pros and cons of staying at the deli, returning home or heading to the coast. The deli had the advantage of familiarity, great accommodation and the possibility of a proper job. Herefordshire had good friends, a supportive family and a dodgy night life. And Cornwall? Well, that was the great unknown.

\* \* \*

Pulling into the station car park, Freddy jammed on the brakes and leapt out of the car. Looking frantically at his watch, he ran up the steps two at a time and crossed the bridge to the London platform. His heart was pounding as he ran along, searching for the train indicator. Had the damn thing been and gone? Had he missed her?

* * *

The banging on the window startled her awake. Kate couldn't believe it – what was Freddy doing on a platform in the middle of nowhere waving his arms around like a madman? She laughed, wondering what he was up to as he disappeared from view.

The next thing she knew he was crouching by her seat, gripping both her hands in his. "I'm such an idiot, Kate, and I'm sorry it has taken me so long to see what has been staring me in the face for months. I love you!"

They looked at each other and laughed as the train began to move.

"Oops."

"What are you doing? You can't come to London with me – what about your job?"

"Don't worry about that. I'll get off at the next stop and catch the bus back." His eyes scanned her face earnestly. "The only thing that matters, the really big question is whether you love me, too. Do you, Kate?

She lifted her hands to his face and kissed him. "Oh Freddy, I've loved you since Day One."

He kissed her again, stroking her cheek and gently pulling her curls through his fingers. "Well, that's a relief." He stood up as a voice on the tannoy announced that the train was approaching the next stop. "I suppose I'd better get off." He kissed her once more as the other passengers smiled and applauded. "Call me!" And with that he left the train.

* * *

Vitaly didn't expect his short-term staff to stay forever, so he and Joseph were gracious when Kate's six months at the deli came to an end and she told them she'd be moving to Cornwall tostart a new life.

Since her first visit – and the kiss – she'd been in constant contact with Freddy who had helped her to find a job at a sea-front bistro that he promised really was a restaurant and not a burger van.

She travelled down with all her stuff the week before the job was due to start. This time, Freddy was standing on the platform waiting for her to arrive, a huge bunch of spring flowers in his hands and a massive smile on his face.

* * *

"Do you think we're really wicked, sleeping together on a first date?"

"I seriously hope so," said Freddy. "Especially when you're only twenty-one. Happy birthday, Kate."

"How did you know it was my birthday today?"

"Ah, I have my sources." He smiled, jumping up to open the blinds so the spring sunshine could flood in and fill the room.

As Freddy climbed back into bed, Kate kissed him. "You are lovely."

"I am. So lovely, in fact, I've even got you a present."

"Hold on." She sat up, pulling on one of Freddy's T-shirts. "Okay, I'm ready," she said, grinning.

Freddy turned and grabbed something from down by the side of the bed. Smiling, he placed in her hands a small box covered in red and gold paper and topped with a star. "Sorry about the Christmas wrapping paper. It was all I had."

"It's lovely."

"I hope so – open it up."

Kate removed the star, pushed a finger under a corner and carefully peeled back the paper. Inside the box she found three smaller packages.

"Which one shall I open first?"

Freddy stroked his chin. "When it comes to presents, I would always go for the biggest one first."

"You're such a boy," she said, grinning. Unfolding the tissue-paper wrapping, Kate found a crystal heart on a silver chain. On either side of the heart were opaque stones in pale blues and greens like sea glass, and tiny silver leaves. A second parcel held matching earrings, which she put on. "Oh Freddy. These are beautiful."

"Do you like them? I thought the stones would remind you of the beach. Here, let me help you with that." Kate dipped her head and lifted her hair out of the way so Freddy could fasten the necklace around her neck. "Perfect. Now open the last package."

Kate eyed him curiously as he picked up the tiny parcel from where it rested on her lap and placed it in the palm of her hand.

"What's this?"

"You'll have to open it to find out."

The last gift was wrapped in blue tissue paper and tied up with silver ribbon. When Kate opened it she discovered a gold key. "A key to your heart?"

Freddy grinned. "I've found a flat to rent and I wondered whether you might like to move in with me. I mean, we did live together for six months, so you know I'm completely house-trained: I can cook, I don't snore too loudly and I've even been known to Hoover."

"We didn't have carpets in Chelsea."

"Okay, I was making that part up. But what do you think?" He looked at her anxiously. "Does living together again sound like fun or not fun?"

"Perhaps, if you ask me nicely," she said, rolling onto her side and grinning.

"Okay," he said, kissing her. "Do you – Kate – take me – Freddy – to be your ever-loving flatmate?"

"I do." She threw her arms around him but he pulled away, frowning. "Is there something wrong?"

"I was only thinking your new necklace doesn't go too well with my Kaiser Chiefs T-shirt."

"You think not?" said Kate, stroking the pale stones at her throat.

"But don't worry, I have a solution. Sit up." Grinning, he caught the bottom of the T-shirt and gently lifted it over her head.

"Better?" she asked, snuggling into his arms.

"Much better," he said, caressing her cheek. "I love you, Kate."

"I love you too, Freddy."

## THE END

If you enjoyed *French Kisses and A London Affair* you might also enjoy *A Summer of Surprises and An Unexpected Affair*.